WHITE LIES
AND OTHER COLORS

J. S. MORETTI

Publisher's Information

EBookBakery Books

© 2022, Jill S. Moretti

ISBN 978-1-953080-34-9

Author contact: jillmoretti@hotmail.com

ALL RIGHTS RESERVED

No part of this work covered by the copyright herein may be reproduced, transmitted, stored, or used in any form or by any means graphic, electronic, or mechanical, including but not limited to photocopying, scanning, digitizing, taping, Web distribution, information networks, or information storage and retrieval systems, except as permitted by Section 107 or 108 of the 1976 United States Copyright Act, without the prior written permission of the author.

While many of the stories in this book are based on historical events, the names, characters, places and incidents are the product of the author's imagination and are fictionalized. Resemblance to actual persons, living or dead, business establishments, events, or locales is coincidental.

Cover: Rock paintings in the Cueva de Las Manos in Patagonia, in Argentina

Dedication

To my long-suffering husband Dave, who would stop singing in the mornings so I could write. Sometimes I only pretended to write.

Acknowledgments

Thank you, Katelyn, for giving me the idea which spawned this novel (and perhaps one in the future), and for your medical/other insights along the way, and to son-in-law Andy for your medical expertise and availability in all things. My thanks to my other daughters, Carolyn and Vanesa, and my mother Janet for your love and support.

To continue in the medical field, I appreciate my colleagues – Connie Keene for plot assistance, Mary Ann Abney for reading this twice in order to pin down the psychiatric, (I may put Susan in here), and Dr. Lilly Wolfgang for eagle eye editing and feedback. Thank you, Dr. Anne Hebert for sharing your ICU expertise and Ellen Perz, RRT for clarity regarding the workings of ventilators. To April Sylvestro, BSN and Reiki Master, thanks for talks about all things spiritual.

To my non-medical doctors – Dr. Grace Farrell, whose marvelous creative writing class gave me courage, Dr. Dave Moretti, who read my book and discussed it even though I didn't read his dissertation on whales, and Dr. Jim Marx for your help with dendrology even though you're a physical therapist (perhaps you belong in the medical field list).

Thanks to Jim Burrough, ham radio aficionado, to Anne Heffron for being my therapist over the years without any credentials, to my patients for their wisdom and inspiration, and to all of my Christmas letter-readers for their patience as they "heard" about this work for years. And finally, thank you to family, friends and classmates who agreed to read a rough draft to provide brutally honest feedback, but didn't. And to I. Michael Grossman, an accomplished author and poet, who, with grace, humor and expertise, turned my pages into a book. Thanks for being my sounding board, honing my editing skills and making it so much fun!

Contents

1. The Session 1
2. Doctoring 7
3. Mama 13
4. The Poet 18
5. Not at Home 27
6. Viet Nam 33
7. Elizabeth 41
8. Elaine 46
9. Jon Con 51
10. Frank 59
11. Trio 67
12. The Medical Office Building 73
13. John 85
14. Best Laid Plans 93
15. Mickey 97
16. The Mission 103
17. Consequences 108
18. Restraint 111
19. Paul 114
20. Discovery 119
21. Conundrum 127
22. Twisted 130
23. Upside Down 143
24. Opportunity 153
25. Annie 163
26. At the Bedside 169
27. Confident 177
28. Uncovering 184
29. Taken 193
30. Resolution 201
31. Disappear 203
32. Aftermath 206
About the Author 213

1

THE SESSION

Annie sighed and brushed the short brown ringlets back off her forehead so she could think. Brow furrowed above her glasses, she scrutinized the faintly illegible faxed sheets on her lap.

"So, you were hospitalized at Westbrook after your father had you evaluated in our ER?"

"Yes."

"Why did he call 911?"

"He heard me talking on the phone."

"And?"

It was like pulling teeth, Annie thought, drawing the story out of the diminutive woman in front of her. She flipped through the pages from Westbrook Hospital's psychiatric unit, located just north of Providence. Psychotic Disorder and Anxiety Disorder Not Otherwise Specified, discharged on the antipsychotic medication Risperdal and Trazodone for sleep.

"I was talking to my aunt." Annie's new patient stared at the blue Oriental rug covering part of the tile floor in the middle of Annie's office which was located in the Medical Office Building, attached to Jonathan Conrad Hospital or Jon Con, as staff affectionately called it. Acronyms abound in medicine. Annie had a view of the community hospital from her window and was grateful every day that she had gotten out of Providence with its traffic and noise and moved forty minutes away to the southern part of the state.

She had to strain to hear her patient and decided to remain silent. Twenty years of psychiatric nursing had honed her instincts, and Annie felt capable of treating most people who walked through her door. She crossed one long leg over the other, her silk skirt dropping to a sequined sandal. She's 48; she's had years of waiting. Finally, the woman looked up at her.

"He didn't like it."

"Your father didn't like you talking to your aunt?"

She looked at the rug again and Annie leaned back in her chair, narrowing her eyes as she studied her patient, noting how her worn sundress hung from her body. Mary Johnson, single, date of birth August 20, 1958. Discharged May 28, 1990 after a four-day involuntary hospitalization and referred to Annie for follow-up. No reference to an eating disorder, substance abuse or cutting. No scars that Annie could see. No tattoos, piercings, not even pierced ears. Luckily there was some information in the hospital record on this 32-year-old waif or Annie would have precious little to go on.

"He didn't like us talking about . . . how we see things."

"You see things."

Mary glanced at Annie. She reminded Annie of the rabbits she would see sometimes on her morning walks, ready to bolt.

"You both see things?"

Nothing. Annie ran long fingers through her hair. Thank God she got it cut as June in Rhode Island can be hot and humid and the air conditioning in her office could be temperamental. She leaned toward the other woman, clasping her hands in front of her. The clock ticked audibly on her bookshelf, sitting on a stack of research articles in a spot where Annie could glance at it unobtrusively.

"Mary, I know this must be very hard for you. You don't know me, and you have no reason to trust me. Trust needs to be earned, earned over time. But we need to make a decision about your medication, if I'm going to prescribe it for you. And I can't do that without getting a history from you. I simply need to understand you and your situation a little better."

Mary pinched her thin lips together and looks defiantly at her. "And my father?"

"As we discussed, this is confidential. The only time I share information is if you plan to hurt yourself or somebody else, or if you know of a child or an elder being hurt. You would have to sign a release of information before I could speak with your father."

"I'm not on the medication," Mary blurted. She glared at Annie, whose expression remained pleasant. This was concerning, as Mary had been discharged from the hospital only 6 days earlier. But not surprising, Annie thought, as it is fairly common to discover that patients had gone off their psychiatric medications. Most people have good reason to do what they do, and Annie was determined to figure Mary out.

"Okay. So how are you doing off of the meds?"

"About the same."

"Which is. . ."

Mary was gripping one hand with the other, hanging on for dear life. "Sleep is worse. And I'm nervous."

"Okay." Annie smiled reassuringly. "That's very helpful to know. I'm sure I can help with that."

Silence. But Mary's eyes locked with Annie's, who decided to push it a little. "Are you . . . seeing more things?"

Mary nearly whispered, "Not more. About the same."

"I see. So maybe you didn't feel like the medicine was helping with that?"

Mary looked relieved. "Exactly."

"Okay! That makes perfect sense. But there are a few things that perhaps you didn't know about the medication. What were you told?"

"That it could have side effects." There was a note of anger which Annie took as a good sign since anger is energizing. Depression leaves people exhausted.

Annie smiled again. "Yes, I'm sure you were told that. What side effects were mentioned?"

"Weight gain. Diabetes. Your cholesterol can go up."

"Mary, those things are certainly possible, but not very common. Weight gain is most likely so I'll track your weight at our visits. Maybe you wouldn't mind gaining a few pounds? I would need to monitor your bloodwork on Risperdal and change to a different medication if we need to."

Annie watched for a response but Mary remained expressionless. Annie softened her voice. "Were you told that you have visual hallucinations?"

Mary gripped harder until the fingers of her caged hand turned red. She had no ring on, no jewelry at all and her face was plain without make-up.

"They told me the medicine would take away the visions, but it didn't."

"I see. Are the visions distressing to you?"

"Sometimes. Usually."

"What can you tell me about the visions?"

Mary remained motionless. Only her lips moved. "I see the future," she whispered.

Annie took this in. "Tell me a little more."

"I . . . see things and then they happen."

"What kind of things?" Annie hadn't seen a description of hallucinations from Westbrook Hospital, and visual hallucinations without a physical cause were rare. The doctor there had looked for a brain abnormality, such as seizures or a tumor, and found nothing.

"I saw the commuter train before it derailed."

"The commuter train?"

"The one in Sarasota Falls."

Annie recalled reading about it in the newspaper several months ago. Three dead, scores injured.

"That must have been frightening."

Mary remained impassive. "Yes."

A quick glance at the clock. Twenty minutes left.

"Mary." Annie leaned in again, her gaze never leaving Mary's face. "You weren't on the Risperdal long enough for it to help you. Could you give it another chance? We could work on this together. I'd really like to help you."

"Could it take the visions away? My aunt says it's not possible. She says I have the family gift."

The family gift? Mary was proving to be fascinating and Annie felt a strong desire to help.

But the job at hand was simply getting her to return again. Annie sucked in a deep breath.

"I can't promise that, Mary, I really don't know. But I can promise that I'll do everything in my power to help you. Sometimes sharing your burden can make it lighter."

Mary searched Annie's face, blue eyes large above high cheekbones. She allowed her hands to drop and leaned back in her chair.

"We could start with your sleep," Annie said. "Did the medicines help with that?"

"A little."

"Okay, then. If you sleep better, you'll feel better. Let's talk about the medications you were put on in the hospital and whether you felt they were helpful in some way. Perhaps we could restart one or both of them, and take it from there. What do you think?"

"My father can't find out."

The complexity of Mary's situation was becoming evident, as Annie knew Mary lived with her parents, working on the family farm. She also knew that her mother was very ill. There was so much more that Annie wanted to know.

"We'll take it one step at a time. If your father is unhappy, you can certainly blame me." Annie laughed a little, trying to lighten the mood. "My counselor made me do it." She used the term counselor deliberately, feeling the word therapist could be threatening.

Mary didn't respond. She stared at Annie who felt suddenly cold; her smile fled and her muscles tensed.

"You don't know my father."

"Maybe I do, Mary. I've encountered other intimidating people in my career. I'm not afraid of your father, but I believe you are."

Mary sat up slightly, rigid. Her straight dark blonde hair had fallen across one eye.

"As I said," Annie continued. "One step at a time. We'll figure out how to do this. How to help you without making your father angry. How to keep you safe . . . maybe we could start with how you got here today. Here," Annie motions to indicate the office, "to see me. It sounds like that was very brave."

"I just got lucky."

"Well, then, let's see how we can keep your good luck rolling. You got yourself here today, and that was really hard, and probably scary, so let's see how we can make it happen again."

A pause. "Okay," Mary said, sounding stronger. Annie breathed deeply and smiled at her.

2

DOCTORING

Edmund Fowler, MD evaluated the screaming toddler in the clinic exam room, listening to his heart, then his lungs, only possible when he sucked in a breath. The screaming was a part of the job that Edmund accepted; he could appreciate the fear driving it and the lack of inhibition in expressing it. Intrusive, idiot parents were another thing entirely.

"Madam, there is nothing wrong with your son. He is fine." Edmund tried to look at the obese, slightly malodorous female who stood next to the examination table, looking down at her son who reached for her, crying, eyes and nose running. Edmund stuffed his stethoscope into the pocket of his lab coat and kept his eyes on the boy. Intellectually he knew he should somehow make a connection with the mother, but he found it intolerable that people continue to conceive and give birth, seemingly without so much as a basic instinct to guide them in fostering the development of these little human beings. God knows what this child came in for; she didn't even know to comfort him. Poor little bugger.

He glanced at her. "You may pick him up." While she did so he picked up the boy's chart and headed for the door.

"But Doctor, today is Friday. . ."

Hand on the door knob, Edmund forced himself to look at her. The little boy had wrapped himself around her and buried his face in her bosom. She held him with one hand under his bottom, the other slipping a neon pink handbag over her head and shoulder which looked heavier than the boy.

Edmund repeated, "He is fine," and swung the door open rather forcefully, heading down the narrow hallway to his office. Nearly all of the "providers" in the large pediatric clinic, physicians, nurse practitioners and physician assistants, would do their charting in the exam room with the patient and their parent (or God knows who else brought them in that day) so as to be available for questions or clarification, but not Dr. Fowler. He simply could not do it and, after many years, he decided he simply didn't have to. Let the pharmacists explain the medication. Let the office staff explain everything else.

It didn't take long for Edmund to flip through the toddler's record and enter his observations. He glanced at the clock. It was a good day due to a couple of no-shows and he gently swung his door shut with one foot. His lanky frame stretched back in his leather chair as he clasped his hands behind his head, disturbing the reading glasses jammed on top. He glanced at his fairly illegible but highly informed scribbling.

"Ignorant twenty-something Welfare Mom brings in her hyperactive, miserable 2-year-old – who's hyperactive due to a diet rich in junk food and miserable due to a steady diet of stupidity and neglect. . ."

Edmund snorted. What he wouldn't give to be able to write the truth in these damn records. What he wouldn't give to be able to speak the truth, as he saw it. But he learned long ago, working in Viet Nam on soldiers who were no more than children, to keep his mouth shut. The last thing anyone wanted was the truth. As he saw it.

He stared off into space for a moment, then shuddered and shook his head, short grey ponytail bouncing back and forth a little. He loosened his tie in order to breath. Twenty-five years! The nightmares had receded long ago but some memories continued to flash in and out like lightning bolts. A soft knock on his door brought Edmund to his feet.

"Dr. Fowler?" The young nurse sporting a ponytail of her own popped her head in when he opened the door. She wore a scrub top with Disney characters marching across it, white pants and sneakers and looked for all the world like an older Mousekateer.

"Your 4 o'clock is ready, just a little early."
"Oh, okay, fine Brenda, fine. Thank you."
"You're welcome!"

No one could be as unceasingly cheerful as this one, Edmund mused, watching her bounce away, a toy otoscope in one hand. She had been pretending to look at a child's eardrum, no doubt, to teach them about the procedure and allay anxiety. He figured she just hadn't encountered "real life" yet, therefore her unfounded optimism. A part of him wished she never would.

Edmund snatched the chart from the plastic holder on the door of Room 3 to see what lay ahead. He was known in the past for insisting that staff use patients' names, not room numbers, to identify them but with God damn corporate health care, as well as the pace and complexity of medical care increasing at breakneck speed, he long ago had given up. He even had to work at remembering his patients' names. On his bad days he visualized them as a flood of human need inexorably flowing toward him like a slow lava river created by some far away eruption.

Edmund immediately identified his next patient by the weight and condition of the medical record. The details of her case popped into his mind as he reviewed his most recent entry. This one was interesting, and challenging. Claire had undergone numerous medical tests, all unremarkable. Her mother was a health care professional, and able to provide a pretty good history. She had brought her daughter to Dr. Fowler for a couple of years, and he had yet to provide a satisfactory diagnosis which would explain her symptoms, although he had done his best to treat them. And she was getting worse. Edmund was just about ready to refer her on to another specialist as the pediatric cardiologist had proved to be no help whatsoever. Dr. Jones had provided the lack of help in a detailed, three-page report which reviewed all of Edmund's work to date, with a couple of add-on tests to rule out a few cardiac abnormalities he hadn't considered. At least Dr. Jones had concurred with Dr. Fowler's lack of abnormal findings in this 6-year-old who appeared healthy but apparently wasn't. And the insurance company had paid that specialist handsomely for it.

Edmund purposefully diverted himself from thoughts of inequities in pay structure and regrets about career paths not taken, and reviewed the little girl's recent lab work. Normal once again. He sighed and closed the record, moving to accommodate another pediatrician heading down the hallway.

"Carl."

"Ed. How's the wife?"

"Fine, just fine, thanks."

Edmund entered the examination room and found a pretty, solemn girl with hazel eyes and long, heavy brown hair held at bay with a large white bow, the ends of which fluttered when she turned her head. Claire sat on the examination table and held her mother's hand. Her mother could be described as pretty also, an older version of the girl with nearly oversized eyes and the same heavy hair swept up and piled high on her head. Edmund recalled the father as being distinctly unattractive, scrawny with small eyes and large glasses. He also didn't say much, deferring to his wife.

Claire had been hospitalized after what was described as a syncopal episode, a sudden loss of consciousness without evidence of seizure activity. By the time she was brought to the ER she looked fine but was admitted for further testing, including the cardiology work-up. No significant findings.

"Dr. Fowler! How good to see you again," Claire's mother Elizabeth exclaimed, smiling. Claire didn't smile and eyed him suspiciously.

"Well, hello Elizabeth, hello Claire," Edmund exclaimed in kind. "I imagine you'd rather not be seeing me on this beautiful day."

"Oh, Doctor, we're just hoping you can make Claire better. She had another fever last night, up to 102.2. And she vomited for no reason at all a couple of days ago. Twice. Her father and I are just so worried."

Edmund kept his eyes on Claire as her mother spoke. The girl didn't seem particularly concerned and waited patiently for it to be over. Edmund had noted this resignation when she was younger, even when she had her blood drawn, something kids fought tooth and nail. Not a peep from Claire.

Elizabeth seemed genuinely concerned. Edmund ran through the usual list of questions to make sure he hadn't missed anything. He asked about travel even though he was quite certain he would be aware if Claire traveled, since he saw her frequently.

He paged through the record, frowning. This fever thing certainly wasn't new, nor was the vomiting. Claire often got dehydrated, but didn't look that way today.

"Any loose stools?" She'd had a work-up for parasites that was negative.

"Why actually, she did have a little diarrhea," Elizabeth said. "I think it was on Wednesday."

"Mommy..." Claire dangled her Rainbow Brite doll by its thick green braids.

"Just a minute, Claire, I'm talking to the doctor."

Edmund dismissed Elizabeth with a wave of his hand. He wanted to hear from Claire. "What do you want to say, Claire?" He sat down on the rolling stool in order to speak with her. Edmund was over 6 feet tall and instinctively knew to meet children eye to eye. He popped his reading glasses on top of his head and cupped his chin in his hand, looking thoughtfully at Claire. She looked at the floor, suddenly shy.

"It wasn't diarrhea."

Edmund could hardly hear her. He was taken aback as Claire had never contradicted her mother before, at least not in front of him.

"What do you mean, Claire?"

Claire glanced at him, and then looked at the floor again. "It wasn't diarrhea, even though Mommy called it that."

"How do you know it wasn't, Claire?"

She bounced her Patty O'Green doll, and said matter of factly, "I know what diarrhea is."

Wisdom from a 6-year-old, Edmund thought.

Elizabeth jumped in. "Perhaps I'm mistaken, or I've forgotten. I've just been so worried. . ."

Edmund found this interesting. "Claire, how have you been feeling lately?"

"Fine," she answered quickly, then looked at her mother. "I guess okay. . . Sometimes not so good. Sometimes really bad."

"She looked pretty awful with the fever, Doctor. She didn't even want to play. And that's not like Claire. She went to bed early."

"Well, Elizabeth, she's looking okay to me. Her vital signs are fine, she doesn't look dehydrated, and her recent laboratory tests are normal. It's possible she had a virus that she was able to fight off, so we can simply wait and see how she does. I do not advocate any further testing at this time. But of course, you may bring her back in if you have further concerns."

"No labwork?"

"Not at this time," Edmund repeated.

Elizabeth took the doll from Claire and grabbed her hand to help her jump to the floor. "All right, Doctor Fowler, we will do whatever you recommend. We certainly want to do the right thing by Claire. Isn't that right, honey?" Elizabeth straightened her daughter's hair bow and smiled down at her. Claire headed for the door, her doll forgotten.

"Yes, go and have fun, enjoy the day!" Edmund smiled at Claire too. There was something about her that was endearing, and he was grateful that he didn't have to subject her to any more procedures, needle sticks or other onerous medical necessities today.

3

Mama

Mary opened the creaky screen door slowly to soften the sound.

"Mary?" Her mother's scratchy voice was barely audible from the living room couch where she had been stationed since she stopped climbing the stairs a few months ago.

"Yes, Mama, it's me. Where's Daddy?" Late afternoon sun slanted into the room as Mary entered and quietly made her way to her mother's side. She leaned over to kiss the hollow cheek and saw that her mother's eyes stayed closed, as if it was too much effort to look at her. Mary's throat squeezed tight and she wanted to run.

"He's out. . . tractor."

"The tractor broke down again?" Mary scanned the tables ringing the couch. No sign of lunch, just an empty water glass.

"Mama, you thirsty? I'll get us some lunch, although it's nearly time for supper. Has Daddy eaten? He won't be in a good mood if that tractor can't be fixed." Mary darted to the adjoining kitchen, thinking she could warm up the pot roast for her father, but her mother couldn't eat it. A small pile of dirty dishes in the sink notified her that her father had already eaten. Bastard. He didn't even get her a glass of water.

She didn't run the water long because her mother couldn't tolerate it too cold. She couldn't tolerate much, and the sight of her on the couch, motionless, brought Mary nearly to tears. Swiping at her eyes with the back of her hand, Mary sniffed and scurried to her mother. She gently lifted her head up and positioned a plastic straw between her lips. Her mother sucked on it but didn't have the strength to bring the water up the tube. Alarmed, Mary snatched it out of the glass and threw it on the floor. She cradled her mother's head in the crook of her arm and brought the glass to her lips.

"Mama," she crooned. "You gotta drink. Just take a little sip, Mama. Come on."

Her mother opened her eyes but looked straight ahead, as if Mary wasn't there.

"Mama?" Tears slid down Mary's face. "Please take a drink, Mama. Please!"

Mary watched her mother, willing her to move, her face distorted through the tears. She carefully laid her head back down and searched for a Kleenex in the pocket of her sundress. The kitchen clock chimed. Her mother looked like an old rag doll, limp, button eyes fixed on nothing, the fabric of her face frayed and discolored. Mary gently placed a hand on her mother's chest. She could hardly feel her breathing. Time stopped as Mary knelt next to the couch and started to pray, heart pounding. She wasn't sure anyone was listening as she mouthed the Our Father, the Hail Mary. . . it seemed no one ever heard her. *Please God, don't let her leave me. Just don't let her go,* Mary thought.

Maybe she should call her father back into the house. It felt like she should do something. He should do something. Something should be done. She realized she was still holding the fresh water glass and carefully placed it on one of the tables, making sure to put a magazine under it so it wouldn't make a ring on the wood.

Mary felt sick and realized she was breathing fast. She made her way to the bathroom and splashed water on her face. She gripped the pink Formica vanity and slowly raised her head, meeting her own eyes in the mirror. Blue, not brown like her father's. Dirty blond hair cut at chin length with her mother's stylist scissors to emphasize her own hollow cheeks, now grown well past her shoulders. Everyone always said she looked like her mother. Who will cut her hair?

Mary didn't shift her gaze, but suddenly it felt like she was abruptly transported to a bedroom she'd never seen before. It was all in pink, right down to the tasseled canopy over the children's bed.

The bed was white with carved wood and a canopy that matched the pink gingham bedspread and ruffled sham pillow. There was a young child lying on top of the neatly made bed and Mary could see her little white face with her eyes gently closed, the spread of brown hair. She looked peaceful.

Other details beyond the bed were blurry. Mary realized with a shock that the child was not moving, like her own mother on the couch, and was sick real bad, just like her Mama. Maybe dying.

Mary sucked in her breath and tried to scan the room, a familiar feeling of helplessness taking hold of her. Where are the parents? Is anyone going to help this child?

She knew from experience that the vision would fade, leaving her in a panic. She didn't know any little girls, and she certainly didn't know how to help this one. Maybe she couldn't be helped. Why would God send her these visions and then not show her what to do? Mary longed to scoop up the little figure and spirit her away to a hospital where people knew what to do. She felt powerless to rescue this little girl, lying there on the bed all alone without even a blanket pulled over her.

Mary knew what it was to lie in bed, alone and afraid, praying for salvation that never came. Praying for a miracle. She had been that child, although she herself had never been close to dying. She had certainly wanted it, in fact sometimes prayed for death to come. Maybe that was a sin, and God was punishing her. Maybe the visions were His idea of a proper punishment. Have the punishment fit the crime.

A surge of anger broke over her, and it broke the vision as well. Mary found herself back in the bathroom, eyes wide in the mirror, hands aching. She let go of the vanity and her hands dropped to her sides.

She took a deep breath staring at her reflection, then turned on her heel and marched to the back door. She swung it open with surprising force and entered the wood porch. The sun was high, the trees full, and Daddy wouldn't come in for hours yet. Mama always loved the summertime.

"Daddy!" Mary hollered. She was glad that her voice sounded strong. Daddy hates a cry baby.

"Daddy!"

Finally, he emerged from behind the barn, a tall, lean, spare man with wild black hair and a greying beard reaching the first button of his shirt. "What the hell, Mary! You know I'm working out here! What the hell is it?"

"It's Mama. She's real bad. We gotta take her to the hospital!" Mary felt sick again but stood firm, glaring at her father.

"Jesus Christ, Jesus Christ!" He shook his head and spit, hands clenched at his sides. "I'm not taking her to no hospital! What the hell are they going to do to her in a hospital? You think they're gonna make her all better in some fancy hospital, Mary? Them doctors are gonna fix her? Jesus Christ!"

He shook shaking a fist at her, glaring back. Mary felt herself shrinking.

"No more of your foolishness, girl, just let me work!" Her father stalked away, disappearing behind the peeling red barn. Yellowed remnants of daffodils and tulips which had swayed gently along its edge surrendered to the tall grass threatening to overtake them.

Mary remembered planting flowers with her mother when she was barely old enough to hold a trowel. Every year since they had eagerly and patiently watched for the yellow, orange and red bursts of color, telling each other that this planting season would yield a better crop, and that they'd be okay. But they never were.

Mary was convinced that hard living had caused malignant cells to run wild in her mother's private parts, and now they spread throughout her body like the fast-moving water of the creek spilling over after a bad storm. She could see the creek in the distance. When it was all stirred up like that, after a heavy rain, she couldn't hear her father's cursing over the rush of the water.

Her mother hadn't escaped him so easily but became a master of blending in to the background and at times disappearing into it altogether. Sometimes when Mary saw that her father was on a rant, kicking at piles of old lumber or even chucking tools across the yard, she would feel terrified and glance around for protection before hiding herself. Her favorite spot was the old elm tree at the edge of their property, far enough away that her father wouldn't bother to look. Mary still considered herself an expert tree-climber, sardonically noting she didn't have much choice but to learn. She'd been five and was sitting on a fat branch, clutching smaller branches when she'd been overtaken by her first vision.

Mary swayed and reached for the rough wooden railing to steady herself. She should have known better than to ask her father for help. *God, I hate him. Too bad he never showed up my visions, in the really bad ones.*

"I'd like that, I really would," she said out loud to herself. Shivering in the sunlight, she turned and entered the rundown farmhouse to tidy up. She'd put water on for tea and would sit with her mother.

4

THE POET

EDMUND FOWLER PULLED into the circular drive lined with flowering vegetation, thanks in large part to his wife of 26 years, Rhonda. At age 51 Rhonda was three years younger than Edmund and five times as energetic. But then, regular tennis matches and daily runs around their upper middle-class neighborhood kept her fit and youthful. Sometimes Edmund felt much older than she as he juggled the demands of his pediatric practice.

He pulled his economy car into the roomy garage next to Rhonda's Jeep Cherokee and shut off the engine. After a moment the garage door ceased its metallic grating and Edmund closed his eyes, savoring the silence. It was early yet, a beautiful evening as the sun slowly retreated, but Edmund didn't move except to slowly lean back until his head rested, ever so slightly against the padded headrest. He felt a bit guilty, avoiding Rhonda's sweet, optimistic self for a few minutes, then told himself it's not her he's avoiding but human contact in general. He just needed a moment.

She opened the door of the house, catching him in the act. "Edmund?" Her voice sounded concerned and he felt foolish.

Edmund swung his car door open with a flourish. "Hello there, sweetheart!" He hopped out, offering a small smile, eye contact. "How was your day?"

"Better than yours, apparently. What are you doing out here?"

"Oh, you know . . . just thinking." Edmund rubbed his eyes and slammed the car door, nearly brushing by her before remembering the quick kiss. His briefcase felt heavy.

"You look tired." Rhonda looked into his eyes as no one can. She was short but always managed to capture his gaze and read his soul. "Maybe we can walk after dinner. It would make you feel better."

"Maybe." He knew they probably wouldn't. She'd serve him a well-balanced and flavorful meal and he'd digest it in his leather chair, surrounded by pediatric medical journals while she did the dishes, humming along with the music they both could agree on. They rarely had the TV on, or went to the movies.

By the time she finished the dishes he'd likely be asleep in his chair and she would be loath to disturb him. She would work on her crafts, write poetry or read, and upon rousing himself late in the evening he invariably would be alone. This gave Edmund a couple of hours to research topics of concern to his patients or review research articles. He was acutely aware that this arrangement suited him more than his wife, but she never complained. It seemed like she let him do what he needed to for his patients. They joked about starving on the money she brought in with her writing, with Edmund reminding her that she added beauty and truth to a world in short supply of it.

He and Rhonda had planned to start a family after he returned from Viet Nam, but by then things had changed, for him at least. He simply couldn't abide the thought of bringing a child into that world, and after a while Rhonda had stopped asking.

Edmund dropped his keys on the Corian counter and removed his tie, tossing it over the back of the recliner. He moved to the sink to wash his hands, then leaned against it, arms folded, studying his wife in turn. "I didn't hear about your day."

"Oh, you know. . ." Rhonda pulled a layered salad out of the fridge and set it down next to his keys, which she snatched to hang on an ornate brass hook positioned next to the garage door.

"The McDonalds are getting divorced. It's hot so we're having salad and a chilled soup."

"The McDonalds?" Edmund pushed back his shoulders. Rhonda got soup from the fridge while Edmund washed up. She placed the tureen next to the colorful twin bowls on the counter and offered him a ladle.

Edmund dished up, carefully streaming a dripping half circle of soup into the bowls.

"You don't seem surprised, Rhonda."

"Well . . . I guess I could see it coming." She attacked the salad with wooden tongs from their trip to Peru and mounded their plates high. Edmund lifted the bowls and brought them to the table, with Rhonda joining him. Mozart's Symphony No. 25 built to a satisfying climax in the family room behind them.

The music reminded Edmund of that small reading room in the Memorial Union at the University of Wisconsin where they had met. He had stumbled upon the intimate, darkened room as he searched for someplace new to study, vowing not to return to the Medical Library for a good, long time. Edmund eyed the small, round carved tables each graced with a green glass Banker's lamp to illuminate the immediate area for reading.

He closed the old, heavy door behind him, shutting out the cattle line of students laughing and chattering in between classes. He was surprised to hear classical music, having never seen a room like this one. Clutching his heavy backpack, Edmund swept his long, brown hair back to scan the room for an available seat. Mozart masked occasional bursts of footsteps across the tile floor. He felt as if he had stepped back in time.

He spotted her across the room, mahogany hair trickling down her back from a loose pony tail, a flowered tunic tracing the outline of her compact body. Edmund eyed her as he threaded his way through the tables to settle relatively close to her, quietly moving his chair so he could see her without turning his head. He folded himself into his seat and pulled out *Practical Clinical Pathology* from his backpack.

Edmond had bookmarked the pituitary gland, the so called master gland for it's orchestration of diverse bodily functions. He wanted to nail down Addison's disease, but he wasn't reading, actually he was reading the same paragraph over and over.

Glancing at the young woman who had captured his attention, Edmund wondered why: she wasn't unattractive, but she wasn't the type of woman that turned heads when she entered a room either. He felt a kinship with the way her studies kept her engrossed.

He watched her slowly lift her head and tilt it backward with her eyes shut and hold it there a moment before moving it slowly from side to side. She brought her arms up, resting her hands on her shoulders and pulled back in a long stretch. Edmund noted the square shape of her face framed by scattered tendrils and the graceful way she moved.

He realized he was staring. He even tried to see what she was studying but he was too far away.

She sighed, glanced at her watch and gathered her book, folder and papers together, noiselessly stuffing them into her own backpack. It took less than a minute for her to stand and sling it over her shoulders and onto her back and Edmund was already on his feet, heart pounding. What was he doing? He slowly made his way to the door while glancing her way to keep her in sight. He couldn't let her get away.

They got to the door at the same time, perfect. Edmund pulled the door open and held it for her to pass through and she smiled at him and whispered, "Thanks." His heart hammered away in his chest as he smiled back, and followed her into the white noise of the hallway.

"Hey!" Edmund called out as she started to move away. He lurched forward and put his hand on her arm, lightly, not grabbing her. She turned in surprise to look back at him and he saw that her eyes were dark brown. They were in the middle of a stream of students, buffeted back and forth.

"Don't I know you?" he said.

She squinted a little as she looked up at him, considering this. "I don't think so."

"I saw you sitting there, back in the reading room, and it just seemed like we had met before." Pretty lame, Edmund thought, but he was too overwhelmed by her to do better.

"No, I'm pretty good with faces. I don't recall yours." Her voice was loud, too, over the noise, but it still sounded nice. Feminine, but not a high pitch. He stood silently listening to her, looking at her. Unsure what his expression was, he hoped he wouldn't scare her off.

"Have a nice day." She smiled again, and turned to leave so Edmund reacted swiftly. He stepped to her side, dodging a couple of students and bent over her, managing a little laugh.

"Maybe I could convince you. Get a cup of coffee with me and I'll persuade you that we know each other."

She studied his face and for the first time he experienced that soul-searching gaze. Despite his sudden, inexplicable longing for her, he felt reassured that she would somehow know that he was okay. More than okay. Maybe worth a shot.

"I'm on my way to class. Sorry."

He caught his breath. "Where's your class?"

"The Humanities Building. Not far. But I have to get going."

"Let me walk with you."

"But aren't your things still in the reading room? You'd hate to have them walk away." She tilted her head, nearly laughing at him. Hope tugged at him as he smiled back.

"I'll chance it."

"Take a chance?"

"Yeah."

They snaked their way to the Memorial Union entrance and Edmund kept a slight distance to avoid bumping into her. She walked rapidly, not wanting to be late, and didn't say anything. He didn't either, and focused on honing his observational skills. Edmund realized he hadn't met many women who required effort on his part, which piqued his interest. Who was she?

They stepped outside into breezy sunshine bouncing off of the white marble steps, making it hard to see. Instinctively he breathed deeper, savoring the air and his unfettered movements.

It took a minute to reach Langdon Street, bustling as usual with people, primarily college students who dodged cars as they crossed the street at random. Edmund had no idea where the Humanities Building was as he had never been there. His humanities credits went back to his undergraduate days and had been mandatory or he would have skipped them entirely.

"So where do we go from here?"

"Straight ahead along the side of Library Mall."

"Maybe I should be carrying your books. I left mine behind."

"I'm fine."

It was a glorious September day and Edmund felt energized and happy. He liked walking outdoors, liked ignoring his studies for once, liked being with someone he wanted to be with. He was aware that he'd have to make up some story about them having met before but the task at hand was to get her to meet him later. And he'd better get on with it before they reached Humanities, wherever it was.

Library Mall was pretty with trees still lush green, a treasure in Wisconsin which was winter barren for months on end. Edmund gazed at an endless variety of people passing them with fresh interest. He didn't get to enjoy campus sights and sounds, as he was usually restricted to a hospital. A twinge of resentment stirred in him.

"What time will you be done?" Edmund tried to sound casual.

"Done?"

"With class."

"Well . . . it's a graduate seminar so it'll be a couple of hours."

"Two hours?" His mind raced. Edmund had planned to study for at least that long and didn't meet with his study group for several hours.

"Two hours." She sounded amused. She looked at the sidewalk but her full lips curved up just a little. So, she was a graduate student. Maybe art. Or some kind of writing.

"What do you study?"

"I'm going for a Master's in Fine Art. Poetry. With a Minor in English Lit."

"Wow." To Edmund it sounded like she was in another world, and then he told himself that was accurate, she was. About as far away from the endocrine system as you could get.

"Wow?" Now she really was laughing at him. He found himself fumbling for words, someone who rarely fumbled with anything.

"That's the Humanities Building straight ahead," she motioned. They were closing in on State Street which bordered the massive building.

"So, you'll get out around 3:30?"

"That's correct." She looked up at him, now grinning.

"Kind of late for coffee and kind of early for supper so maybe we could get some ice cream? I can come back here in two hours. My treat."

"Hmm . . . ice cream. It's a lot of running around for you, returning in two hours. Are you trying to avoid your own studies, um, whatever your name is? The person I've never met before in my entire life?"

He couldn't help but laugh and she joined him. He was relieved he didn't have to make up some stupid story. She was on to him.

"It's Edmund. Ed. I don't really like either name."

"Edmund." She rolled it around in her mouth like a hard candy she was tasting. He was glad it didn't rhyme with anything. If she rhymed words at all. Poetry, for God's sake!

"Well, Edmund, I'll meet you here in two hours, for ice cream. It's hard to say no to ice cream. You don't need to come with me further. I'll see you then." She summarily dismissed him with a wave of her hand and started crossing the street.

"But wait, I didn't get your name," he shouted over the traffic.

"Rhonda!" she yelled back over her shoulder, not breaking her stride.

Their lives had been intertwined since that day, and Edmund still marveled that she put up with him at all. Now as he sat across from Rhonda in their dining room, his stomach brought him back. He reached for the salt, arranging his meal like a surgical tech lining up instruments for a minor procedure.

"What do you mean," he asked, "you could see it coming?"

Rhonda was focused on her salad. "Hmmm?"

"The McDonalds. Divorce."

"Oh. Well, she's been unhappy for years. I could see it. Couldn't you see it? But then I ran into her in the market and we were talking and she broke down in the produce section. Over the onions, actually, which is kind of ironic."

"Really! She just started crying in the market?" Edmund could hardly visualize such a thing. He couldn't recall the last time he had even teared up.

"Well, we were talking. We must have been there for half an hour. Joyce has been in therapy and she just . . . told me a lot of things she's never said before. Not to anyone but her therapist, she said, and maybe Tom, as far as I know."

"What kind of things?"

"Well . . ." Rhonda repeated, lowering her eyes to the jumbled assortment of cheese, nuts and vegetables. "She feels like she's lost herself. Like she doesn't know who she is anymore." Rhonda jabbed at her salad. "She didn't know what was wrong or what to do." Lifting her gaze, Rhonda met his eyes. "Edmund? Are we okay?"

He felt a tightening in his abdomen, mirrored in the strings of the symphony playing. "Of course we are," Edmund said reflexively, decisively. Then he laid his spoon down and in a softer tone, repeated, "Of course we're okay." She didn't move, looking at him.

"Rhonda, you don't think . . . are there any problems here? With us? Is there anything I should know?" The tightening crept into his chest; his anger surprised him. He was angry with Joyce. He doesn't need this after a long day! Joyce McDonald can go to hell for all he cares.

"I was just thinking . . ." Rhonda mused. "Maybe I could benefit from talking to someone. You know, a counselor. This is about me."

"Rhonda!" he looked at her in amazement. "Psychotherapy? What are you talking about?"

"Just for me," she repeated firmly.

"You don't know who you are anymore?" Edmund tried unsuccessfully to avoid sarcasm. He was just so tired. And now this.

Rhonda didn't reply and Edmund knew better than to push her. They ate in silence with an unusual degree of tension between them. Finally, Rhonda asked him about his day and he began talking about Claire. Sometimes he just had to vent, and he trusted Rhonda's discretion. At times she was helpful, offering a fresh perspective. And she was well acquainted with discussions of bodily functions and fluids over dinner. Edmund briefly reviewed Claire's current circumstances, and she listened with apparent interest.

"And then Claire said," he continued, "'I know what diarrhea is, and it wasn't diarrhea, even though Mommy called it that.'"

"How old is she? Isn't she 5 or 6 years old?"

"She's six now."

"Sounds older. I'm sure she does know what diarrhea is, the poor thing. She's had every symptom in the book."

"Someday I should compile a time line of all of her symptoms," Edmund said thoughtfully. "But maybe what she really needs is a therapist," he added sardonically, still annoyed with Rhonda's desire to see one.

"How does her mother deal with Claire's illness?"

"Elizabeth? She does fine. She rattles off Claire's symptoms so well that I get a clear picture of what's going on. Or at least as clear as it can be. And she seems to appreciate how hard I'm working on all of this."

"I mean, isn't it upsetting to her that her daughter is sick all the time? Claire's an only child, right?"

"She seems to take it as well as anyone could. She's very invested in her daughter. Very attentive, and worries about her constantly."

"And Claire's father?"

"Well, I haven't seen him much. I think he works a lot."

"Even when she's in the hospital?"

"I've met him a few times, yes, when she's in the hospital. He seems caring enough, but Elizabeth is a respiratory therapist and acquainted with medical jargon, so she's the mouthpiece."

"So she shoulders the burden of Claire's illness? That's a lot. Maybe at this point Elizabeth should be seeing a therapist."

"Maybe we all need a therapist."

Rhonda didn't reply.

5

NOT AT HOME

"**W**HY ARE YOU doing this?" Elizabeth asked loudly. She handed Claire her doll and motioned for her to go to her room. Tony looked at his wife, bewildered. He had told his daughter she could go out to play, outside, where germs thrived in hidden bird droppings and unpredictable dogs roamed the street. At least that's how Elizabeth saw it.

"Why would you let her go out there?"

"Because it's a beautiful day and she . . ." Tony stopped talking and turned away, running one hand through unkempt hair trailing down his neck before taming it under his Red Sox cap. He readjusted his glasses. Tony knew better than to go against his wife's wishes when it came to Claire.

Elizabeth's round face showed an odd mix of anger and calculation... what, he didn't know? He never knew what she was thinking. But she clearly had an agenda and although he knew what it was, it just didn't make sense to him. He was aware that Claire was old enough to explore and climb and, God forbid, play with other children, but Elizabeth kept her reined in like a champion race horse who could not risk injury. And for all of her precautions, Elizabeth carted that little girl to the doctor's an awful lot.

Tony shook his head, looking down at his feet like a reprimanded schoolboy. He was 30 years old yet he felt those feet start to shuffle almost of their own accord, taking him out the back door of their modest ranch house and onto the small, sunny strip of grass which served as a backyard.

He let the door slam behind him, which was unusual. More typically, he would quietly shut out the sound of his wife, or his daughter.

Tony checked the pockets of his baggy overalls for cigarettes, found half a pack and pulled one out. He noticed as he lit it that his hands were shaking, kind of like his insides. He inhaled, making the tip glow red as he walked toward his Chevy pickup. Squinting, Tony appreciated the brief sun and solitude.

Reaching his vehicle, he held out his hands, fingernails dirty due to long hours working in the garage but now steady. Crawling in, cigarette clenched between his lips, he fumbled for the key so he could head to work and a day filled with people and things he could understand.

∾

Annie sat quietly in her office with Mary, periodically glancing down at her sketchy nursing assessment and follow-up notes. Mary was trying to regain her composure and failing; she was clearly in crisis and Annie hoped she wouldn't have to rehospitalize her. She held out a box of tissues.

"I'm sorry," Mary whispered, rocking back and forth, arms folded across her chest as if to keep herself from breaking.

"Don't apologize, Mary, you need to cry. You just lost your Mama," Annie said softly, using Mary's term for her mother. She noticed a tightness in her own throat. So sad, and potentially dangerous for Mary. Annie leaned in.

"I just don't know what to do!" Mary cried out suddenly, mouth twisting.

"What to do?" Annie repeated, needing clarity.

"I can't stay there. Not now. Not with Mama gone!" Mary's words filled the room. The white noise machine whirred in the hallway.

"Are you afraid?" Annie didn't mention Mary's father. She didn't need to, recalling their first session, and there might be other factors that put Mary at risk. Annie watched her closely.

"I don't know . . . I don't know how I feel. Bad. Really bad," Mary muttered. She seemed to collapse in on herself, staring at the blue rug. Annie decided to push it.

"Mary, are you more afraid of your father now that your mother is gone?"

Mary's head jerked up and she glanced at Annie. "I really don't know."

"He's hurt you in the past." It was a statement of fact.

"In the past." Mary was back to whispering, tears held at bay.

"When you were little?" Annie kept her language vague so that Mary could fill in the blanks. She was pretty sure Mary had a traumatic past that would affect her recall of specific time and events.

"Yes." She was back to one-word answers.

"Did he hit you?" Annie started with the easiest form of abuse to talk about.

"No, he never hit me. He hit my mother a couple of times."

"Did you witness that?"

"Yes."

"How old do you think you were when you saw that happening to your mother?"

"I don't know."

"Before Kindergarten?"

"I never went to Kindergarten."

"Oh." Annie decided to go off topic for a moment. "But you went to elementary school?"

"My father wanted me home schooled. He thought Kindergarten was stupid. I went to first grade but then stayed home. My mother taught me. And I worked on the farm with her."

"I see." Annie shelved the business of home schooling for the moment. "You grew up with a father that hit your mother, at least on occasion. That sounds pretty rough. But he didn't hit you."

"No, but his yelling was so . . ." Mary took in a deep breath. "Scary. I would hide."

"Was your mother able to protect you?" Annie hoped there had been even rudimentary protection for Mary growing up.

"No . . . she would hide, too."

"Hide with you?"

"No."

Annie formed a picture of a terrified child hiding herself all alone, aware that her only protector was hiding, too. She softened her tone, looking intently at Mary's face.

"Did your father ever touch you in a way that made you feel uncomfortable?"

Mary sucked in her breath, making a whooshing sound. Her eyes darted toward Annie, then away, like an animal hiding in the brush. Annie needed Mary to say it out loud.

"It's common, Mary, unfortunately. I hear it a lot." Annie tried to normalize the terrible thing that should never be normal.

"Yes," Mary whispered.

"Has he done that recently?"

"No."

"And you never told?"

"No . . . my mother couldn't take that. She had enough to deal with."

"And I understand you don't have other siblings? Your parents didn't have previous relationships?"

"No."

"I see." Annie leaned back against the couch, giving Mary a moment to process the disclosure, which was monumental for her. She considered the risk of recalling this disturbing detail of her relationship with her father which could further destabilize Mary's condition, especially since she had buried it for years. But Annie needed to know what they were dealing with in the wake of the loss of her mother.

Mary resumed rocking, clutching herself. Silent tears coursed down her cheeks and she squeezed a wad of tissues.

"Mary," Annie said gently. "Are you able to sleep? Are you eating?"

"No . . . maybe a little. I got a couple hours last night. It helped knowing I could see you today."

"And the eating?"

"No."

"Do you ever get dizzy? Vomit?"

"No. I do drink water. I know I have to."

"That's good. But you need to eat a little. Are you taking your meds?"

"Yes. They help me fall asleep."

"Okay. I'm glad to hear you didn't stop your meds." Annie paused, thinking of how to proceed. She had to tread carefully. "We need to talk about your safety, Mary. With your mother gone, there could be a risk that your father will . . . act differently." Vague language, sort of a fill-in-the-blank with Annie feeling she couldn't assume anything. She certainly didn't want to alarm Mary with visions of what could happen. The poor woman had enough of her own visions.

Mary didn't fill in any blanks for Annie, repeating, "Act differently?"

"Yes." Annie wasn't about to offer more and simply looked at Mary expectantly. She watched her start to struggle with fear as her breathing became rapid and shallow.

Avoiding Annie's gaze, Mary said, "I don't know what that man will do. I hate him."

No ambivalence, Annie thought. Mary's feelings toward her father could mobilize her into action to protect herself. It was certainly better than paralysis.

"You said you can't stay there."

"I can't stay there, I won't!" Mary's defiance was heartening but Annie still wasn't sure how much she could expect from her.

"There's a women's shelter in this area. You could go there." Annie kept it simple, wondering how Mary might react.

"A shelter," Mary breathed. "I didn't know there was such a thing. Of course, I never would've left Mama. But now . . ."

"Unless perhaps you have family who would take you in for a while?"

"No."

"Your aunt?"

Mary's chest heaved. "He would look for me there! It would be the first place he'd look and he'd bring me back!"

It occurred to Annie that Mary had the look of her cat when he'd race to the back door from the woods at the sound of yelping. A coyote kill.

"You could get a restraining order against him," Annie said. "It would offer some protection for you and your mother's sister." Annie was careful not to guarantee protection; Mary's departure could escalate her father's violence.

"What's a restraining order?"

"It's an order issued by the court in cases of stalking or domestic violence. Your father would be told not to come near you or contact you."

"But what if he did?"

"He'd be arrested."

A pause. "And then what?"

"There are no guarantees, Mary. We would take it one step at a time. However, it seems pretty clear you can't go back there."

"No."

Mary seemed to contemplate this information as her breathing slowed. She sat up, unlocking her arms, hands loose in her lap. She remained silent until moving to throw the wad of tissues into the wastebasket, overhead, with a precise flick of her wrist. She made the shot from several feet away and commented, "Just like chucking potatoes."

Turning to Annie, Mary said, "My aunt will take me in."

6

VIET NAM

Rhonda scanned the Medical Office Building directory, feeling like she was on Edmund's turf. She tried to look like she was interested in a surgeon, a cardiologist, a nephrologist, anything but the Behavioral Health Clinic located on the third floor. It was down the hall from orthopedics; maybe she could fake a limp. Maybe not, since she always took the stairs. She marched toward the stairwell like a soldier on a mission.

She was quite aware that the pediatric practice was on the first floor and she could be spotted by one of Edmund's colleagues, or his staff, people she had gotten to know over the years. Maybe she'd see one of his patients, or even Edmund himself. But she had booked the appointment for 11AM, knowing Edmund was probably running late and trying to finish his morning patients with enough time for lunch. Rhonda was also aware that Behavioral Health would waive her co-pay as a professional courtesy to Dr. Fowler's wife, which hardly seemed fair, as Dr. Fowler certainly could afford payment for . . . her treatment. Good lord, what was she doing here anyway?

Despite her short stature, Rhonda climbed the stairs two at a time. She enjoyed feeling her legs work and showing them off with a short skirt she had worn for many summers. She absently pulled her fitted shirt over her taut abdomen, trying to avoid thinking about what her new therapist might ask her. She had obsessed about that last night, staring into the dark with her thoughts swirling so fast and so hard she could almost see them.

Yanking the office door open a little too hard, Rhonda scanned the waiting room. She had never given up her maiden name, but it was a small community, especially for a doctor's wife. Relief loosened the knot in her stomach. No familiar faces, no one offering her more than a passing glance.

Rhonda sat down and reached for the *Providence Journal* which was scattered on a nearby table. She hadn't gotten to read it yet and liked to keep up with current events. The front page story caught her eye:

```
Two-Plus-Four Agreement Talks to pave the
way for political reunification of the
two German States under German Chancellor
Helmut Kohl after the collapse of the Ber-
lin Wall last year'.
```

Rhonda shook her head imperceptibly. She still felt disbelief at the history shattering events under President Reagan, who she hadn't liked and hadn't supported but . . . the memory of him in West Berlin, the actor in the role of a lifetime with American flags waving behind him: "Mr. Gorbachev, take down this wall!"

Rhonda scrutinized a photograph in the paper of mostly young people attacking the wall with hammers and chisels an ocean away, seeing herself in them, with her friends a generation ago protesting the Viet Nam War in Washington. They had been tearing down the war with peace signs, not hammers.

Rhonda recalled being filled with dread the day Edmund enlisted, although she knew he had his own battles to fight. His letters captured a tiny slice of the war in sickening detail while she had soldiered on, writing poetry and prose, teaching at the University. The work had seemed paltry and meaningless.

When she found her voice, it was writing op-ed pieces, magazine articles and anything she could get published to criticize the war. Rhonda had contemplated getting arrested at one of the rallies before it happened. Rhonda Gibbons, cuffed and charged with a crime. It was shocking but not unexpected, and done in good company.

Rhonda stared at the newspaper in her hands but didn't see it. She saw Edmund and herself at the airport upon his return, he jetlagged and grubby, she feeling awkward after their initial heady embrace. She had been surprised at the sight of him, brow lined deep, grey at the temples, seemingly wise in the ways of desperate men. Good lord, had she really brought him flowers?

As time went on, Rhonda lacked recognition of the jigsaw puzzle that had become their lives. She wanted him to talk, but he pushed it down, deep and dark, and didn't let her in, even when the nightmares woke them both. Sweating, shaking, breathing hard, he would get up and tell her to go back to sleep. He'd silently stalk about the house. Even if she got up with him and made him tea, tried to hold his hand, he'd shake her off without so much as a glance. "Go back to bed. I'm fine." He was the doctor, the healer. Healer, heal thyself.

With a start Rhonda realized that the therapist would probably hear some of this, about old wounds that may still be festering. She was aware, having done her own research, that PTSD could occur in people close to trauma but not directly experiencing it. But it had all happened so long ago and she herself had never had a nightmare. Could the war still be thrusting its cold tentacles into their lives?

A woman entered the waiting room from the clinic hallway after her session, preparing to leave. Rhonda's heart sank. It was her next-door neighbor Shirley, the last person she cared to meet now, in this place. Rhonda thought of Shirley as medium: medium stature, medium build, medium looks with medium brown hair of medium length. Shirley faded into the background until she spoke, and she spoke a lot, about everybody and everything. Rhonda lifted her newspaper higher, to no avail.

"Rhonda?" For a medium person, Shirley had a large voice.

Rhonda lowered the newspaper and mustered a smile. "Shirley! How are you?"

Shirley cackled, "I'd say I was fine, but here I am, and we both know what that means! How are you, Rhonda?"

"I'm fine. Nice to see you, Shirley." Rhonda tried to resume reading the paper but Shirley plopped down in the chair next to her, whispering loudly. "I see Ruth here and she's fantastic! Who do you see?"

Rhonda was rescued as the door to the interior hallway opened. A woman no taller than herself but nearly two decades older smiled at her. "Rhonda?" She readjusted her glasses and motioned with one hand. "I'm Ruth. Come on in."

Shirley hissed, "You're gonna love her, Rhonda!" and winked at Ruth, who seemed to be making a mental note that the two women knew each other.

Rhonda threw the newspaper aside, grabbed her bag and followed. The baseball in her throat made swallowing difficult. Rhonda was amazed at how nervous she felt, noting that seeing Shirley in the waiting room made everything worse. At the same time, she wondered how much this grandmotherly woman might be able to help her.

Ruth walked briskly down a short hallway into a cozy office with a multicolored area rug and a mismatch of comfortable chairs. A bright Central American wall hanging dominated one wall across from a knock-off of Monet's *Poppies* and a couple of diplomas. "Please have a seat. Anywhere."

"Thank you." Rhonda ignored an enormous chair that threatened to envelop the sitter in favor of a rocking chair with a rainbow crocheted throw tossed across its back. Ruth stationed herself at her desk and swiveled her chair around to give Rhonda her full attention. "So," she said, "before we get started, it seems you know someone in the waiting room?"

"God, yes," Rhonda said without thinking. "I mean, it was awkward, seeing her here."

"Yes, I am sorry about that, but it's a small community. I can try to schedule you on different days so you don't run into her again."

"That would be wonderful. Thank you."

"Of course. Now, what brings you in today?"

"Oh," Rhonda said, feeling somehow caught off guard. She gripped the smooth round ends of the arms of the chair and crossed her legs, trying not to rock.

"I guess it's just . . . I guess I'm just not happy. I should be happy but I'm not." The words hung in the air long enough for Rhonda to register their shock value. She couldn't believe what she had just said. Of course she was happy, but there were things. Just some things getting in the way.

"You're not really happy?" Ruth clarified, as if it was the most normal thing in the world. Her pleasant expression bore a small smile but her eyes penetrated Rhonda from behind her glasses.

"It's not that I'm not happy. I'm a happy person, really. I'm pretty easy to please, actually . . ." Her voice trailed off. Rhonda realized she had no idea how to explain how she felt.

"You said you should be happy."

"Well, I have everything I could want. My husband is a pediatrician who works in this building, and he's very generous, and we have a good life together." She was talking too fast.

"Your husband is a pediatrician?"

"Yes, Edmund Fowler. Do you know him?" Rhonda's heart beat faster.

"No, not really. I treat adults, and we've never crossed paths." Ruth smiled again and Rhonda felt a current of relief.

"It's a big enough place," she fumbled, "that you wouldn't run into him, necessarily."

"Yes."

Silence. Rhonda knew it was her turn to speak. She wasn't used to being at a loss for words. Words were her trade, her livelihood, although it was damn lucky she had married a doctor with a good paycheck or she'd be waiting tables to make ends meet.

"Sss . . . so," Rhonda stuttered. "It's just the way it is. If you can't change something you have to accept that. Move on."

"Move on?"

"Oh, I don't mean leave the marriage. I love Edmund. I just wish. . ." Rhonda glanced down at the rug.

"It sounds confusing." Ruth's voice was reassuring, soothing really. "You love your husband, he's good to you, you have a good life together, but yet there's something. Something you have to accept."

"Yes. I just wish he was around more."

"I'm sure that you do."

"And he works too hard."

"I can only imagine." After a pause Ruth continued. "So, you don't see him as much as you would like? How is that for you?"

"Lonely." Rhonda blurted it out and felt immediate relief. She would never dare tell Edmund this and she felt she couldn't admit it to her friends either. "But what can I do? I can't tell him not to treat his patients. They need him."

"You need him."

"I don't get to need him. I'm not sick."

"I see." Ruth nodded her head. She was no longer smiling.

"This is a common problem," Rhonda said. "I know a couple of doctors' wives and we commiserate sometimes about how little we see our husbands. However . . ." She swallowed hard around the baseball and continued. "Edmund and I never had children. I think it would be different if we did have children."

"Did you both want children?"

"Initially, yes. We talked about it when we decided to get married. And even before that."

"And then?"

"And then Edmund went and enlisted in the Army, on his own. He felt he had to go to Viet Nam." Rhonda heard the angry edge.

"How did you feel about it?"

"Well, I guess I'm not sure. No one bothered to ask me."

"You couldn't tell him not to go. Because he had to treat his patients?"

Rhonda thought for a minute. "Maybe there's a theme here," she said slowly. "Maybe there are other things I can't tell him, and other things that I'm not asked."

"Maybe." It felt like Ruth was validating her pain.

"It's ironic, you know," Rhonda continued. "I'm a poet. A writer. I say things for a living. I try to speak the truth."

"But this is different."

"Yes."

Rhonda processed Ruth's perspective as she gazed out the window at wisps of clouds skittering against a sapphire sky. It was her own perspective, she silently corrected herself. Ruth didn't really know her. But in a short time, Ruth had learned volumes about her. What else had she buried?

"Rhonda, were you or Edmund infertile?"

"Oh, no. I mean, I don't really know. When he came back from Viet Nam, he no longer wanted children. Actually, it was a matter of not trying. I stayed on the pill and he wouldn't discuss it much. He knew I wanted children, but by then things were different. We were different."

"Different in what way?"

"I was young and idealistic, and had become an anti-war activist. I put my heart and soul into that, and saw an ugly side of this country. Imagine regular people spitting on Vets after they came home from that nightmare! Edmund sent me weekly letters detailing a little bit of what he was going through. It was horrifying. I think he had to get it out somehow and writing it down helped him. I thought it kept us close, and I wrote back as much as I could. It certainly affected my own writing.

"But I constantly worried about Edmund," Rhonda's expression darkened. "Sometimes I felt like I was already a widow. I wondered how I would deal with that, and played it over and over in my mind. The flag-draped coffin, me dressed in black, crying. I was only 27 years old. I'd see my parents there with me; would I go back home with them for a while? What would I do?"

Rhonda glanced at Ruth who said nothing, so she went on. "Edmund did come home to me but . . . sometimes I thought we'd be better off writing letters to each other, the talking was so painful. There I was, ready to share in his experience, to help in some way, the way I had when he was gone. But he'd have none of it. He was . . ." She searched for the right word. "Distant. He was home yet he was still so far away. No one had prepared me for that. And no one had prepared him for coming home. You wouldn't think he'd need that. But he wasn't told he was shipping out until 36 hours before it happened. One day he's in a war zone amputating some young boy's leg and the next he's flying home to his family, to me. He was really, really unprepared. A big part of him stayed there. He honestly questioned going back, but I wouldn't hear of it. I wouldn't let him."

Rhonda took a deep breath. "I threatened to leave him."

Ruth sat motionless, her eyes scanning Rhonda's face. "You felt you had to."

"Yes," Rhonda whispered. She started to cry. She kept crying and cried like she would never stop, and Ruth wordlessly handed her the tissues. Rhonda wiped her eyes, her nose, and held the box gently with one hand so as not to crush it, the other gripping the arm of the chair until her fingers grew numb. She uncrossed her legs and rocked with her head bowed, a small part of her brain noting that this was why Ruth had a rocking chair.

7

Elizabeth

EDMUND RAN HIS hand through his thinning hair, down to the ponytail. He sat relaxed next to Claire who was lying in a pediatric hospital bed. Looking up, he met her mother's gaze; Elizabeth was smiling a little. Strange.

"Dr. Fowler, are you telling me Claire didn't have a seizure? Then what was it?"

"No, Elizabeth, I'm saying we simply can't confirm a diagnosis of epilepsy. The electroencephalogram showed no unusual activity, as did the MRI of her brain. She's exhibited no unusual behavior here in the hospital which could suggest seizure activity. I will discharge her on phenobarbital to prevent any further episodes, however a pediatric neurologist in Providence would be the next logical step. I understand you're willing to have Claire evaluated further?"

"Oh yes, of course! We need to get to the bottom of this."

"I recommend Dr. Zambrano, or really anyone in his practice. They're all good."

"Could you transfer all of her records before we get there? It's a bit of a drive and I want to be prepared."

Edmund smiled. Probably due to Rhode Island's small size, its natives were famous for their avoidance of travel. "Of course, but it's only 40 minutes or so, without factoring in traffic. Dr. Zambrano's office staff can give you directions from the highway. Parking, however, could be an issue so take a city map along. Better yet, take your husband."

Edmund watched Elisabeth's reaction as he took one of his cards out of his pocket and scribbled the neurologist's phone number on the back.

She took it, glanced at it and clutched it to her chest rather dramatically. "Oh, Dr. Fowler, thank you! Claire and her father and I all thank you for being such a good doctor. What would we do without you?"

"There, there," Edmund said reflexively. After several years of caring for the family, Edmund had become accustomed to Elizabeth's ways. Usually, he wished all of the mothers he dealt with were as concerned as she. But today he covertly observed Claire who was staring down at the covers on her bed. She didn't look at him, or her mother, or the TV. She sat still, as if trying to blend into the rainbow colors of the bedspread.

Edmund realized she was acting less and less like a normal six-year-old in light of feedback from the hospital nursing staff. They described her as withdrawn, likely in response to Elizabeth's overprotectiveness. Elizabeth refused to leave her daughter's side, despite their urgings for her to take a break. She would say it was her duty to assist Claire in every possible way, down to washing her face and hands for her in the morning.

When staff suggested to Claire that she do certain things for herself, Elizabeth reacted strongly, as if she and her daughter were being attacked. One nurse also observed an interaction between Elizabeth and her husband in which Elizabeth became very angry at his perceived interference with Claire's care. They argued in front of Claire until Tony backed off, muttering he was going to get a cup of coffee. He left the room and never returned. Claire hadn't seemed to notice.

"Really, Elizabeth," Edmund said suddenly. "I'm quite serious that Tony should accompany you to Dr. Zambrano's office. I think he should be there."

Elizabeth looked down at Edmund with a blank look, taken off guard. Her eyes narrowed briefly and then she smiled. "I doubt he can get off work, Dr. Fowler, but I'll certainly make a point of inviting him. Thank you for your kind concern. Maybe Claire and I will explore Providence in July, depending on how she's feeling. Claire, honey, you get to go to Providence!" Elizabeth smoothed her daughter's hair, still smiling. Claire didn't look up.

"Elizabeth, I've been thinking," Edmund said. "This is all so very stressful for you. You take the brunt of it, Claire's illness and now this hospitalization, what with your husband's work schedule and all. Also,

I haven't noticed a lot of family support. What if you saw one of our therapists so you would have someone you can talk to. It's not easy raising a bright, independent child like Claire under these circumstances."

Elizabeth froze with one hand on Claire's head. After a moment she said slowly, carefully, "Why Dr. Fowler, I'm surprised you think I need . . . therapy. But I'll consider it, of course."

"We have a couple of nurses, Elizabeth, who have an advanced degree in nursing. One of them is Annie Clark, who has expertise in comorbid conditions, meaning physical illness plus, uh, emotional problems." Edmund knew he was floundering.

"You're concerned I have emotional problems?" Elizabeth didn't even blink.

"I'm concerned that this all is becoming a bit much for you. Just go and talk to her, Elizabeth. Give it a try. I'm hoping you'll feel relieved, and perhaps less alone."

"Well . . ." Elizabeth absently stroked her daughter's head.

"I'll speak with Annie on your behalf. Let me do one more thing for you." Edmund smiled at her.

"You mean for Claire."

"Well, anything that helps you will ultimately help her."

Elizabeth shrugged. "I guess you're the doctor."

∾

"Mary, you're not using the Trazodone for sleep?" Annie was paging through her record, reviewing their past sessions, realizing she needed to check on Mary's medications.

"I don't need to. I sleep fine at my aunt's house. We're like two peas in a pod," Mary said with a wave of her hand.

"That's wonderful." Annie smiled at the woman, noting her improved appearance which probably reflected a better mood. She had ditched the baggy sundress for short shorts and a sleeveless top that complemented her slender frame. Mary appeared self-conscious as she tugged at her shorts to pull them down. Annie commented, "You look nice today."

Mary blushed. "My aunt got me some clothes. Said I needed something new and we went shopping together. She said it was time to have more fun."

"You didn't shop much with your mother, Mary?"

"We were always working. We worked hard, until she took sick, that is. Then I worked twice as hard because she couldn't."

"Do you ever miss being at the farm? It's a big change."

"God, no. My father's on that farm! My aunt says I never have to go back there. I never have to see his face again."

"When you came to see me last time you were pretty frightened that your father would follow you. It took a lot of courage to go to the police station and get a restraining order against him."

"My aunt went with me. She told the police he had hurt me in the past and he'd do it again. I think the police officer could see how scared I was. He was really nice to me."

"So your father is abiding by the restraining order? He's not trying to contact you? You don't notice him driving by your aunt's house?"

Mary paused, "It's been fine."

Annie looked up from her notes. "Fine?" She waited.

"He calls me some times," said Mary.

"He calls your aunt's house?"

"Yes."

"When does he do this?"

"When she's at work." Mary's words tumbled out. "I do the housework and cooking and I'm looking for a job. I think I'll get hired as a waitress at the new diner in town. I'd really like that."

"Your father calls when he knows you're alone."

"Yes." Mary looked away.

"Do you answer? Do you speak to him?"

"Yes." A whisper.

"Is he pressuring you to come home?"

"That's not my home!" Mary rocked back and forth and her eyes darted about the room.

"What does he say, Mary?"

"He says we're going to lose the farm if I stay away! He says he can't keep it going all by himself. He says we'll lose everything."

"I see." Annie took this in. "What else does he say?"

Mary's eyes filled up. "He says he misses Mama, and he misses me! We both lost her!" Mary collapsed with anguished sobs. Annie moved to sit close to her. They sat together as Mary cried, shoulders shaking.

"I'm so sorry, Mary. You miss her so much."

"She was everything to me."

"I know, I know."

After a time, Mary took a couple of deep breaths and mopped her face with tissues. As she quieted Annie waited for her to speak.

"He didn't really love her, you know."

Annie nodded.

"He was horrible to her. Horrible to me. We both hated him but Mama never said it. I could feel it. She was scared of him just like I was."

"I'm sure she was."

"She did her best. You may not think so, but she always . . . did her best."

"It was terribly hard for you both."

"Yes. Yes," Mary nodded her head slowly. "But now she's in heaven." Dabbing her swollen eyes with a tissue, she offered Annie a slight smile. "And I'm with my aunt!"

8

Elaine

Elaine Noble still didn't feel well, which was unusual for her. Since losing her sister to cancer and finally getting her niece Mary away from that monstrous father of hers, she felt a little vulnerable. Glimpsing her mid-fifties self in the mirror, pale and disheveled, Elaine shivered. What was unheard of was for her to cancel her classes for the day, but she had done it, not believing she could get up in front of a hundred college kids and lecture on electrical circuits without passing out. God, she felt awful.

Carefully putting the thermometer down on her bedside table, she considered her options. With a fever over 103 degrees, perhaps she should call her doctor. No, he'd just want to see her in the office and Elaine knew she couldn't sit for all of eternity in a waiting room. She threw off the bedcovers impatiently and swung her legs over the side, pushing herself to a sitting position. The room revolved around her. In a cold sweat she realized she was dehydrated and should drink something with electrolytes in it. Orange juice has potassium and fructose, but the thought of it made her stomach turn. *Maybe just ginger ale*, which she kept in the pantry for emergencies. Having lived alone most of her life, she was prepared for anything.

Lurching to a standing position, Elaine reached for her bureau. Hanging on, she took a tentative step toward the stairs.

Damn, if I'm this unsteady, how can I make it down to the kitchen? Maybe I should wait for Mary to get back from the market. No, I really can't wait. She was suddenly, overwhelmingly thirsty. And having had only water yesterday left her weak.

With enormous effort, Elaine pulled her soggy nightgown over her head and threw it on the floor a few feet away so she wouldn't trip over it. The room was settling down around her so she reached out and grabbed the afghan lying on top of the bed and wrapped it around herself, shivering. The colorful, rough yarn scratched her skin.

Clutching the afghan around her neck with one hand and bracing herself with the other, she took a couple of slow steps until she reached the landing at the top of the stairs. With one hand on the wall, she dropped the afghan to the floor, inching forward with her free hand to grab the railing. She stepped carefully down and slowly, slowly lowered herself until she was sitting on top of the afghan, dressed only in her underpants. God help her if anyone came to the front door, but she wasn't expecting deliveries and her neighbors left her alone.

Freezing, Elaine yanked at the edges of the afghan, drawing it up around her. Thankfully it reached to her chest and she gathered it into a knot in front of her. Using the railing, she inched herself forward and down each stair, one at a time. She would not give up. She figured she couldn't go back up anyway and just sitting there was intolerable, so the only way out was down.

By the time she reached the bottom step, Elaine was exhausted and questioning her own judgment – maybe this wasn't such a good idea. Maybe she should've waited for Mary to come home.

Elaine briefly smiled at the thought of Mary. It was surprisingly reassuring having her around, and she was a lot stronger than she looked. Elaine wondered what her neighbors would think if they saw her handing Mary keys to her home and to her new Land Rover Discovery.

Elaine thought of how similar they looked; on more than one occasion Mary had been taken for her daughter. The whole thing had felt like a surprising, interesting and gratifying turn of events for them both, Elaine thought, despite the grief they shared.

After sitting for a minute Elaine readied herself for the journey through the kitchen to get to the pantry and the lusted after can of soda. As she reached up to claw at the railing, her stiff neck aching, she froze. There was a man outside the window on her front walk, squinting in the bright morning light. He was looking in her direction but she was pretty sure he couldn't see her huddled one step above the floor. Elaine recognized the greasy, black hair, the beard, even though she hadn't seen him in several years.

A jolt of anger cut through her, quickly replaced by fear. If Mary showed up now, who knows what could happen? What was he doing here? What did he want? This asshole was blatantly breaking Mary's restraining order in the middle of broad daylight, on her property. Who did he think he was?

In disbelief, Elaine watched him approach her front door as she hunkered down against the wall. If the door wasn't locked, she couldn't get to it in time and she certainly couldn't reach the phone across the living room to call for help.

Heart pounding, she heard his heavy boots scrape on the cement steps, then the rasp of the door knob as he turned it. Instinctively Elaine pulled the afghan higher above her breasts, eyes wide, staring at the door. He twisted the knob violently, seeing it was locked and perhaps hoping he could break it. Elaine realized that with her Land Rover gone from the driveway he probably thought Mary was alone in the house. Maybe he was primitive enough to think he could come into her home while she's at work and drag his daughter off!

"Over my dead body," Elaine muttered under her breath, and with a herculean effort hauled herself to her feet and stood, swaying, waiting for the room to stop spinning. If only she wasn't so weak.

Gripping the stair rail and her afghan, she saw he had moved to her front window and was peering in. Furious, she glared at him, trying to resurrect some measure of authority as university professor, homeowner, sister-in-law and protector. She was aware of the threat to herself now that he had been caught violating the restraining order; he probably believed he could intimidate Mary, who wouldn't turn him in. Elaine would have no such compulsion and in fact would relish the opportunity.

It seemed like eternity as Elaine did her best to hold her ground despite the sensation of standing on deck in a squall. Jack abruptly turned and strode away down her front walk and then the driveway, fisted hands at his sides. Blood pounding in her ears, Elaine turned and crept toward the kitchen, legs nearly buckling beneath her. When she finally got to the ginger ale, she felt like she had been rescued from a life boat after days at sea. The soda gave her the strength to make it to the couch after hanging on to the kitchen counter, then the wall and the desk before finally collapsing in a bright yarn heap. She barely heard the key in the lock a half hour later, followed by Mary's screech, "Aunt Elaine! Are you alright??"

∾

Staring out the front window, Mary wondered what to do. Aunt Elaine was tucked safely in bed after drinking Gatorade that Mary had brought home, then plodding up to bed one step at a time, leaning on her. Now Mary was left alone with her thoughts, and a tidal wave of fear rolled from the pit of her stomach.

Aunt Elaine had told her in a few words about her father's trespass, in fact, his violation of her restraining order and how she had felt too sick to even call the police. She had told Mary they would talk about her father once she was feeling better, and perhaps they could ask her friend Paul for help. He was a police detective who apparently owed her aunt a favor.

But Mary didn't want to involve the police. Somehow, she knew they couldn't really help since her father would still be free to do whatever he wanted, whenever he wanted just like always. Nothing would change, except he would be furious at her for contacting the police, and the thought of him furious made her heart pound. Mary sat down abruptly. The overstuffed chair with the flowered upholstery was nicer than anything Mary had known growing up. She wished she had seen her aunt's house earlier.

The furnishings in Mary's room, the balance of color and fabric, left her wondering if Aunt Elaine and her mother really were sisters. Of course Daddy had no concept of redecorating, and putting money and time into the farmhouse instead of the farm seemed ridiculous to him. Mary trying to calm her stomach with the deep breaths that Annie had taught her.

When she got upset like this it felt like she still lived there. Mary remembered how many times she felt rooted to the spot, listening to

Mama's soothing voice through her bedroom door at the top of the stairs, trying to make out if it was safe. Mary could almost feel herself squeezing Pink Bear.

The nights were the worst, when Mama was sleeping. Pink Bear stood guard as Mary tried to keep awake. She would strain to hear the near-silent turn of the door knob to her bedroom, the quiet creak of floor boards under the weight of the monster with the huge hands. She would see its shadow, feel the covers slowly pulled back, exposing her body. She could hear him breathing, and feel her nightgown pulling up, clenching her eyes shut as he touched her bare skin in the dark. She would hear the terrible whispered reminder not to make a sound, that if she cried or moved, as sure as he was her father, he would make her mother pay. And she didn't want that, now did she?

A sticky summer breeze rustled the mini-blinds, which clacked gently. They were pulled down half-way to block the heat of the day, but Mary was suddenly cold. She also felt a little sick, but that was nothing new. She had let herself remember. Bad idea.

Mary rose from the chair to get a drink of water. She decided to persuade Aunt Elaine to drop it. No police involvement, not even her aunt's friend Paul. Let sleeping dogs lie. Don't poke the bear.

9

JON CON

THERE WAS SOMETHING about Annie's new patient that triggered a red flag. Elizabeth was pleasant, and appeared to be forthcoming, but clearly did not "own" her feelings. In fact, Annie had very few patients who were as divorced from their internal experience as this woman was – she detailed a truly awful situation with her six-year-old as if she were describing the proverbial day at the beach. Not that Elizabeth took her daughter to the beach; she had uncharacteristically pale skin for living in Rhode Island in August. She also described a phobia of germs and kept her only child under close wraps. In fact, Annie had to use a diagnosis of phobia for billing purposes, as Elizabeth denied feeling depressed or anxious and she offered no other psychiatric symptoms. The reason she gave for treatment was that "my pediatrician had wanted me to see you".

At the conclusion of their second session, Annie felt increasing concern for Claire, whose life and her mother's seemed to revolve around her health, or lack of it. A recent visit to a pediatric neurologist had apparently found nothing to explain her seizure activity, which was not captured on EEG despite a 24-hour recording. Elizabeth knew her daughter's medical history well and could cite the name and dosage of her antiepileptic medication. She said that Claire had ongoing bouts of vomiting, diarrhea and headache which predated the antiepileptic medication.

Annie felt it was helpful that Elizabeth worked part-time as a respiratory therapist so she had experiences and contact with people outside of her family. However, working in a hospital where she saw very sick people in the ICU or the Emergency Department could feed her fears about Claire.

Annie also felt concern about Elizabeth's mother-in-law. According to Elizabeth, her mother-in-law had mixed up Claire's medications on more than one occasion, and had refused to watch her when she and Tony had a last-minute change in work schedule. Elizabeth had implied that her mother-in-law could be drinking, and she also took a lot of prescription medication.

Annie made a mental note to try to get Elizabeth's husband Tony into a session with her to obtain his view of things. However, she needed to continue to build trust with her patient before suggesting something that could feel threatening.

"So, Elizabeth, when do you get time for yourself?" Annie inquired.

"Oh, I don't know." Elizabeth threw her a big smile. "I'm a mom first, and then a wife and employee. Tony knows this, by the way. Children are so vulnerable and innocent; they need protection and love and guidance. So Tony comes second, I'm afraid, since we had Claire, but he's okay with it. There just aren't enough hours in the day!"

"Your mother-in-law watches Claire while you're at work three days a week?"

"Oh, just for a few hours until Tony gets home. I'm blessed to be able to work evenings. And a smaller hospital is enough for me."

"And the commute?"

"It's not bad."

"But you never really got to my question about what you do for yourself. For a little me-time." Annie returned the smile.

"Oh, I don't know," Elizabeth repeated, looking up at the ceiling. "I love to read, and sometimes I let myself do that. Thirty minutes in front of educational TV won't hurt Claire, I tell myself."

"We all need a break."

"What do you do when you need a break, Annie?"

The question took Annie by surprise and she looked up from her notes. Elizabeth was smiling.

"I'm blessed to have lots of interests," Annie said carefully. "But let's get back to you. Anything else, Elizabeth? Do you exercise?"

"I used to walk with Claire in the stroller, of course, but for the last few years we walk around the block or window shop. Claire likes that."

"But she may slow you down a bit. Last week you told me you used to be a runner."

"Oh yes, the price of parenthood!" Elizabeth laughed but it never reached her eyes. Annie felt like she was being scrutinized, and wrote the word "guarded" to describe this woman who seemed to be less and less forthcoming.

"By the way, Elizabeth," Annie said as she changed the subject. "You had previously indicated some concern about your mother-in-law's behavior. Do you worry when she's alone with Claire? Before your husband gets home?"

"Oh no, not really," Elizabeth brushed off the question, "she's fine. She would never hurt her granddaughter."

"Even unintentionally?"

"She's not that stupid," Elizabeth said swiftly.

"But she is . . . erratic."

"Hmm . . . I never thought of her that way."

"Unpredictable, perhaps?"

"Let's say eccentric. She makes me crazy, but she wouldn't hurt Claire."

Annie had asked Dr. Fowler if Claire had ever been brought to the Emergency Room with an injury. He indicated this had never happened. Additionally, she had met all of her growth and developmental milestones within a normal time frame.

"She makes you crazy?" Annie echoed.

"Oh, sure, the usual things, I guess."

"Such as?"

"Well, she's a nurse's aide. But she doesn't work. She says she can't because she's in pain all the time from a back injury. But I know she can. When nobody's looking, she moves just fine. She spends her days on the couch and expects my husband to drop everything and run to her side. I think she's addicted to pain pills and her doctor keeps ordering them. She lies to him to get more."

"Have you or your husband spoken to her doctor?"

"Tony refuses. He just won't do it."

"Did he tell you why he won't speak with her doctor? It sounds like a bad situation."

Elizabeth shrugged. "You know men. They don't talk."

"So, your mother-in-law may be impaired on pain pills?"

"She's fine when she's with Claire. She would never hurt her granddaughter," Elizabeth repeated coldly. Annie let it drop.

"I guess I'm wondering, Elizabeth," Annie visualized tiptoeing around potential land mines. "I'm wondering how it must be for you, worrying so frequently about . . . things? Not having anyone but Tony to confide it? As you said, men don't talk."

"Well!" Elizabeth leveled her gaze at Annie with arched eyebrows. "I must say, Annie, the way you put things, I just never think of it that way. I have my family, and they need me, and every day I get up and do what's right by my daughter and my husband. I deal with my mother-in-law the best that I can."

"It sounds that way," Annie affirmed. "And your mother? She's in Florida, right?"

"I don't talk to her. The woman is insane."

"You left Florida and never looked back?"

"That's right. I never go back there."

"But your sister is still there? Your younger sister?"

"She lives with her. As long as she lives with our mother," Elizabeth rolled her eyes, "we won't be doing much talking. It's just the way it is. I've accepted it."

"But weren't you close to your sister growing up?"

"Not really. She's 3 years younger than me. I was always the one who had to take my mother's crap and she was the little angel who could do no wrong."

Elizabeth's voice had hardened and she stopped herself, putting on a gentler tone. "Annie, you're really nice and everything, but I just can't see how these questions are helping my situation. My daughter's sick and that's all there is to it."

"Which must be hard for you," Annie tried to sound persuasive. "It would be hard for any mother, especially a mother who wasn't treated well growing up and chose to leave her mother and her only sister."

"Like I said, Annie, I never looked back. I'm better off without them." The hard edge was back and Elizabeth shifted gears. "So, I'm not sure this is helping me or Claire, but I'll tell Dr. Fowler that you tried. You did a good job."

"What if you came back for one more session? I do think talking to someone could be helpful, Elizabeth."

"I'm really not sure it is." Elizabeth had abandoned the smile.

"I'd like to tell Dr. Fowler that we gave it our best effort, Elizabeth. I appreciate you signing a release of information form so I can speak with him. You do so much for your daughter and your husband. Please do just this one thing for yourself. One more session. Then I can refer you on if you'd like, to another therapist."

There was a pause before Elizabeth retrieved the smile. "Okay then, one more session."

"Thank you, Elizabeth."

༒

Ruth and Annie sat across from each other in Annie's office, clutching early morning cups of coffee from Java Hysteria. They had known each other for several years. It was a symbiotic relationship in that Annie helped Ruth's patients who needed medication, and Ruth offered years of clinical social work experience for Annie seeking a fresh perspective on a therapy patient.

Every now and then Annie consulted the hospital psychiatrist or even referred a patient to him for medication management. She appreciated her ability to provide both psychotherapy and medication management at Jon Con.

"So! You have a patient to discuss in this wee hour of the morning," Ruth said with a grimace. "If I retire, who will be here to discuss patients with you before your day begins? And who else can you bribe with a simple cup of black coffee? Thanks, by the way."

"You love it and you know it," Annie retorted. "And I don't see you retiring any time soon. You're one of the best therapists around, so let me know what you think of my new patient. Well, not so new. I've seen her for a few months now. Let's call her 'M'."

"'M' it is. How old?"

"32. Single. Until recently lived and worked with her parents on the family farm. Dad's abusive, verbally and sexually, although she hasn't been in a sexual relationship with him for several years. She never told anyone, and moved out recently after her mother died of cancer."

"That's rough," Ruth nodded sympathetically. "Was she able to prepare for her mother's death?"

"At some level. She threw herself into caring for her mother, who was ill for a couple of years, and also tried to keep things going on the farm. However, she had a short-term involuntary psych admission at Westbrook Hospital before she was referred to me."

"Depression?"

"Psychosis. She didn't meet criteria for a depressive disorder but did receive a diagnosis of anxiety. Apparently, her father overheard her talking with her aunt on the phone about one of her visions and called rescue."

"She has visions?"

"Yes. It seems her aunt has them, too. Her mother's sister, that is. She referred to the visions as the family gift. 'M' is close to her."

"What does your patient see in, um, these visions?"

"She claims to see the future. She said she saw the commuter train derailment in Sarasota Falls before it happened."

"Really!"

"Really."

"In living color?"

"Well, the visions are detailed and this one was quite distressing to her when it happened. She's been on Risperdal for two months without improvement and I've increased it twice."

"Delusions don't respond well to antipsychotic medication," Ruth mused.

"Yes, but this isn't a classic delusion. She may be delusional about having hallucinations," Annie said wryly, "but why would she be having visual hallucinations? She's not having seizures, as far as I can tell, and her imaging was fine at Westbrook. She has no neurologic symptoms, in fact, I sent her back to the neurologist for another look. He just thinks she's crazy. But she's not. She's not even anxious, since moving in with her aunt. She seems to be grieving her mother appropriately, and that's another thing she shares with her aunt. That and these . . . visions. Which are more than visual hallucinations, it's like she's living it when she has them."

"I take it your patient isn't highly educated."

"No, home schooled, then worked on the farm."

"Is her aunt educated?"

"She teaches electrical engineering at the University."

"Really!" Ruth repeated. "Married?"

"No, they're both single. "

"'M' has had other visions?"

"Yes, one in which she saw a little girl lying on a bed. She felt the girl was sick, and it bothered her that she was alone. She said it really shook her up. Somehow she felt the girl could be dying."

"Well, you have to admit, at one time 'M' was a little girl, alone in bed, and probably feeling sick herself, what with her history of incest."

"I thought of that. But she provided a lot of detail about the Sarasota Falls derailment; she really made it come to life. She claims she saw it two days before reading about it in the newspaper. She never talked to anyone about the derailment and couldn't even talk to her mother about the vision, as her mother was sick herself. So 'M' called her aunt. She was so distraught that during the call she became careless, and her father overheard the conversation."

Ruth's brow descended over her eyes as she mulled this over. "Do you think her father was truly concerned about her? Or was her psych admission something else entirely?"

"I think it was a display of power. He used the crazy card when 'M' went to the police to obtain a restraining order against him, bringing up her recent psych admission. But her aunt was with her and was believable when she vouched for 'M'."

"So, she got the restraining order?"

"Yes. He's violating it by calling her, of course."

"No surprise there." Ruth shook her head. "I assume you're working on that with her."

"Yeah, we're working on a lot of things. She's making progress but as you can imagine, she'll need weekly sessions for a while. So, what do you think of these visions, Ruth?"

Ruth considered the question. The fingers of one hand supported her chin, nearly hidden under the sagging folds of her cheeks. Annie had learned to take this petite woman seriously; she was an expert witness in the Rhode Island court system and defended her patients with wise ferocity.

"Well, males in some Native American tribes went on a vision quest as a rite of passage. However, they fasted four days and went into a trance state before they experienced visions," Ruth said thoughtfully. "Does 'M' go into trance? Does she dissociate?"

"She does lose time when these visions occur, but only a few minutes. She doesn't seem to dissociate from present time when she's not having a vision. Her memory seems coherent. But there could be gaps in childhood memory. I haven't worked with her long enough to figure that out."

"And you don't really know how bad the abuse was."

"Not at this point. We've had to focus on the present because she's had so much going on. And we need to work on her feelings of safety with me and some coping skills before we go digging up her past."

"Of course, of course." Ruth smiled impishly. "There are more things in heaven and earth, Horatio, than are dreamt of in our philosophy."

"Oh great, a Shakespearean quote. How very helpful, Ruth!" Annie laughed.

"By the way, Annie, do you ever feel, at an intuitive level, that 'M' is, uh, confabulating?"

"You mean taking me for a ride? That hasn't happened since I was new at this game." Annie laughed again. "But no, not at all. She's more avoidant than attention-seeking, and I don't see her as personality disordered. Not yet, anyway."

"Always a good thing to rule out. Well, 'M' is certainly interesting. You'll get a clearer picture of this over time, Annie. But do keep me in the loop. I'd like to know how all of this unfolds."

"Of course, absolutely. Like you said, who else can I talk to at this hour?"

10

FRANK

RHONDA SIZED UP the man standing beside her. She was a good judge of character, and she liked him. Not pushy, not selling himself, with an easy confidence. She also couldn't help but notice his strength after years of landscaping work.

"So, Frank, you come highly recommended. This would be a lot of work. Could you accommodate us?"

"Well, Mrs. Fowler . . . "

"It's Gibbons. Please call me Rhonda."

He smiled a little and she noticed his smile tilted to one side. "You're right, it would be a lot of work. Why did you wait until September to install a waterfall in your back yard? And to do this amount of landscaping?"

"Because I realized I need to be happy," Rhonda answered impulsively, then blushed as he turned to look at her. "And my husband agreed to pay for it. I prefer this over Aruba." A clumsy attempt at humor.

Frank turned his attention back to the rolling expanse of lawn interrupted by Rhonda's substantial vegetable garden. "So, you'd want my guys to work around your garden? I assume you'd want us to leave that alone?"

"I'm sure that's possible. I've been working on it for years." She gestured toward the large wooden box in the far corner of their property. "I made the compost bin myself. It feeds the garden."

"Well, it depends on what you want back here. I think your vegetables must have been beautiful this summer, but they don't fit with a formal garden scheme."

"I'm not very formal." Rhonda felt good, hearing praise for her years of hard work from this stranger who knew his way around a garden.

"How many years have you lived here? The front yard has been nicely developed as well, and your flower gardens are really wonderful."

Another wave of appreciation. "We've been here 22 years. As you can see, gardening is one of my passions."

"Do you entertain a lot? Will you need to accommodate a lot of people here in the back yard?"

"Not so much. We don't have a lot of family in the area and we're pretty quiet. At least my husband isn't all that social."

"So, this space will be primarily for you and your husband."

"And the wildlife. I'd love a couple more butterfly bushes."

"Yeah, I see a couple of bird feeders. You have a real nice spot back here. Secluded."

Rhonda glanced at him. Frank was looking at her again, weathered face creased into a smile, eyes a startling blue. She looked down, blushing again. What was wrong with her?

"Yes, we enjoy it." She sounded a little stiff. After a moment Rhonda felt him shift his gaze back to the yard.

"You'd like to sit by the pond, you said. I'm seeing a couple more boulders over there," he pointed. "I would put some flat rocks around the edge of the pond and make a stone wall for you to sit on. I'll have to build up the area to create the waterfall and would install tall grasses, flowering shrubs and plants. Whatever you like. We can do a mix of perennials so you always have some color.

"You'd have plenty of sun. Then I'd extend your patio with your table, chairs and umbrella nearby, stone steps leading to the pond, with ground cover and mulch. Low lighting after nightfall, it would be nice to be able to see the stars when you're out here at night."

"That sounds amazing. I was also hoping for water lilies in the pond."

"Of course. Do you have any interest in a koi pond?"

"That I'm not sure about. Perhaps you can guide me about what a koi pond would entail, the upkeep and that kind of thing."

"It would be my pleasure." Frank smiled his crooked smile, flashing those blue eyes at her. Rhonda felt suddenly energized, heart beating faster before she reined herself in, telling herself to calm down and wondering if she looked ridiculous.

"I can submit a plan for your review in a couple of days," Frank said. "Then we can discuss the cost, depending on what you want. I can recommend flowering plants that do well in Rhode Island, and you may have your own ideas."

"I'm reliably here in the afternoons, and you can stop by any time. It's when I work," she said.

"You work from home? What do you do?" He looked genuinely interested.

"I'm a writer. Freelance, poetry."

"No kidding. I don't know any writers. Should I have heard of you, Rhonda Gibbons?"

"Only in some literary circles, I'm afraid," Rhonda laughed. "I did teach a writing course at the Neighborhood Guild."

Frank looked at her a bit longer than was socially acceptable and this time she didn't look away. It was a nice feeling, being seen. She hadn't felt this way in a long time.

"It was nice to meet you, Rhonda." Frank turned to leave. "I'll call you before I stop by with the plans." He headed around the house toward his truck parked in the circle driveway and Rhonda followed.

"You don't need to," she said rather loudly as he strode away.

"Yes, I do. I can't afford to waste time," he said over his shoulder.

"Okay," Rhonda said simply, and watched Frank as he climbed into his truck with lithe, quick movements. With a small wave goodbye, she turned on her heel to enter her quiet, orderly home, alone with her thoughts that were anything but orderly.

～

"No, no, no . . ." Mary whimpered, twisting her head from side to side as if she was back on the psych ward. Elaine, the early riser, happened to be passing by in the hallway and heard her through the bedroom door. She hesitated and then knocked gently. "Mary? Can I come in, honey?"

"No, please! Please!" It sounded as if Mary was still asleep, and Elaine decided to intervene. She opened the door as Mary sat bolt upright in bed staring, chest heaving. Elaine instinctively sat at the edge of her bed and drew Mary toward her, hugging her, rocking her as Mary collapsed against her, sobbing.

"Oh, Aunt Elaine, it happened again! I saw her, the little girl, the one I told you about. Why did I see her again? I think she's dying and I can't help her and she's all alone! Oh, God!"

Elaine held her close. She made shushing noises and stroked her hair, as if Mary was the child she used to know.

After a few minutes Mary pulled away, wiping her eyes with balled fists. "Why does this happen to me, Aunt Elaine? Why me? I know you see things sometimes." She looked at her aunt. "Do you have these horrible visions of people hurt and dying that come true? My God!" She folded her arms over her stomach and bent over them.

"I see things," Elaine said slowly, "voluntarily. That's different. I allow myself to see without focusing, and go inside myself to learn more information about whatever the question is. I see things that have happened already, for the most part. You can learn to control these visions coming to you, Mary."

Mary stared at her. Elaine decided it was time to forge ahead and explain a few things, now that Mary was safe and sound in her home and Elaine could help her assimilate them.

"Sometimes police use psychics in this way. So does the FBI," she said.

"I never heard of that," Mary breathed. Elaine smiled, aware that Mary had never really been exposed to life, despite her best efforts over the years to give her books, magazines, anything to prepare her for a future on her own. Elaine had found out accidentally from her sister Linda that such reading materials had not only been banned from the house by Jack, but burned in the back yard in front of Mary, who eventually became adept at smuggling them in.

Elaine quickly replayed Linda's descent into hell - the surprise visits to the farm early in Linda's marriage which distressed her so much that eventually Elaine stopped coming. They would talk by phone when Jack was in the barn or tending to his crops. Linda would practically whisper, even though he was out of earshot. The phone receiver would abruptly slam into its cradle, leaving Elaine afraid and angry.

She began meeting Linda at the grocery store in town once a week. Linda would look about furtively while they strolled around the store and talked. She would wonder out loud if her husband had followed them there, which was ridiculous as Jack only had one vehicle, a dirty pick-up truck he used on the farm.

Later on, Linda took more risks, once she had a child. Elaine would take Mary for an hour while she shopped for food. They'd go out for ice cream or hot chocolate, depending on the weather, or just sit on a park bench and talk. Elaine could see how bright she was, and with the innocence of youth Mary would make casual remarks about life with her father that enraged Elaine. Over time she became more and more guarded, cautiously picking her words and looking at Elaine for a reaction.

Elaine knew her sister couldn't leave after years of trying to get her to move out, and to live with her. Also, it never got to the point where Elaine felt justified in taking Mary from Linda in order to get the girl away from Jack. With her savings Elaine knew they could have disappeared and started over someplace. But leaving Linda alone with Jack after losing the only light in her life had seemed cruel and Elaine couldn't bring herself to suggest it.

She remembered pleading with Linda after their mother's death to attend her funeral, all the while knowing it wouldn't happen. Elaine went alone.

"Aunt Elaine?" Mary interrupted her thoughts. "How come you never gave me anything to read about psychics, if there are others who . . . are like us?"

"There's not much out there, I'm afraid, or I would have. You never spoke to your mother about these visions?"

"Not for years. She wasn't very receptive."

"No?"

"It was like she just couldn't go there. Maybe she was afraid my father would find out and think I was crazy, or use it against me. But now I've been held for days against my will on a psych ward because of them. It did make me feel crazy, as I couldn't explain any of it. All I got were drugs. I'm still getting drugs," Mary said bitterly.

"You were held against your will because of your father. I wish you would have called me."

"I couldn't. I felt like he had won. And despite being really doped up I was scared. They kept calling it anxiety. It was all I could do to hold myself together enough to get out of there so I could take care of Mama. I was so afraid she would die."

Mary looked at Elaine. "Have you ever helped police solve a case?"

Elaine was silent for a moment and then smiled. "Just once."

"Once?"

"Yes, as a favor to a friend. A good friend."

"Who?"

"The police detective I told you about. I haven't seen him for a very long time."

"Why not?" Mary asked.

"We had . . . sort of a falling out."

This surprised Mary. "What kind of falling out?"

"Let's leave it at that," Elaine said brusquely. "Right now I'm more concerned about you, Mary."

"But were you able to help him solve the case?"

"Yes, I was."

"How, exactly?"

"I was able to tell him," Elaine thought for a moment, "where the body was. It was a homicide."

"Really! You saw the body? In your mind?" Mary could hardly believe it.

"Yes, after I obtained some of her belongings from him. From the detective. I went to the police station and held her sweater."

"And then you saw her," Mary breathed. "Wasn't that terrifying?"

"Unpleasant, yes. A bit disturbing. I was able to take him, Paul, to the field where she had been buried. But we went alone, since his police colleagues weren't too receptive to the idea of a psychic helping them."

"You went alone? Weren't you afraid?"

"No, I knew we were safe." Elaine left it at that. She didn't want to overwhelm Mary by telling her she could sense the killer was not in the area.

"You took the detective right to the spot where she was buried?"

"We had to look around a little bit. But I had seen specific landmarks in my mind which made it fairly clear. Then we found the freshly turned earth."

Mary looked alarmed. "You didn't dig her up, did you? Right then and there?"

Elaine smiled again. Sometimes Mary seemed much younger than her years. "No, honey, Paul came back with a specially trained dog and other law enforcement professionals. He made it look like the dog found her body."

"You didn't get the credit, Aunt Elaine? They didn't see how you helped them?"

"I didn't need any credit. I knew what I did."

"And the detective knew what you did."

"Yes, Detective Rice is his name." Elaine glanced away. "It took a while, to gather evidence and build a case. Are you assuming it was a male who committed the crime?"

"Men are violent."

Elaine tapped her cheek with one finger. "We need to introduce you to some more men."

Mary laughed. "Well, there is one who comes into the coffee shop an awful lot. And I always seem to wait on him. Isn't it funny?"

"Do you like waiting on him?"

"Yes," Mary said, looking down with a rush of color to her cheeks. "He seems nice. But sometimes it's hard to tell, isn't it, Aunt Elaine? I mean, how do you know if you can trust men? Or anyone, for that matter?"

"You go by how it feels, in here." Elaine laid her hand gently over Mary's heart. "Your intuition never lies. But sometimes we just don't want to listen to it. You may notice that it doesn't go well for us when we ignore our intuition."

"You're so right, Aunt Elaine! I used to know when my father was ready to explode, way before Mama! I used to motion to her," Mary made a gesture with her hands, "to stop talking, and she would stop, because it just made him mad. I was right every time."

Elaine saw her opportunity. "But now you need to use that internal voice to guide you in other ways, with people you want to trust."

"Well," Mary said, "I had a good feeling about the lady who hired me at the diner. The owner's daughter, Cindy."

"And that's going well."

"Yes, she's been very patient with me, since I never used a cash register or waited on people before. She taught me how to remember what people order. She's so fast, and so efficient, I really like how she works. And she's always kind. Always."

"That's important."

"That's critical. I can't work in a place where people aren't kind. I couldn't."

"Yes, that's very important. I like your passion, Mary. You're beginning to decide what you want to do, not just what you have to do."

"Well, I'm not a college professor."

"Not everyone needs a college professor, but most people need a kind waitress in the local eatery. I'll bet people talk to you, Mary. Do they ever tell you things they should be telling a therapist?"

Mary looked surprised. "I never realized that, Aunt Elaine. But you're right, sometimes they do. And I'm happy to listen to them if I have time."

"And if you don't have time?"

"I tell them I'll come back if I can and I usually do. But even if I don't, they seem to appreciate it. I can tell."

"You can tell . . . by how it feels?"

"Yes."

Elaine couldn't help but hug Mary, wondering which one of them was benefiting more from finally getting her off that damn farm. Linda would be happy if she could see Mary now. Maybe she could.

11

Trio

Edmund felt happy, managing to leave work early and drive home through the fading brilliance of a perfect October day. Red and yellow leaves spun gently to the ground in a glass bead curtain of color.

He sang along with Elvis on the Oldies Station, something he usually resisted, not caring to admit he was on the other side of young. He glanced at himself in the car mirror, and thought briefly about a couple of women who had seemed attracted to him. Outside of a little ego boost, he never took the bait.

Rhonda had put up with his idiosyncrasies all these years, he mused, and still looked good in a swim suit. Edmund rubbed his midsection, noting a bulge above his belt. Maybe Rhonda would take a walk with him today, or maybe he could even jog a little.

He used to run, wearing reflective gear in the dark after work, even though their subdivision was quiet and pretty safe. He really needed to get outside again.

Sometimes after lunch at his desk Edmund would walk quickly around the parking lot at the Medical Office Building, just to clear his mind, when the waiting room wasn't stuffed to the gills with children and parents all wanting a piece of him.

Edmund turned up Rock Around the Clock and swerved into his driveway faster than usual. He circled around to the front door and shut the engine off, intending to take Rhonda out to dinner someplace. He realized he didn't surprise her enough, change it up once in a while. Had he become so utterly predictable?

Rhonda's poetry surfaced in his mind. It was about as far away as you could get from Latin-based medical terminology. Edmund had always felt that medical language sheltered the doctor from equal footing with the patient. In treating kids, he saw their uncanny ability to sniff out a phony. If you really didn't care about them, you were in for a fight.

She had been quite focused on her poetry recently and seemed frustrated, stymied in her drive to get published. Maybe that happened to creative people in the latter half of their careers, but Edmund felt powerless to help her. Maybe she needed a surprise.

She wasn't in the kitchen as he had expected, in fact the stove was cold and the countertop barren. No dinner prep here. Edmund strolled around the roomy, comfortable house intent on finding her. She didn't seem to be anywhere. Finally, he heard her outside, on the patio. He headed for the sliding glass door leading to the back yard and stopped cold.

Rhonda was standing next to an attractive man in jeans and work boots; she was talking animatedly and laughing that laugh of hers. Ordinarily Edmund would stride out that glass door, hand extended to greet the newcomer. Except this guy didn't seem like a newcomer. He and Rhonda had an easy camaraderie that caused Edmund to shrink back from the door into the shadows as if he'd been slapped. They clearly hadn't heard his car in the driveway, and he hadn't activated the garage door as expected. Hell, he wasn't expected at all, not at this hour, anyway. Is this what went on when he was at work?

Edmund watched them with his heart thumping, standing close together in the waning light of that gorgeous day. He could feel his pulse in his throat. He took in the backhoe parked on the grass, the modest truck and trailer in the driveway, the shovels and freshly dug earth.

This must be the landscaper, here to work in their backyard, here to install a goddamn waterfall for his wife, and for him, behind their house. Edmund searched his memory, trying to recall if Rhonda had told him the work was starting in earnest today. Maybe. Maybe he hadn't paid attention since it was her project, after all. It belonged to her and this guy who looked like he had stepped out of a Marlboro commercial.

The landscaper looked animated as well, as much as Marlboro men get animated, and Edmund watched him lean in to his wife to say something that made her laugh again. The goddamned energy efficient patio doors blocked out their words, but Edmund observed the intimacy of their conversation. It looked like they were dating, for God's sake. Edmund felt sick.

He tried to talk himself down off the ledge as he watched them. Maybe this wasn't what he thought it was. Maybe he was reading a whole lot into what he was seeing. Maybe it was the project that bonded these two, and nothing more.

Edmund took in a long breath and let it out slowly between clenched teeth. He couldn't stand here forever, staring. He strode to the glass door and slid it open, plastering on a news anchor smile.

"Well, well," he said heartily, extending his hand. "You must be our landscaper."

"Edmund!" Rhonda exclaimed, stepping back. "You're home early." Edmund couldn't read her expression but her body language said it all.

"Edmund, is it?" the landscaper asked, taking his hand in a firm grip and looking him in the eye. "I'm Frank. Frank Zambrano."

"End of the alphabet," Edmund said stupidly, measuring this man. Up close he was even better looking, with a strong jaw and closely cropped curly dark hair. He could be several years younger than Rhonda. Edmund wondered briefly if the lack of grey or a receding hair line made him look younger than he was.

Frank laughed a little. "Yeah, yeah. Last to be picked for anything."

"I didn't see your truck when I pulled up."

"Oh yeah, I backed it up over there, to unload some tools." Frank motioned to it. "I'm always careful about the lawn, by the way, try not to leave unnecessary tracks."

"We appreciate that." Edmund tried not to sound sarcastic.

"Frank is pretty much done for the day," Rhonda said. She sounded louder than usual. "But I was commenting on how much progress he's made after only two days here."

"Two days?"

"Yes, he was here yesterday. I didn't mention it because you got home so late. You were tired."

Edmund felt irritated. "Well, Rhonda, I'm not sure a backhoe in our yard constitutes idle conversation."

"I had told you Frank would be starting this week. You just forgot."

He hated her soothing tone. But she was right, he had been pretty quiet last night, preoccupied with other people's problems, and had settled in to his chair after eating for a brief time before sleep caught up with him. Edmund found himself wondering what she did while he was sleeping in the evening, something he had never really considered. Maybe she was lonely.

His mind vaulted to a scenario in which she and Frank spent time on the phone together, planning their project and then talking about other things.

Edmund silently chided himself. Rhonda couldn't have known this guy that long, as they were just getting started. Frank had come for an estimate, and two days of excavation. Hardly a torrid affair. Edmund wished he had paid attention to Rhonda's ramblings about recent events, as perhaps he recall with more detail. He should have listened to her.

"Well, I better get going," Frank said. "It was real nice to meet you, Edmund. I appreciate working here and I think your backyard is going to look real nice with the pond, some plantings and the waterfall. I'll bring in some extra rock, and also take advantage of that large boulder over there." He pointed to a vague dark shape at the periphery of the yard. "But I guess Rhonda filled you in on the details."

Edmund felt caught off guard. "Yes, some details. I think it'll be great," he agreed lamely.

"And we all need to get dinner," Rhonda said rapidly. "You both must be starving."

"Thanks again for lunch," Frank said, smiling at Rhonda, who avoided his gaze. "I'll see you late morning tomorrow as I have a few things to do in town."

"That'll be fine," Rhonda said.

"Whenever," Edmund said. He stood with them awkwardly until Frank turned to go. He impulsively placed his hand on Rhonda's shoulder and gave it a squeeze, realizing he didn't touch her enough. In an odd way he missed her.

"Goodbye," Edmund said, wishing he could say good riddance.

"Have a good evening," Rhonda said, smiling at the retreating figure. Edmund realized how much she smiled, at everyone. Maybe this was no different.

"You, too," Frank said as he strode away.

Edmund turned to enter the house with Rhonda. She glanced up at him. "How was your day, honey? Pretty good, I would assume, if you were able to come home early."

"It was fine. But I'm more interested in your day, Rhonda. This is pretty exciting, and I know you've been looking forward to breaking ground."

"Oh yes, Edmund, it is exciting! I can't wait to see it finished, to see the garden path and to watch everything bloom next spring and summer. And I think Frank is a good fit for us. He seems to understand what I want before I even say it." Rhonda sounded happy.

"Oh, yes, a good fit," Edmund said, unable to delete a trace of sarcasm. She looked up at him quickly. Edmund searched her face in the waning light. "But only time will tell."

Rhonda reached out to grab the patio door. "Well, we are under a bit of a time crunch, since I didn't get my act together and hire someone sooner. We're playing beat the clock against the weather. He's hopeful he can get it done before the ground freezes. Frank has another landscaper with some time available in a week or two who can work here with him, so that will help."

"And what will this project of yours cost us?"

"A lot," she said impishly. "But I have faith that we can recoup the cost when we sell."

"Or not," he smiled back at her.

"It'll be worth it, you'll see. Instead of falling asleep in your chair after a hard day, soon you'll be sitting next to a waterfall gazing at the stars. And feeling relaxed!"

"Actually, honey, I plan to start running again. I was hoping you would come with me for a fast walk tonight, to break me in a little."

"Of course, I'd be happy to! What brought this on?" Rhonda looked at him curiously.

"I've been thinking about it for a while."

"You never said anything."

"I'm noticing I'm a bit out of shape. It took me a while to get around to making a commitment, but I left work with the intent of starting today."

"That's wonderful," Rhonda said enthusiastically. "All of my nagging is finally paying off! Where shall we walk? Around the subdivision? We can snack a little before we leave."

"Yes, and I can see we'll be going out to dinner tonight." Edmund avoided saying he had planned on that, too. Too late to show this woman a little consideration, but he planned to be a lot more considerate in the future. And maybe lose a few pounds.

"Sorry, honey," Rhonda said, surveying the empty kitchen.

"Don't be ridiculous. It's clear you've been working." He looked at her grubby jeans and noted the work shirt she never wore, buttoned low. Her thick, reddish-brown bob was held back by her bandanna to hold it at bay.

"I want to hear more about the whole thing, this project of yours, over dinner," Edmund said. "And I want to catch up with you about your writing. I haven't heard about it for some time."

"And I want to catch up with Claire, and hear how she's been doing." Rhonda yanked open a cupboard door. "Grapes, cheese and crackers. Go find some flashlights and let's get going."

12

THE MEDICAL OFFICE BUILDING

"It's been a couple of months, Elizabeth, since you've been here. How have you been?"

Annie sounded pleasant but her gaze was no-nonsense. She held people accountable, and Elizabeth's third session was delayed since she had failed to schedule an appointment. Annie knew she was still trying to "hook" her into treatment.

Elizabeth followed suit with an unblinking gaze. "Why Annie, I've been just fine, thank you." Her voice reminded Annie of sugar maple sap running downhill. "My Claire, on the other hand, hasn't been at all well. We just saw Dr. Fowler, who said he had spoken with you. He encouraged me to see you again."

"Whatever works, Elizabeth, to get you in here!" Annie exclaimed with a laugh before getting down to business. "It's good to see you again. I hope Claire is okay?"

"Well, she's not eating and her energy isn't good. She gets a lot of tummy pain and of course that makes it hard to eat."

"Oh dear. Is she losing weight?"

"A pound or two. Dr. Fowler's scale doesn't always agree with mine but we go with his reading, of course."

"A pound can be a lot for a six-year-old. Is she tall?"

"No, pretty average, like me. I'm five foot five."

"I see . . ." Annie's voice trailed off as she looked down at her notes. "If you'd like we can discuss Claire's nutrition, such as healthy foods that may appeal to her."

Elizabeth's eyes narrowed. "Oh, I've been around that bush before, Annie. I doubt there's much you can teach me about feeding my child."

Annie realized her mistake. "Of course, Elizabeth, I'm sure you've tried just about everything to get Claire to eat. She eats fine when the pain isn't bothering her?"

"Yes," Elizabeth said stiffly.

"Do you like to cook? I must admit, I don't enjoy it at all. I hear from a lot of moms that they prepare more than one meal at a time for their children and that would make me crazy."

Elizabeth smiled and Annie felt she was forgiven. "I do like to cook and I must say, I'm pretty good at it," she said smugly.

"That must help your situation enormously."

"Some," Elizabeth said, nodding her head in agreement. She sat back in her chair and looked at Annie expectantly. It was going to be a long session, Annie thought.

"Did your mother do the cooking when you were growing up, Elizabeth?"

"Yes. Back then you never saw a man in the kitchen, unless he was a professional chef or something."

"You grew up in the 60's."

"Yes."

"Betty Crocker casseroles?"

"Lots of 'em," Elizabeth laughed. Annie felt a twinge of hope.

"Which were the favorites? Green bean casserole made with condensed mushroom soup topped with a can of French-fried onions?"

"Hmm, so many to choose from. I used to like the hot tuna noodle casserole made with frozen peas and crushed potato chips on top."

"Oh yes, that was a good one. I'm older than you but I remember bananas wrapped in deli ham slices baked in a mustard cheese sauce. The bananas got mushy as they cooked."

"Oh my God, I never even heard of that!"

"It was a classic. I actually grew to like it." Annie tried to keep the mood light. "I was wondering if your mother taught you to cook."

"God, no. What's all this about my mother, Annie? I don't actually call her that, you know. She's not much of a mother. I call her Martha, which gives her more respect than she deserves." Elizabeth spat out the words.

"Mothers are pretty important people when it comes to how we function in the world, and why we do things. I've met some moms who are good at mothering because they try to do everything the opposite of how their own mothers did it."

"Well, I guess I'm right there with them. All of those good moms!" Elizabeth declared.

"What is it that you do with Claire that would be opposite of what your mother did with you? I mean, Martha?"

"I don't hit her," Elizabeth responded. "I have never hit that child."

"So, you were hit? Martha hit you?"

"It was a long time ago."

"Over twenty years. Maybe twenty-five."

Elizabeth was silent and Annie gave her time to think, hoping they could continue on this track. Instead, Elizabeth reached into her bag and pulled out a piece of tan construction paper, folded into quarters. She handed it to Annie.

"I just remembered this. I did this drawing when I was alone, just like you said. I tried to recall what it was like growing up in that house. I did one and then I stopped. It was enough to show you."

Annie unfolded the paper. What she witnessed was concerning. It was a pencil drawing of a small girl without hands. The girl's mouthless, distorted face looked terrified. Unable to speak or scream or fight, she was powerless. Hovering over her was a depiction of evil, rendered all the more frightening in its simplicity, drawn as it was from childhood innocence. A stick figure in the corner with long hair and circles for breasts bore an angry expression. No trees, no birds, no house, no hope.

Annie felt Elizabeth's eyes upon her. She gently folded the paper and looked up. "Thank you for doing this, Elizabeth. It must have been very hard for you."

"I didn't let it in. You can't let it in."

"I'm sure it would be frightening to let it in. But that means you're not letting in other emotions, good ones. It's impossible to keep out only the bad feelings. When we go numb our lives suffer for it. I can help you with this, Elizabeth. I know you've never been in treatment before. We could go slowly and carefully to help you with the pain as you let it go."

The contempt in Elizabeth's voice surprised Annie. "What's this 'we' stuff, Annie? How much did you suffer? Did you have a mother who hit you every time you cried? Do you have a child who could be dying? Do you even have a child?"

The barrage hung in the silence between them.

Lip curling, Elizabeth proclaimed, "I thought not."

∽

The wind hooked the door of the MOB and nearly pulled it out of Mary's hand as she left the building. As usual, she was lost in thought after her session with Annie but the whoosh of chilly air brought her abruptly into the present. She held the door open for a young child entering with her father. Mary admired the child's thick dark hair as she walked by. Her own hair was thin and straight. She looked down at a mass of curls held off to one side with a large bow, askew and threatening to escape with the next wind gust. The father glanced at Mary and muttered, "Thanks," as he took hold of the door.

Suddenly Mary felt a shock run through her as she realized the child looked familiar. It wasn't so much thinking the child looked familiar as feeling it viscerally. Mary's mind careened through the possibilities. Could this be the little girl from her visions? If not, why was Mary feeling like this? Aunt Elaine had always told her to trust her intuition. But this child looked fine, not sick at all. And her father seemed okay, at least he was there with her. Which was more than her own father had done.

Mary watched them through the glass door, trying to shrug off the feeling. She didn't want to act crazy when everything seemed fine. The little girl was hanging on to a whimsical doll with vibrant green hair. Her vulnerability touched Mary, who impulsively grabbed the door handle and re-entered the building. She rummaged around in her pocketbook as if she'd forgotten something, or lost her keys.

The pair down the hallway from her took no notice. The girl ran ahead of her father and pulled on the door of the outpatient lab. Mary wondered which one of them needed testing. Without much of a plan, she followed and entered the lab with as much confidence as she could muster, pretending to look for her keys which she had pushed down into the depths of her bag.

There were only a few people waiting for lab work; there was a sign-in sheet and patients were called in order by the lab tech. Mary would have at least a few minutes to try to talk to the dad and find out . . . what?

She moved about the room, pretending to scan the seats for her keys. The girl picked up a picture book from a table with magazines, and Mary could hear her talk about the pictures, not to her dad, but to her doll. Her Dad stared rather sullenly at the rug.

As Mary approached them he didn't look up. "Have you seen any keys?" Mary asked in a friendly tone, pretending she was at work and he was just another customer. "I guess I dropped them someplace." She counted on the fact that the other people in the room probably didn't want to get involved, since they knew she hadn't just been in the waiting room and she hadn't gotten any lab work done. She could feel their eyes on her.

The girl's dad looked at her briefly. "No keys," he mumbled and the girl looked up from her book. She had wide hazel eyes in a little round face, and given how unattractive her father was, she was surprisingly pretty. Mary remembered the white chalk skin.

"I guess I'd better look on the floor," Mary said, dropping to her knees. "Hey, honey, could you help me? I have to look under these chairs." Mary had decided to involve the girl and her dad as a way to start a conversation, and to observe her more closely. The girl threw the book aside, holding her doll by one braid as she jumped up to help.

"Oh, thank you, sweetie. What's your name?" Mary smiled at her.

The girl looked solemnly at her father. "It's okay," he said.

"Her name is Claire," the dad said to Mary. He got up and moved his chair, glanced behind it and sat down, not offering to search further.

"Claire. Now that's a real pretty name," Mary said to her.

Claire didn't smile but dropped to her knees by Mary. Maybe she wasn't used to adults crawling around waiting rooms. Mary placed her hands on the dirty rug and leaned on her arms to peek under the chairs. "Do you see anything shiny?" she whispered.

Claire did the same and Mary was glad that her father didn't seem to care. Claire had forgotten the doll in her hand and carefully set her up straight in a chair.

"Oh, good, we don't want your doll to get dirty. What's her name?" Mary hoped to get Claire to talk and was rewarded with a whisper. "Holly."

"Holly," Mary repeated. "Holly has very green hair." She spoke to her the way she had heard adults speak to children in the diner.

"I got her at Christmas time," Claire said a bit louder.

"Oh, how wonderful. From Santa Claus?"

"Number 22!" the lab tech called behind them and Mary was reminded that their time together was short. Feeling more and more that this was the girl from her visions, she felt frustrated, wondering how to help her. Her father seemed distant. Desperately Mary reminded herself that God had given her this gift for a reason and now He was bringing the three of them together.

Claire had been distracted by the lab tech and watched an elderly man follow the tech into the inner hallway. The older man carefully placed his walker in front of him, step by step as the tech stood by patiently. Mary noticed the people waiting for lab work in the middle of the afternoon were older, probably retired.

"Are you getting tested today, Claire?" Mary reverted to whispering, hoping to find out something about her health without her father hearing. She casually moved a chair to get a better view underneath it, not looking at Claire.

"Yes." Mary could barely hear her.

"Oh, that's not much fun, I guess."

"No." Claire suddenly crawled from chair to chair with exaggerated movements and Mary wondered if she was trying to distract herself. Maybe she was feeling anxious about an impending blood draw.

"Perhaps you're good at it," Mary offered.

"Yes," Claire said and then added, "I'm the Queen of the Lab!"

"Mary looked at her blankly. "You are?"

"That's what they call me. I don't wiggle and they always get my blood because I stay still and don't cry. Marge calls me the Queen of the Lab!"

"That's enough, Claire," her father spoke from across the room. Mary decided to try and engage him.

"I hope you don't mind if she helps me look for my keys." She smiled up at him. Claire kept crawling.

The dad shrugged. "Ain't no problem."

"Thanks," Mary said. She plopped on the rug. "Claire seems bright. Only child?"

"Yeah, and she's around adults a lot. Picks up big words. Her mother has been home schooling her."

"How wonderful." Mary tried to keep the conversation going.

"Well, there are advantages but her mother don't like her playing with other children. Germs and God knows what."

"Oh," Mary said. It seemed Claire's Dad didn't agree with some of his wife's child-rearing practices. Maybe she could get him to vent to her, like people did in the coffee shop. "It does sound like she's used to getting her blood drawn."

"Yeah, we're in here way too much. Marge is one of the lab techs. Claire really likes her. Usually, my wife brings her but she had to work." He looked dejected and Mary decided to push the envelope and sit in a chair a few seats from him. She was beginning to feel foolish sitting on the floor. As she brushed off her blue jeans, Mary remembered what Aunt Elaine had said about people who want to confide in her.

"Claire looks healthy and she certainly has energy. She's adorable. I hope she's okay," Mary said quietly as they both watched Claire get up and retrieve her doll.

Claire's Dad followed her lead, speaking in low tones as he pushed his heavy glasses up with one dirty finger. He seemed relieved to talk. "I don't know if she's okay. She always seems fine but her mother is convinced something is wrong with her. Claire has these episodes during the day that the doctors can't explain. First it looks like fainting, then it looks like a seizure. She even saw a heart doctor, then a neurologist. There's nothing wrong with her heart or her brain. There's nothing they can find."

"Number 23!"

A pregnant woman came in to the lab and Claire's Dad looked at her for a moment. He sighed. The woman took a number and sat down, smiling at Claire who was swinging her doll around and humming. The older gentleman returned with his walker and prepared to leave with a woman who was probably his wife. Only one more person waiting and then Claire would disappear into the back of the lab, and Mary would lose the opportunity.

"I'm so sorry. That sounds awful." Mary kept her eyes on Claire's father who kept his eyes on the floor. He raked his blackened nails through his hair.

"Thanks."

They sat in silence together, watching Claire's antics. Then he spoke. "What about your keys?"

"Oh, yeah, don't worry, I'll find them. I can always walk home and get the spare set, I don't live far away," Mary lied. She rose swiftly to hold the door open for the elderly man and woman and then sat down closer to Claire's father. "Do you live near here? So, you don't have to travel too far for Claire's bloodwork?"

"In Narragansett. Not far."

Impulsively Mary stuck out her hand. "I'm Mary Johnson. I work at the diner near here, the Rise and Shine Diner. You should bring Claire in sometime for pancakes, I can have the cook make one into Mickey Mouse for her. I work there five days a week and would love to see her come in."

He shook her hand briefly, but smiled. "Well now, Mary, that's real nice of you. Maybe we'll do that. Although I work a lot and most of the time Claire is with her mother."

"Okay, well, maybe it will work out. Maybe her mother could bring her on by?"

"I doubt that'll happen. But I tell you what . . . it will happen. I'll make it happen." Claire's Dad tapped the chair with his fist for emphasis. "Maybe my mother could bring her in to the diner. Claire needs a friendly face and somewhere fun to go. She's always stuck in these goddamn medical situations. She even gets hospitalized with nothing to show for it. Nothing but a lot of bills."

"I tell you what," Mary used his words unconsciously. "You get Claire in to the diner and I guarantee she'll have a good time. Just ask for a Mickey Mouse pancake and I'll tell my manager to keep an eye out for her, in case I'm not there. We'll make Mickey Mouse with blue M and M's for eyes and a big whipped cream smile, just for Claire. But I didn't catch your name."

"Tony. Tony Brunero."

"Nice to meet you, Tony."

"Nice to meet you, too, Mary."

"Number 24!"

An obese woman with a grey bun lumbered to her feet and made her way toward the lab tech, audibly wheezing. Alarms sounded for Mary, who didn't know what else to say. Then she realized with a start that Tony was looking at her. Not just looking at her but . . . looking at her with interest. Not like a married man should be looking at her. He averted his gaze by looking down at her barren left hand and Mary saw her opportunity. If she feigned interest in him (hard enough to pull off as he was that unattractive) maybe he would see her again. And she could somehow get involved enough to learn more about Claire and more about this family. Maybe she could prevent the vision from even occurring.

"It would be nice, Tony . . ." Mary began and stopped.

"What?" He looked straight at her.

"It would be nice if you brought Claire in to the Rise and Shine Diner. Not your wife or your mother, but you."

He continued to look at her and then smiled. It seemed as if he was out of practice, smiling as he was. "Well," he said, "maybe I could call you to see if you're working on the day I want to bring Claire to the diner."

"Oh . . . okay. Of course, call me first. So, I can see Claire again." Mary took a deep breath. "And you." It was like scraping the words from the bottom of a pit. His expression told her she had hit pay dirt.

"Maybe the lab lady can give us a piece of scrap paper so you can give me your phone number."

"Uh, yeah, that would be fine. I don't have anything to write on." Mary dug in her bag, fingers touching her keys. "I do have a pen." She located it without dragging the keys up with it.

"That's great. I really do look forward to seeing you again, Mary."

"You too, Tony. And of course, Claire."

∽

"What are you trying to say, Rhonda?" Ruth queried, peering at her from behind her glasses. She waited patiently as Rhonda collected her thoughts.

"I guess I'm saying that the attraction is mutual, between me and the landscaper - his name is Frank – but I don't intend to act on it. It's just nice to feel . . ." Rhonda searched for the right word. "To feel this alive again."

"No one intends to act on it," Ruth replied brusquely, "which is how people justify continuing the relationship."

"Geez, Ruth, you don't mince words, do you? Please, just tell me what you think!" Rhonda felt like she was caught with dirty magazines and Ruth smiled at her affectionately.

"I wouldn't speak so plainly if I didn't think you could handle it," she replied.

"You know I love Edmund. I would never hurt him."

"You have no intention of hurting him. But things happen."

"You don't know me well enough, Ruth, to know how strong I am. I've simply decided to appreciate whatever comes my way without hurting anybody, especially Edmund."

"What if you wind up hurting Frank?"

Silence as the two women looked at each other. It was clear Rhonda hadn't considered this. To her the flirting seemed harmless enough and she was surprisingly resistant to giving it up. She always did the right thing and dammit, she always supported everyone else. Especially Edmund. But despite popular opinion, her raison d'etre was not merely to support his work.

Rhonda knew how confused Edmund would be if he was privy to her thoughts. She could never explain this to him. As if reading her mind,

Ruth introjected, "How much of your unhappiness has been apparent to your husband?"

"Hmm . . ." Rhonda chewed on a fingernail. She never did that. Her nails were like her, no polish, no nonsense, cut short.

"He seems less distracted lately. More in tune with what I want to do. He took up running again, which is really great. He was starting to develop a paunch and fall asleep in his chair in the evenings. Now he stays awake and sometimes we talk. So maybe I'm more prominent in his thinking lately, maybe since I started coming to you."

"Yes, or maybe since Frank showed up to do your bidding," Ruth said with a trace of irony.

Rhonda's brown eyes widened. "You don't think . . ." she stammered.

"I don't think what?"

Rhonda recalled Edmund and Frank together. "You don't think Edmund can tell that Frank and I are, that Frank and I have this attraction?"

"I'm sure I don't know," Ruth stated flatly. "But it's certainly possible."

Rhonda's mind flew to their last encounter. Frank had given Edmund an update on the pond and how he planned to construct the tiny waterfall. Edmund had seemed interested and was pleasant with both of them. Rhonda felt a tightening as she realized her self-talk made it seem like she and Frank were a couple. What was she doing?

Then she saw Frank's side-smile, like an afterthought, like he was realizing how special she was. He could really see her, and he didn't look away. Her heart skipped and she felt embarrassed, realizing how she must look to Ruth. A desperate middle-aged woman who had to seek attention outside her marriage, even though her husband clearly adored her. How pathetic.

But she didn't feel middle-aged, and she didn't think she looked middle-aged. The fact that Frank was probably younger than her fueled the fire. After years of giving, what if she took a little? Something innocent, since Frank knows what he's doing as well as she does. And she has no intention of letting it go too far; she and Frank can enjoy a harmless dalliance as long as it lasts. Perhaps it could strengthen her relationship with Edmund if it made her feel more desirable. Which it clearly did. She had even noticed a difference in bed with Edmund. More passion.

"Rhonda?" Ruth broke Rhonda's reverie and she realized time was growing short. "What if Edmund did find out? Or suspected something was going on and confronted you?"

"Nothing is going on," Rhonda retorted.

"There is such a thing as an emotional affair, Rhonda."

"I've never heard of that." Rhonda knew it wasn't true. She had looked with disdain at women in this position over the years. Now she understood.

Ruth didn't address this directly but after a few minutes quietly indicated that time was up. As she gathered her things, Rhonda avoided her gaze and Ruth said gently, "Rhonda, you are a wonderful woman. You will do what you choose to do. But you're playing with fire."

"I'll call to schedule my next appointment, Ruth. I have a busy month coming up."

13

JOHN

Sunlight warmed the diner, which was initially constructed from an old railroad dining car. A short aisle had been added to the long, sloping corridor to create an L; black and white floor tile lent a modern look. Booths on either side were wide enough to accommodate families or groups of customers seeking a hot cup of coffee, quick food and the solicitous attention of bustling women in uniform.

The counter with six red vinyl stools set atop shiny metal stems usually appealed to singles, most often men. Half-circles of white light were hung just high enough so nobody hit their heads. Single retirees who woke up early had already read their papers, so they watched the goings-on with interest, a reprieve from the TV or the dead quiet at home.

Mary pulled her thin white sweater tight across her black dress which ended several inches above her knees. With its contrasting white collar, sleeve cuffs and apron, Mary felt like she matched the floor. Goosebumps prickled her skin despite the yellow glow seeping through the windows. She wished she didn't have to wear stockings every day as they didn't keep her warm, but she appreciated her tennis shoes as she rarely got to sit down. It was early yet but the diner was nearly filled to capacity.

At this hour of the morning Mary waited on a lot of men going to work, mostly blue collar, all ages. It seemed the harder they worked, the more they ate. Some came in groups of three or four, and called her by name. Most were respectful. The ones that weren't were well known to the waitresses, who bailed Mary out during uncomfortable exchanges with a wink and a raucous comeback. Leave 'em laughing and move on seemed to be their motto, but it was difficult for Mary to do as she got overwhelmed and tongue-tied. She wished Mama had prepared her better since the Golden Rule didn't seem to apply here.

Luckily, she was used to early mornings from the farm and liked the wake-up shift, sending folks off to start their days with a full belly and a smile. She never smiled at Ernie, however, and avoided his eye contact. He was one of the worst of them and seemed to thrive on suggestive comments at any hour of the day.

Ernie came in today and as luck would have it, Mary had to wait on him. A large man, he seemed to fill the booth. As Mary approached with two coffee pots, one red handled and the other green, his eyes slid slowly down her body.

Ernie drawled, "So, Mary, how are you today? Did you get a good night's sleep? I could give you a few pointers, you know, on how to get a good night's sleep."

Mary's stomach churned. "More coffee?"

"Yes, indeed, little lady. Fill it up. I'm sure you could fill up more than just my coffee cup." He laughed.

Mary poured while keeping as much distance as she could from the man who seemed to sweat in all kinds of weather. Tendrils of blond hair snaked down from his receding hairline to stick to a wide forehead. Mary kept her eyes on the cup as if worried about spilling, a real possibility as she started to shake.

The bell above the door jangled and she glanced up. Mary caught her breath, seeing a youngish man, maybe mid 30's, enter and scan the diner. He sported a suitcoat with the collar turned up and had his hands in his pockets. He took them out and blew on them before taking his usual seat at the end of the row of stools.

The man was tall enough to need to spread his legs a bit to avoid hitting the black and white checkered wall beneath the counter. He spotted her, smiled and Mary smiled back.

None of this was lost on Ernie, who abruptly reached out to grab her wrist. Shocked, Mary nearly spilled the decaf. "Well, well, now," he snarled. "You know that guy?"

Mary stepped back and Ernie let go, the coffee pot still intact. His beefy hand hung in the air, with its mat of damp blond hair. It happened so quickly Mary felt frozen, staring at that hand. She thought no one had noticed until she heard a voice behind her. "Mary? Are you okay?"

The tall man was right behind her, talking to her but looking at Ernie with an icy expression. "Are you handling the counter today?" he asked. "I'd like to order."

Mary turned to face him, trying to block him from Ernie's view. "I'm fine. I can take your order, Sir."

He had kind eyes, which she saw were quite blue and they crinkled at the corners as if he laughed a lot. He wasn't laughing now. He turned on his heel and strode back to his seat. Mary followed him still shaking, stepping behind the counter to place the pots back on the warmer. She rubbed her wrist where Ernie had touched her, feeling his sweat.

Mary washed her hands, using a lot of soap, rubbing well up her arms. Then she snatched the order pad and pencil out of the pocket of her apron and approached the man, even though she wasn't covering the counter today.

"I can take your order now and thanks for waiting. And . . . thanks."

"You must take a certain amount of abuse, working here," he said, replacing the menu into the clip on the jelly tray.

"I don't know if I'd call it abuse," she said carefully, not wanting to endanger her job. "Most people who come in here are real nice."

"I guess there's one in every crowd." He dropped his voice and looked into her eyes. "But I'd like to introduce myself. My name is John Smith."

"Oh!" Mary said. She didn't know what to say.

"Yes, I know it sounds like I'm making it up, but I really am John Smith. There are a lot of us." His eyes crinkled even more as he smiled and offered his hand. She took it and they shook; it was warm but dry and Mary wished she could keep hers there.

"It's very nice to meet you, John. I know I've seen you in here before. I'm good with faces," Mary said, flustered. She had very little experience with men in suits, except during her hospitalization, and briefly wondered what he was doing here in the diner. She also wondered what he saw in her, to introduce himself like that and to intervene with Ernie. He must encounter a lot of women who get to wear suits, or at least dress up, women with well-applied makeup and more than clear nail polish.

"I have an unfair advantage since you wear a nametag." He was still smiling and his longish hair was brushed straight back off his face. Mary wondered if he used gel. She wondered if it was time to get herself to a hair salon as Aunt Elaine had told her to do. She self-consciously ran her hand through her bob, wishing it was summer and she was blonder.

"But it doesn't give me your last name, which isn't fair since you know mine," he continued.

"Oh!" Mary said again, then felt foolish. She was terrible at this.

"Mary, table 6!" Sally, another waitress, hissed as she rocketed past hoisting a heavy tray of food. Mary realized she had never finished her coffee rounds and now was taking John's order out of order. He seemed to realize this too, as she said, "Johnson. Mary Johnson."

"Well, Mary Johnson, I'll just have the Monday Morning Special, with orange juice, please. And no rush. I can read my newspaper."

Mary jotted this down, thinking in her current state it would be just like her to forget it. She thanked him, looking once more into those blue eyes before rushing off to place his order and attend to her customers. But she couldn't help herself from glancing in his direction as she worked.

He seemed in no rush to get to his job; maybe he was in a high position in a company, an executive, or maybe in sales, working his own hours. She noticed on one pass with the pots that his shoes were sort of worn, not polished. That made him more approachable somehow.

She wished he drank coffee so she'd have more of an excuse to talk to him. When she asked him about his Monday Morning Special of eggs, ham and grilled potato he smiled again and indicated it was great, just great. But she couldn't linger.

Mary found herself smiling more today, something Sally noticed as they passed by each other. The women who worked at the diner tended to be older and experienced; the younger ones often took higher paying jobs at restaurants close to the ocean.

Mary was still uncomfortable with their teasing but recognized it was part of the job as they did it with the customers and with each other. Most of the customers clearly enjoyed it, and some days it got a little wild with the louder ones, but the waitresses seemed aware of some kind of invisible boundary to contain it.

They had a whole different demeanor with the female customers while remaining just as pleasant. Maybe this was the kind of thing people learn in school, or in families that talk to each other. Mary made a mental note to ask Annie about this.

Ernie was long gone, having left shortly after eating, all the while trying to catch her eye and failing. But she could feel him watching her and it made her want to vomit. After what felt like forever Ernie had gotten up, lifting his grey sweatshirt hood over his large head and pulling up his ill-fitting blue jeans to cover his backside. He had to turn sideways to pass people in the aisles and Mary made sure she was nowhere near the cash register as he paid his bill. She noticed John Smith kept his eyes on his newspaper as Ernie passed, and the two men didn't speak.

The breakfast crowd was thinning and Mary watched John Smith leave as well. This time she tried and failed to get to the cash register in time to talk with him. But he furtively looked her way as he counted out the bills, leaving a tip on the counter. Cindy, the owner's daughter waited on him and said something that made him laugh, some crazy thing and then he was gone.

Mary's day ebbed and flowed. She busied herself to keep from thinking but it was her nature to be introspective. She thought about the people she had waited on, and wondered about their lives. She wondered more than once about John Smith, but that distracted her too much and she forced herself not to. She wondered if she'd ever learn easy conversation with strangers, the repartee that colored the diner experience. Some days she felt like the bus boy, keeping her head down and just doing her work. These were the poor tip days, days when she couldn't get Mama out of her head.

Thoughts of Mama led to thoughts of Daddy and today Mary tried to shake them off. She was living her own life and he would have to live his.

Because of her visions, Mary was a little superstitious. When she heard Daddy's noisy pickup truck pull in, Mary panicked, feeling as if her magnet-like thoughts had drawn him to her. She watched his boots hit the blacktop as he got out of his filthy truck. He pushed the door shut violently, risking losing it as the vehicle was God knows how old. There was no mistaking her father's lean frame and powerful stride, notable for a man in his early sixties.

Mary's heart slammed in her chest so hard she felt she couldn't breathe. Jack brazenly approached the diner, not like someone who could be arrested for being there, thanks to Mary's restraining order. Her legs gave out so she slid into an empty booth near the front door. She was breathing fast, eyes fixed on him like a cornered animal. There was no escape.

A portion of her brain which was used to assessing danger noted that his hair was more matted than usual and had new streaks of grey. His beard was no longer trimmed and his jeans had a tear at one knee, things Mama used to attend to.

Jack opened the door of the diner so forcefully that the little bells attached to it danced wildly. He stepped in, looking right at her. In a few heavy steps he was towering over her, hands balled up in fists at his sides, his quiet voice laced with threat. "You're coming with me."

The diner escaped into the background and Mary saw only him. Looking up at her long time jailer's ferocious eyes and thin lip line, she struggled to catch her breath and quell her heartbeat, hanging onto the edge of the table as if it anchored her. There were no words, he was here and she was lost. All was lost.

"Can I help you, Sir?"

The cheery voice traveling down the aisle seemed surreal as it was attached to Sally, the least threatening woman in the world with her soft smile and dumpling body sculpted by years of free grill food. She arrived at their booth and Mary noted with surprise that Sally's eyes weren't smiling at all, in fact they were a gross mismatch to her face. Mary knew in an instant that Sally understood the threat, and she was dedicated to action. She seemed to fill up the space next to them.

Jack stared at her. "No help needed here. Go back to work."

"Sir, you are delaying one of our best waitresses. You can speak to Mary after her shift is over."

"Well, now," Jack drawled slowly. "Mary here is my daughter and she's coming home with me to work on the farm like she should be doing. She don't belong here. I've come to take her back."

Sally's eyes flickered to Mary, sitting frozen in the booth below him. "She would need to give two weeks' notice. She hasn't told us she's leaving. She would have to keep working here for two more weeks."

Jack snorted. "You know what you can do with your rules, lady." His voice dropped and he leaned closer to Sally, eyes boring a hole beneath unruly eyebrows. "I said she's coming home. Now."

"I have a restraining order against you!" For a moment Mary couldn't identify her own voice as the words came out. She had never challenged this man but she was terrified he could hurt someone.

"Is everything okay over here?" Cindy appeared behind Sally, eying Jack and taking it all in. "We don't want any trouble. Sir, I am going to have to ask you to leave." Her voice was loud enough that other diners took notice. Jack ignored her and looked down at Mary, coldly reevaluating her. Then he hissed, "Mary, get your ass up out of this goddamned booth and come with me!"

Mary flinched as if she'd been hit and started to tremble. She forced herself to look into those eyes, so close, and her throat closed shut. She was unable to speak.

"Sir, we can notify police of your presence here," Cindy said. "Several of them come in regularly and they've been mighty helpful to us."

Jack fixed his stare on the two women and Mary noticed bulging veins standing out in his neck. His expression had darkened and he seemed to be thinking about what to do next. A male voice from down the aisle seemed far away, "You ladies need any help over there?"

Mary could tell it was one of two truck drivers who frequented the place as she had waited on them many times, including today. One was a large man, albeit out of shape, but he could still pose a threat and seemed ready to do so. Out of the corner of her eye Mary glimpsed other customers staring. The din of voices and clinking cutlery and dishes had ebbed as people became aware of the showdown. A few booths away a young mother whispered to her big-eyed toddler as he watched them, gripping a forkful of egg.

Jack leaned over Mary, so close she could smell him, and said evenly, "This isn't over." Cindy and Sally moved aside to let him pass, never breaking their gaze. It seemed the entire diner watched Jack amble to the door as if he had all the time in the world. He opened it with a parting shot over his shoulder, "You all have a nice day."

Mary watched him retreat to his truck and imagined his fury. She had seen it in his cold demeanor, in his step. She remembered him backhanding her mother if she ever dared to stand up to him. Her mother would go reeling across the room and land on the floor and Mary would rush to her side.

Her fear came down a notch, but Mary knew she wasn't safe. She wouldn't be safe until it was over, somehow, maybe with him dead. She didn't know what else to think.

14

BEST LAID PLANS

It was so gradual a change that Tony didn't notice it. Claire remained in the background of his thoughts and his existence. He worried a lot about money and wished Elizabeth would work more. His mother was willing to watch Claire but Elizabeth was insistent on home schooling her. That left her with a couple of evening shifts per week after she listed all of the reasons her mother-in-law shouldn't, couldn't watch Claire more frequently.

In his heart Tony knew she was wrong. Elizabeth's constant circling around Claire reminded him of a fierce mother hawk, except he couldn't quite see Elizabeth pushing Claire out of the nest. Tony tried not to look too far ahead. But one thing looming in the future was higher heating bills as an early New England snow was predicted, even though it was only November.

As Tony sat eating a bowl of Wheaties across from his daughter, he saw that Claire wasn't eating her Sugar Pops, her favorite cereal. The circles under her eyes stood out against skin the color of Tony's newspaper and she seemed thinner. Now that he thought about it, Claire hadn't been as active either. He realized all this with a pang of guilt. Claire sat looking at the red and white flowered tablecloth which hid the pockmarked wooden table her mother had offered when she downsized her house.

"Ain't you hungry today?" Tony spoke quietly, as Elizabeth was right down the hall.

"No," she said simply.

"Do you feel sick?"

"I guess . . . I really did throw up today."

"You really did?" Tony was also realizing how little he spoke to his daughter, even when he drove her places.

"I did this time." Claire nodded imperceptibly. It seemed as if she didn't want to move, even her head, but rather sat waiting patiently to be excused from the table.

Tony had been thinking about Claire ever since he met Mary at the lab. Thinking of Mary made him excited and he thought about her a lot. He had a strong intention of taking Claire to the diner for pancakes, telling himself they both could enjoy an outing. But that seemed impossible with Claire looking sick, and Tony still hadn't found an excuse to take her out when it didn't involve some kind of doctoring.

"So, you two all done with breakfast? Why, Claire, I don't believe you touched your Sugar Pops, honey. Do you have a fever?" Elizabeth laid her hand on Claire's forehead, shaking her head and clucking her tongue.

"She said she threw up," Tony offered. "How many days has she looked this sick?"

Elizabeth looked at her husband in surprise. "Why, good God, Tony, you noticed! Usually, you question my decision to take Claire to the doctor but this time we're actually in agreement! She's been worse for 3 or 4 days, now."

As if on cue Claire heaved a sigh. "Can I go back to bed?"

"Why yes, honey, no lessons today. You need to rest until we see Dr. Fowler tomorrow afternoon." Elizabeth acted as if seeing Dr. Fowler would fix everything and they just had to wait.

Tony saw his opportunity. "Do you want me to leave work early tomorrow and come by and pick Claire up at the doctor's? You need to get to work, right?"

"You're offering to leave work early?" Elizabeth crossed her arms over her chest for emphasis, turning to her husband. "You must think she's really sick."

"Just trying to help out. What time is the appointment?"

"We should be done by 2 o'clock. Is that too early for you?"

Tony had already stopped by to see the hours on the door of the diner and saw that they closed at 3. He could get there and see Mary and maybe pretend Claire had just started looking sick. Claire could lay her head in his lap, something she hadn't done in years, and he could tell her to stay quiet. She did what he told her to do. Maybe he could get some sympathy for a change. Maybe he and Mary could talk. He'd have to call her and see if she was working tomorrow.

"No, I can get there by 2 o'clock. You can get to work on time. We don't want you losing your job, Elizabeth." Tony spoke forcefully and ignored the look that Elizabeth gave him. He picked up his lunchbox and headed out the door a bit early so he'd have time to call Mary from work. Her phone number nearly burned a hole in his wallet.

༄

As John Smith left the diner thoughts of Mary distracted him from the cold. There was an innocent quality to her that he found appealing, given his line of work. She wasn't loaded down with jewelry, no wedding band, and her blue eyes were large even without makeup.

He thought it was refreshing that she apparently didn't spend much time in front of a mirror, getting ready for the day. Maybe she had more compelling things to think about. And she was surprisingly strong despite her nearly ethereal appearance; he had watched her from his perch at the counter, careful not to look like some kind of stalker. He wondered if she'd always been a waitress.

Turning the key in his Subaru, John started to shiver. Eating breakfast in a suit and tie still felt awkward, like he was playing a part he hadn't rehearsed. But he felt it was important, as a small business owner, to project an image of professional competence, reassuring to those seeking out his home security business.

John picked up his clipboard to review the address of his first sales call. This was another homeowner who got skittish after suffering a break-in. He was all too familiar with the scenario.

Grander homes and estates were certainly more lucrative, John thought, and it seemed the more he charged, the more trust he got in return. He had a funny relationship with trust. When he had worked as a cop there were a couple of times women had trusted him way too much. They were victims of domestic assault, and thought he could somehow save them as soon as he gave them a little bit of attention. Maybe it was the uniform. But they always seemed to return home, for yet another beating. He never knew why they would do that.

The car heater worked overtime. Staring at the console, John felt the familiar tension twisting his gut into knots. Why was he thinking of all this now? He had given it up long ago. The Force, and then his girlfriend. He had his business degree. He knew how to get people to listen to him, especially the very rich in their isolated homes along the coast. So go do it.

John spotted the paper on the floor of his car. He sighed. His brother had written that he just couldn't travel East to see him right now, what with kids and job and such. *Would he be home for Thanksgiving? Of course he'd be there for Thanksgiving. It was that, or Chinese takeout.* Keeping busy usually worked for him most the time, but holidays alone were a killer.

Putting his car in gear, John put these thoughts aside in the same way he had banished disturbing images on the Force. He had a full day ahead.

Passing the large windows of the diner on his way out of the parking lot, John quickly scanned them for a glimpse of Mary. He'd give anything to have had his badge when he confronted the asshole who was bothering her. But it went okay. He wondered if she got bothered like that a lot.

Driving along Ocean Road with the sun bouncing off the waves like a frenetic, sparkling ping pong ball, John felt good. He'd risk it with Mary and ask her out. Even if she was involved with somebody, John felt he had a chance with her. He had seen her glancing his way more often than she needed to, even before the run-in with the asshole. Maybe this would be his last weekend of going it alone.

15

MICKEY

SHE KNEW WHAT she needed to do, so Mary extended herself, even though it caused ripples of nausea to course through her body. Now that she had found Claire, who was suffering and possibly in danger, Mary couldn't let her go. If that meant coming on to her father to establish a connection, then so be it, although Mary was going on pure instinct when it came to attracting a man.

She forced herself to smile at Tony, gateway to Claire, who was lying on the seat of the diner booth with her head in his lap. It was not lost on Mary that Tony had brought his daughter in for pancakes even when she was clearly too sick to eat. And he didn't seem attentive to her, which made Mary furious, but she swallowed it and channeled her anger into unbending resolve.

Sticking her notebook in the pocket of her apron, Mary asked Tony if she could get him some coffee. It had been a week since she had met them in the outpatient lab and Claire was looking bad. Mary would have been truly alarmed at her condition even without the privileged information her visions gave her.

She submitted an order for a Mickey Mouse pancake and hoisted the nearly full pot of coffee, thinking she'd have to dump it at closing. There weren't a lot of people in the diner, just a couple of stragglers finishing their lunch. It could easily be managed by the other waitress, Debbie Lynn.

Mary worked hard; she doubted that her coworker would object to her sitting with Tony and Claire awhile. Nobody said anything when

Debbie Lynn sat with her husband for pieces of time when he showed up at the diner.

As Mary poured the steaming black liquid into Tony's cup, she could feel his eyes on her. It took effort not to step back, but she forced herself to stand so close she could almost feel his arm as he held up his coffee cup. He smiled up at her.

Grateful for a lousy cup of coffee and a pancake, Mary thought. In a few quick steps she replaced the pot on the warmer and sat herself down across from Tony and Claire. Although Mary was no expert in parenting, she noted that Tony kept his hands on his warm coffee cup, ignoring his daughter. She was such a sad little thing.

Tony's eyes were clearly visible through his thick glasses only when Mary looked straight at him. She noticed they were a pale blue, and tired. He kept his voice low, intimate. "It's so nice to see you again, Mary. I've been thinking about you."

Chest tightening, Mary tried to swallow around her dry throat. She looked at Claire, lying on her side, head positioned so as not to crush her hair bow. "I'm so glad you made it, Tony. Was it hard to get here?" Mary looked at him and nearly shuddered. She looked back at Claire.

"Yeah, well, what with work and everything." He adjusted his glasses.

"And Claire not feeling well makes it hard, I guess. You still don't know what," Mary paused, wondering what to say since Claire could certainly hear them. "What it is?"

"Her doctor just keeps running tests. Tests and more tests. Claire saw him today. He don't have any answers." Tony sounded disgusted. "At the garage where I work if you kept bringing your car back in because something was wrong and we never seemed to fix it, there'd be hell to pay. And we certainly don't get paid like the doctors."

"It sounds terrible," Mary said, tapping into her sympathy for Claire.

"It's not fun." Tony followed Mary's gaze to his daughter and almost as an afterthought patted her head. "Is it, Claire?"

Claire, who had clear instructions from her father not to speak, looked up, confused. Tony gazed at Mary.

"Do you work at one of the garages in town?" Mary inquired.

"Yeah, Farrell's. Right off Main Street. They been good to me."

"That's wonderful. How long have you worked there?"

"About ten years now. I got a job as a cashier at Benny's right out of high school but it didn't pay much, and I always liked cars. I like things you can put your hands on, and understand that way, you know?"

"So you're a mechanic?"

"Not officially. I pump gas, but I also do some work on cars. Ricky Farrell, the owner, taught me a few things. He's a good guy."

Dennis, the diner cook, was visible from the back kitchen as he slid a plate under the warming lights and dinged the little bell. Mary smiled at Claire.

"That's your Mickey Mouse pancake, honey. I'll go get it." Claire didn't move and Mary added with false enthusiasm, "I'll be back in a flash. Don't go away!"

She slid out of the booth and stepped up to the high counter, as they called it, thinking fast. She knew where Tony worked, but not where the family lived, and if Claire was truly in danger that would be key.

Mary lifted the plate with its single large pancake gaily decorated with M & M's, whipped cream and a cherry nose. The mouse ears were perfect. Dennis had three children and always did it up right for the kids. But this little one, barely visible in the booth with her father, needs much more, Mary thought.

She scooched back into the booth, brandishing the heavy plate as she exclaimed, "Here it is, Claire!" Tony took it from her and put it down in front of his daughter.

Claire pushed herself up from the shiny red vinyl seat with one arm and inspected the pancake. She didn't smile, and after a moment whispered to her father, "I'm not hungry."

"Just one bite, Claire? Mary ordered this especially for you," Tony said in a hearty tone. She shook her head slightly and laid back down, not even minding her hair bow.

Mary wondered if he felt guilty for bringing Claire. They should have gone straight home from the doctor's office. Mary saw the little pink bed from her visions and asked suddenly, "Does Claire's bed have a canopy? Maybe she'd like that, since she's sick a lot. She could use her imagination to turn it into a boat and sail away."

Tony's eyes widened. "Claire does have a canopy bed. I thought it was silly, but her mother insisted. How did you know?"

Mary felt cornered. "I didn't know. I had a canopy bed when I was little, that's all."

She was such a bad liar. Her father would've cut off his thumb before buying her something like that. "A lot of little girls have canopy beds," she said lamely.

Changing the subject, Mary decided to try to align herself with Tony. "Claire's illness must make it hard on your marriage. I read someplace that the two things that couples fight about are finances and how to raise the children."

"Well, you got that right," Tony retorted. "Have you ever been married?"

"No, never had the pleasure."

Tony made a sound Mary had never heard before. He looked down at his near empty coffee cup. "Well, I can tell you, that's another thing that ain't easy. People can change once they slip that ring on their finger, at least that's what my wife did."

Mary wondered how anyone could've married this man and then wondered what his wife must be like. "What do you mean?"

"Elizabeth is hard to live with sometimes." Tony was looking down at his daughter, choosing his words. "We had problems before Claire got sick, and then . . ."

Mary jumped in. "I understand." The last thing Claire needed was to feel guilty for being sick.

"I think you do understand." The way Tony was looking at her made Mary's heart beat fast and she wanted to run. But she figured he'd answer just about any question she put to him.

"Do you and Claire live near here?" Mary intentionally left Elizabeth out of it and tried hard not to look away from Tony.

"Yeah, not far."

Mary needed an address. She tried to look coquettish, a word from one of her mother's old novels. "Where, exactly?"

Tony, paused and then grinned. "You planning on a visit, Mary?"

"Well, no, but since we're friends, and maybe we're going to be good friends, I just wondered."

Tony kept grinning. "We live on Pickens Street in Narragansett. The little ranch house with brick along the bottom and yellow siding. Do you have an apartment, Mary?"

"I live with my Aunt, here in town. I can't afford an apartment." Now that she could find Claire's house if she needed to, Mary was itching to extricate herself from the conversation. "I'd better get back to work, Tony. The diner will close soon and I have a lot to do."

"We could wait for you, Mary. Wait right here until you get off work."

"Oh no, Tony," Mary said quickly. "That's not allowed. And you really need to take Claire home and put her to bed, the poor little thing."

They looked down at Claire who didn't move.

"But I'll see you again, right, Mary?" Tony said in a low voice. "We're friends. Maybe next week? When do you have a day off?"

Mary lifted Mickey Mouse as she stood. The plate was a bit heavy but she felt immediate relief being above Tony, who offered up his coffee cup. "I don't have my schedule yet." She forced a smile, wondering how she looked, and took the cup from him. "You have my phone number."

She made her way to the counter where she deposited the uneaten pancake, trying to look rushed. Placing Tony's coffee cup beneath the countertop into a plastic tub of dirty dishes, Mary saw that Debbie Lynn had put fresh paper napkins in all of the dispensers. Damn her efficiency! There really wasn't much to be done as she couldn't start sweeping the floor until all of the customers had left.

Out of the corner of her eye Mary saw Tony encouraging Claire to sit up and slide out of the booth. Claire took Tony's hand and stood, then slowly walked with him to the cash register. He didn't rush her. Mary felt him watching her as she picked up the coffee pots and backed into the kitchen to dump them out.

Debbie Lynn was laughing at something Dennis had said and Mary whispered loudly as she walked past her, "Can you ring that guy out?" Debbie Lynn gave her an odd look but exited the kitchen and Mary heard her say, "Are you two all set?" Away from Tony, away from Claire, Mary began to tremble. She fished out the order pad from her pocket with her stub of a pencil and wrote, 'Yellow sided ranch with brick, Pickens Street, Narr.'

Dennis was scraping the cooling griddle with a metal spatula to clean it and the jarring sound felt oddly reassuring. Mary felt safe with Dennis. She busied herself washing the coffee pots and then the sink, scrubbing as if she could scrub away the sight of Tony looking at her. By the time she rinsed them he was gone from the diner and gone from her thoughts.

16

THE MISSION

WHEN IT FINALLY got down to doing something about the obsessive thoughts circling his brain like killer whales on the hunt, Edmund felt strangely calm. It was like watching himself in a movie; he had no lines but his actions were mentally rehearsed and he performed them smoothly, almost mechanically. Despite the danger it was a relief to be doing something, not caged at home in the evenings with Rhonda. She'd sit across the room reading or working on her poetry while he obsessed about her relationship with Frank. Rhonda and Frank. He just couldn't believe it.

Edmund couldn't shake the question of whether she was falling in love with him, Frank the landscaper, while he shared a house with her, a bed, a life. He wondered what they talked about, what they could possibly have in common, what Frank knew about Rhonda that he didn't know. Every day as Edmund pulled into the garage after work he wondered if he was interrupting anything, if they would look at each other and separate themselves before he could find them together. It made him crazy. He literally thought he might lose his mind.

Edmund knew he was distracted at work and the staff was beginning to comment on it. "Dr. Fowler? Are you okay?" from Nicole, the pony tailed nurse. "Hey buddy, what's up?" from Carl, his closest friend in the practice. "You haven't been yourself."

At times Edmund thought about what that meant, not being himself, an aging pediatrician who no longer believed he could impact the world one child at a time - a doctor considering retirement as a solution to his professional challenges. A man who had let his body go until a recent feeble attempt to start running again. *God! How did I get here? No wonder Rhonda was looking at Frank. Not that either one of them let on,* Edmund thought, *no slip of the tongue.* But he knew Rhonda. He had a strong feeling she was keeping something from him.

I really have nothing definitive to go on, and I don't believe I could catch them together; it just wasn't going to happen. But I need some kind of proof.

He didn't know how much longer he could go on like this, consumed with the thought of the two of them together. He worried, and shuddered to think what could happen. *I could lose it somehow. Confront Frank? Look like the jealous, raging husband? Drive Rhonda away for good?*

All of which led Edmund to this place in the Medical Office Building late at night after parking in the hospital employee parking lot. He knew everyone would be gone, even the cleaning crew. Over the years he had been in and out of his office at all hours; Edmund was quite sure no one would see him quietly let himself in to the building. Once he got in through either of the entrances, Edmund had access to any practice in the building. Prescriptions pads and sample medications from pharmaceutical companies were locked up, but nothing else was and there had never been any trouble.

A lone security guard patrolled the adjoining hospital at night but there was never a reason to have him include the MOB in his rounds. As the security guard was older than Edmund and too heavy to run far, there was little fear of discovery from that end.

Edmund had brought along a tiny flashlight and a bag of supplies including disposable latex gloves. No fingerprints. He had checked his equipment and was reassured that it would work. He just had to find a spot to set it up.

Red exit signs cast a demonic pall in the hallways and Edmund tread lightly in his black work shoes. He was dressed all in black and was aware he'd need a good story if confronted, but none had come to mind. He sprinted up the back stairs to the third floor. He knew where the Behavioral Health Clinic was, but once he got there he wouldn't know which office belonged to Ruth. God knows he had offered to attend one of Rhonda's sessions with Ruth but Rhonda had never allowed it. She would joke that he could get his own therapist and the subject would be dropped.

In the waiting room, Edmund's flashlight played off of artificial flowers clustered in tall vases on the floor, rows of chairs with end tables holding tidy stacks of magazines, even a couple of artificial fichus trees in the corners, all of which reminded him that the Clinic treated only adults. No tiny chairs or low tables, no picture books. Edmund remembered talking to Annie, the Clinical Nurse Specialist, about Elizabeth Brunero and a couple of other parents from his practice but he had never referred anyone to Ruth. Rhonda seemed to like Ruth and had recently resumed seeing her after several weeks' hiatus. She had said she was too busy with the backyard project to keep up with her therapy. Maybe she was too busy with Frank.

Edmund silently turned the knob and pulled the interior door to the clinic open enough to allow the red glow to escape from the inner hallway. It glinted off his flashlight so he clicked it off and entered. Offices similar to his own but minus medical equipment flanked him on either side; they were bigger and he could make out rugs, artwork and coffee tables placed in front of couches or easy chairs.

Edmund carefully stepped into the first one on his left and looked around, needing his flashlight again to locate diplomas on the wall. It was Annie's office. The window had no blinds as it was three stories up. No charts on the desk, no coffee cups, just a gooseneck lamp arched over a Rolodex by a *Nursing Drug Handbook*. Pens and pencils sprouted from an oversized coffee mug, and a busy corkboard with reference materials clung to the wall above. Edmund glanced around briefly before striding out and across the hall to the next office.

An enormous arm chair hogged one end of it and there was a rocking chair and an armless slipper chair positioned around an area rug. Off to one side Edmund noticed a small desk and chair; two diplomas hung above so he could verify that this was Ruth's office. Despite being windowless and dark, Edmund could see it could be cozy and inviting. A sign reading *"Inspire"* hung over the door.

So this was where Rhonda confided in Ruth, things she would never divulge to him, things she had kept to herself over the years. Hidden longings, shrouded truths? He could picture her in the easy chair, looking vulnerable while she reflected on her life with him, maybe crying and saying . . . what? That while he was myopically focused on his career, his reputation, his ego, she had asked for nothing? Until now.

Edmund shook his head spasmodically as if he could pry the thoughts from it. He really was driving himself crazy. Focusing on the task at hand and grateful for the distraction, his attention was caught by the ticking of a wall clock. Edmund pulled an RF microphone from the bag he carried; it was bit bigger than a matchbox. He decided the basket of artificial English ivy adorning the bookshelf above his head was a good spot to hide it, away from the ticking clock.

He placed it behind the ivy, tucking it in so it was nearly invisible. As he stepped back to inspect his work, the clock's ticking became more audible and more annoying to Edmund. His mind traveled to "The Tell-Tale Heart" by Edgar Allen Poe, parts of which he had memorized in high school. A line from the poem echoed in his mind:

"Now I could hear a quick, low, soft sound, like the sound of a clock heard through a wall'."

He thought to himself, *Here I am alone at night with that sound getting to me, just like in the poem, where the narrator goes mad and kills the person he loves.*

For an instant Edmund pictured confronting Rhonda with his fears and talking to her. Just talking. But he couldn't take that chance. He might be wrong, and risk losing her to his jealousy, or even driving her closer to Frank. This way if there was no affair, it would be apparent over time. And he might learn something else that could help him with Rhonda, help them get back to the intimacy they used to share.

After a quick tour of the clinic, Edmund decided to place the RF receiver and cassette tape recorder in the closet at the end of the hallway. He placed it on a high shelf behind a stack of old psychiatric records. He could retrieve the tapes and plant new ones the night before Rhonda's sessions, which she marked on their calendar in the kitchen. Although he could set a timer for the beginning of Rhonda's session, he might capture other people's sessions as well, but Edmund didn't care. He didn't plan to listen to people talking to Ruth about their pathetic lives. If the recorder was discovered, it would not be linked to Ruth's office, and he could remove the microphone if anything happened to the recorder.

Gently pushing the closet door closed in the dark, Edmund pushed thoughts of getting discovered, even arrested, into the dark recesses of his mind. He simply wouldn't think about it. He had chosen this course of action and therefore he was committed to it. It was conceivable he could lose his marriage in the end but by God, he'd go down fighting.

17

Consequences

Around the time Rhonda was ready to take a break from the poem she was working on, the doorbell rang. *Glad I got to the dishes after lunch,* she thought, pulling open the heavy front door. It was Frank, the collar of his tan pile-lined leather jacket turned up against the November wind. He had come to settle the bill for the landscaping after one more walk-around to make sure Rhonda was happy with everything. Since she had been involved at every step, and essentially worked beside him for the life of the project, walking around it again was a mere formality. But he had insisted and she wasn't about to say no.

They both knew there was more at stake than their financial agreement, and Rhonda had avoided thinking about the possibilities that lay ahead. She wasn't ready to give up their relationship, which up until now felt intimate without being physical. Not that she hadn't thought about touching him, and letting him touch her. Sometimes she could think of little else. But she wasn't ready to launch a full-blown affair with Frank, replete with dangerous liaisons and shadowy consequences. Her confusion blanketed her life which up until now had felt reassuringly predictable.

Rhonda bit her lower lip as she admitted Frank into the foyer, trying not to look like a kid in a candy store. He seemed enthralled to see her; she could tell by the way he kept his eyes on her, as if looking at her was the only thing he needed. It had been so long since Edmund looked at her that way. Rhonda drank it in.

"Maybe you should close the door, Rhonda," Frank said, turning down his collar, his frame silhouetted against the light streaming in. He could still make her blush, and she hurried to push it shut. Rhonda wasn't used to having Frank in the house and she found it unsettling but also intoxicating. She was glad she had decided on the form-fitting striped sweater with shoulder pads. Even her moccasins were in style, something she usually didn't care much about.

Frank isn't dressed for yard work, Rhonda thought to herself as she watched him shrug out of his coat, exposing a button-down shirt under a cable knit sweater. In place of his work boots he wore Nike's. Frank handed her his coat silently, and she hung it up in the closet despite knowing he had come to walk around the back yard in raucous 40-degree weather. She could hear the wind disturbing nearby trees and the scratch of bushes against the house siding. She really should trim them today.

"It's good to see you again, Frank," Rhonda said a bit awkwardly. That smile of his, and those Virginia bluebell eyes, kept her off balance.

"I've been thinking about you, Rhonda."

She caught her breath and hoped he didn't notice. Despite knowing this moment would come, and wanting it to, Rhonda still felt confused. Stupidly, she smiled up at him and said, "I can make coffee."

"I don't want coffee." They were still standing in the foyer, close, and he stepped closer. She could smell his woodsy after shave as he wrapped his arms around her. Rhonda's arms flew up and she rested her hands on his broad chest. He was so different from Edmund, she thought as her heart hammered away.

Drawing her in with his face close to hers, Frank closed his eyes and Rhonda hesitated, then felt his warm, dry lips against hers. Suddenly she pushed against him with all her might and stepped back.

"I'm sorry!" she said loudly. "I can't! I just can't." He was still close and Rhonda had to look away. She found it hard to catch her breath.

"But Rhonda . . ." He sounded as confused as her and she glanced at him, eyes wide.

"I thought we were falling in love," he said.

His pleading expression tugged at her heart and she realized suddenly that Ruth was right. She was hurting him. He kept his hands up, open, but didn't touch her.

"No," Rhonda said firmly. "This isn't love. I'm sorry, Frank. I need you to leave."

"Rhonda," Frank stepped closer. "Please . . ."

She ducked around him and retrieved his jacket from the closet, feeling its weight, smelling the woods scent. She held it out to him at arm's length, meeting his gaze without flinching.

"I'll mail your check," Rhonda said. She knew she'd never forget the look on Frank's face. It was like she had stabbed him with her kitchen knife.

He didn't move. After a heavy moment, Frank took his jacket, threw it over one shoulder and reached for the door. Hand on the knob, he turned to face her. "Keep my number, Rhonda."

She said nothing. She couldn't look at him. He jerked the door open and stepped out. Rhonda watched him leave, feeling a mix of guilt, sadness and relief. Quietly shutting the door and leaning against it, Rhonda looked at the ceiling and thought of Edmund.

18

Restraint

"You were very brave, Mary, but I'm worried about you," Annie said, clasping her crossed leg and leaning in. She allowed her expression to convey a fraction of the concern she felt. "What if your father had accosted you in a deserted parking lot? Or waited for everyone to leave the diner? Don't you occasionally lock up at the end of your shift?"

Ironically, she and Mary had celebrated this increase in responsibility at the diner. Now it seemed to be a bad idea.

Mary avoided Annie's gaze. "I'll tell Cindy I can't lock up anymore," she said.

"That's not a solution and you know it. You have to go to the police, Mary. You have witnesses. Your father can't ignore your restraining order."

"What would happen to him?"

"He'd probably get arrested, or pay a hefty fine."

"Even if they lock him up, it won't last forever."

Annie knew Mary was right, but she cautioned, "Your father needs to suffer some kind of consequence. His behavior could escalate."

Mary pleaded, "Please, Annie, let me talk to my aunt. She's friends with a local police detective and has wanted to talk to him about my father but I wouldn't let her. Maybe he can help us. This detective has dealt with him before."

Annie frowned. "Does your father have a police record?"

"I don't think so. Maybe he's been charged with disturbing the peace once or twice."

Annie could feel Mary's eyes on her as she took a deep breath, staring at the floor. Finally, she said, "Okay, I agree with talking to your aunt. But please, let me know what you two decide to do."

In truth the decision rested with Mary; Annie knew she couldn't contact the police on her behalf. But she felt it was only fair that Mary notify her aunt of her father's most recent threats. And maybe her aunt's friend, the police detective, could be of some help.

"There's something else." Mary's voice jarred Annie out of her reverie.

"What, Mary?"

"I'm having visions of . . . of me." Mary's hollow cheeks had filled out since she had left the farm but her blue eyes still dominated her face. Right now they were enormous.

"What do you mean?"

"I see myself in these visions and I don't know where I am but it's dark and I'm outside and I'm so scared." Mary spoke fast. "I see a little house in front of me but it's dark too, and I see myself walking toward it even though I'm terrified and . . ." She buried her face in her hands.

Gently, Annie prodded her. "And?"

Mary looked up, tears in her eyes. "And that's it. That's all. That's all I get. But it's going to happen, Annie, I know it is. My visions always come true!"

Annie considered this. "Have you had a vision about yourself before?"

Mary dropped her eyes, thinking. "No, I haven't, actually. That's why this is so frightening."

"But Mary, if you're in the vision, then you have control over it. You can choose to walk up to that house or not. Especially since you would have gone to the house, wherever it is, on purpose."

"But why, Annie? Why would I go to a place that makes me feel so frightened?"

"The house was unfamiliar to you?"

"Totally. I've never seen that house before."

"Were there any numbers on it?"

Mary thought hard, and then shook her head. "I didn't see any numbers."

"Can you describe it?"

"Just a small one-story home. It had a tiny yard with other houses close to it. I'm not really sure what color it was, it was so dark without any street lights nearby. But it was painted a light color, I could tell that much."

Discussing the details was designed in part to make the whole thing seem real and less nightmarish; Annie could see the tension draining from Mary.

"And there weren't any sidewalks," she added. "Just a narrow, cracked cement walkway leading to the front door."

"Any vehicles parked in the driveway? Maybe you caught a license plate number."

Annie watched Mary try to recall this detail. She intuitively found herself believing Mary, and believing her visions. What if they were real? Annie thought she had better nail down how much Mary dissociated from current reality.

"No," Mary shook her head. "No vehicles in the driveway."

"Are you certain," Annie tread carefully, "this was a vision and not a memory? Is it possible, Mary, that what feels like a vision to you is actually a memory, at least in this instance? A very frightening memory that is still incomplete?"

"I know the difference between a vision and a memory, Annie," Mary said swiftly. "I have plenty of memories of my father coming to me at night, and him screaming at my mother, and threatening her, and threatening me, things that I would just as soon forget. Those aren't visions." Voice shaking, Mary stared at Annie.

Annie replied, "Okay, I'm sorry, Mary. I'm really sorry for what you had to live through, and the challenges you still face. But I'm impressed with the way that you stick with me as we work together on this. You're very brave. And I can see you work hard as you set out to claim a new life. I will help you in whatever way I can."

19

PAUL

"I haven't told anyone this, but . . ." Mary's Aunt Elaine paused, searching for the right words. She hadn't seen Paul for some time, and she wanted to make her intentions for reaching out to him clear; she wasn't asking him to meet her at the Main Street Café on a whim. They had ordered coffee, exchanged pleasantries, and now he sat looking at her as if to remember every aspect of her face. She was aware of the laugh lines surrounding her eyes, the grooves cupping her mouth. At least her weight was nearly the same as it had been 20 years ago. She squirmed a bit and looked down at her cup, encircling its warmth with her hands.

Elaine remembered – how could she forget - long ago "checking" with her gynecologist to see if she was in good shape to conceive. Paul had wanted children even more than she did, as all she really wanted was Paul. But the engineer in her was examining every detail of their relationship to ensure their happiness, to proceed as expected: courtship, marriage, children. A life she hadn't dared to hope for, growing up as she did in the home that she did. Elaine couldn't believe that she had found a guy like Paul, given what her mother had settled for.

Elaine vividly recalled emerging from the doctor's office, plodding blindly as she searched for her car, feeling half the woman she had been going in; stopping at the far corner of the medical office parking lot, she fell to her knees. Elaine could still see aspen mingling with oak beyond the blacktop, giant acorns strewn about holding the promise of life. She sobbed behind a Pontiac, hands covering her face, pressing against her eyes until she saw swirls of color. How had her body failed her so completely?

A part of Elaine's brain worried that she'd be seen, the college professor weeping in the parking lot. She really didn't care.

But Paul . . . what of Paul? Unapologetically, she dried her swollen eyes with her sleeves, swiped at her nose and struggled to her feet to brush herself off. Her crotch felt tender and swollen after the protracted examination.

Elaine forced herself to recall where she had parked. Yes, down from the entrance along the left side, half-way to the end of the row. There it was, she could see her car. She could find her keys at the bottom of her expensive bag, a treat for working long and hard for other people's kids.

Tears fought their way back up as Elaine took the back roads, longing for the quiet solace, the cold comfort of the home she had created. Pulling in, she contemplated the children's swing chair she had put up on the back deck. The two extra bedrooms seemed unnecessary, newly painted with primary colors. New England red in the dining room. She'd probably tone it down.

Inside, Elaine moved slowly to her flowered wing chair where she could look out across her front yard, noticing that the marigolds ringing her youngest maple tree needed attention. She picked up the phone and dialed. Hearing Paul's no-nonsense voice made her heart hurt.

"Hello, Paul Rice here."

"Paul, it's Elaine. We have to talk."

They met and she recalled it hadn't gone well, returning to the moment and lifting the cup to her lips, breathing in the comforting familiarity of coffee.

"My brother-in-law tried to break in," she said, "after my niece Mary moved in with me."

Paul looked incredulous. "He did what?"

Elaine knew her brother-in-law Jack was known to Paul since his violent temper had gotten him into trouble when he came to town. Paul had been one of the police officers who had arrested him a couple of times.

"I was home, and gratefully Mary was out doing errands. Jack rattled my door knob, which was locked, thank God, and then stomped around before leaving. Mary has a restraining order against him so I was shocked that he'd show up on my property."

"You didn't call the station?"

"I was too sick with the flu to do anything. After Mary got home, I felt I had to tell her, to warn her. I just don't know how to keep her safe. She didn't want me contacting you, and I respected that. But then the bastard went to her work place and tried to get her to come back to the farm. He told Mary that he couldn't keep it going without her."

"Where did this happen?"

"At the Rise and Shine Diner in town where Mary works as a waitress. She's trying hard to get her life on track since her mother died. Jack is making it impossible to do so. He seems obsessed with Mary and she's terrified of him."

"So, she told Jack no, she wouldn't leave with him and that was it?"

"You know Jack better than that. He was very threatening. One of the waitresses and the owner's daughter, Cindy, intervened. They let Jack know they would call the police if he interfered with Mary working. Then a male customer, a big guy, asked if they needed any help. Mary was astonished that these people would come to her aide since she hadn't worked there very long. She also feels safe with the cook, another tall guy who's been protective of her."

"But Jack could do some serious damage if he got angry."

"Absolutely." Elaine felt her voice rising. "And Mary shouldn't have to live in fear, damn it! I'm not sure what her father's intentions are but . . ." Feeling powerless made her angry so she took a minute to calm down. Paul watched her closely.

"Jack kept my sister a virtual prisoner on that farm and I believe his abuse had something to do with the cancer that killed her. If he should show up again looking for Mary, I'm not sure what could happen."

Paul suddenly smiled. "Don't tell me you still have your Dad's old pistol, the one that's been jammed since 1971?"

Elaine laughed. "Yeah, actually I do. I figure if anyone does break in, I can brandish it and scare them off."

"Well, at least you couldn't actually fire it. But that's not a good plan. Why don't you let me talk to Jack?"

"Talk to him?" Elaine was surprised. That didn't sound like a good plan either.

"I can be very persuasive. Don't you remember, Elaine, how persuasive I can be?"

She looked at Paul, revisiting his features. Deeper lines in his forehead, greyer at the temples but overall, he was still the same rugged Paul. Something stirred in Elaine, a feeling she had buried deep.

"I do remember that, Paul. As I recall, it got us into trouble on one or two occasions," she said impishly. He could always bring out a side of her she didn't share easily, the carefree, girlish Elaine behind the college professor.

"As I recall, Elaine, you always went along with me. Until you didn't."

A shadow crossed his face and she asked quickly, "Are you seeing anyone, Paul? Did you ever get married?"

"No." He kept looking at her. "Are you with someone?"

"No." Elaine scrutinized the paper placemat advertising local businesses as if it interested her. She couldn't describe the sudden flood of feelings; they confused her and she felt decidedly uncomfortable.

"Thank you for helping us," she said. "Mary and me. We both appreciate it."

The words hung in the air between them until Elaine finally looked up. She looked into those eyes and couldn't look away. The two of them sat together, not speaking, until Elaine offered lamely, "I really should go. Please keep in touch. And stay safe."

Paul reached to cover her hand with his and Elaine stopped breathing. It felt so warm and familiar. "Okay," he said. "But it seems I stay safe unless I'm seeing you again. That's dangerous."

Elaine pulled away to reach for her pocketbook. She fumbled for the ten-dollar bill she had stashed in the zipper pocket. Laying the bill on the table, she rose and stammered, "Goodbye, Paul."

Wheeling around, Elaine wiped away tears with the back of her hand as she weaved through the tables to get out. Pushing through the door, the sunlight attacked her, so she took the wheelchair ramp.

Elaine made it to the anonymity of her Land Rover before breaking down completely, sobbing while rummaging around in her bag and watching the door in case Paul came out. She flipped the visor down to obscure her face.

Banging the glove box latch with the side of one hand, Elaine saw it fall open. Damn him! Seizing her sunglasses, Elaine jabbed her key into the ignition and cranked it toward her. The engine started right up like it always did and she shifted gears, watching the café door in the rearview mirror.

20

Discovery

Shirley Nelson, next door neighbor to the Fowlers, carefully backed her aging black Volvo out of the driveway, glad to get out of the house on the day after a particularly hectic Thanksgiving. She liked to cook, and God had blessed her with a good husband and a good family to cook for, but she was done with the kitchen for a while. She thought of Fridays as "Shirley's Day", meeting with her therapist, Ruth, early and then taking herself out for breakfast and shopping. She never missed an appointment with Ruth, who helped her stay glued together, as her husband Jim put it. Ruth described Jim as a patient man and Shirley had to agree.

Approaching Dr. Fowler's house next door, Shirley spied Rhonda putting a large envelope into their mailbox at the curb. Despite having her car windows up and the heater blasting, Shirley called out a hearty, "Hello, dear!" and slowed down to wave energetically.

She was tempted to stop and chat a little, as both of their houses sat on large lots and she rarely saw Rhonda in the front yard this time of year. Given the pressures of her career, Rhonda didn't chat much; she always seemed to be on deadline.

But Shirley didn't want to be late for Ruth and besides, Rhonda had waved and turned and was scooting to her front door, bent over with arms crossed over her bulky fisherman's sweater to block out the frigid wind.

Such a nice couple, Shirley mused, pushing the gas pedal with a plump foot squeezed into low black pumps. She wore the black wool pants which made her look thinner. *Too bad they never had children.*

Shirley's life had revolved around her son, James Junior, until he had grown up and moved away to start his own family several years ago. This was a natural, expected but not necessarily easy transition for Shirley, who often wondered why Jimmy felt he had to move quite literally across the country to the West Coast; it gave her and Ruth "grist for the mill", as Ruth put it. Shirley still wasn't sure what her boundaries, or lack of them, had to do with it but if Ruth felt they were important then she would talk about boundaries.

Shirley parked closer to the door of the Medical Office Building than usual and marveled at all of the empty spaces. The lot appeared to be about half full. She figured there were probably more patients traveling on the long holiday weekend and fewer who wanted to see their doctors.

Coming off the elevator onto the third floor, Shirley charged down the hallway like a miniature Spanish bull seeing red. She was preoccupied with the upcoming session and fretted that she might be late, although she rarely was. What would Ruth think of her?

As she approached the clinic door, she saw that it was dark. Then she realized that although the hallway was lit, all of the office doors she had passed were dark. The clinic was closed; she must not have an appointment.

Suddenly the door at the end of the hallway opened and Dr. Fowler emerged, decked out in a striped royal blue tie which complemented a light blue shirt under his white lab coat. A black stethoscope was looped around his neck. From where she stood, Shirley could tell he was as surprised as she was to see him, and they gawked briefly at each other before Dr. Fowler strode up to her.

"Why, Shirley! What are you doing here? All of the medical practices on the third floor took the day off. Pediatrics, however, remains open as parents like to bring their kids in on a day they're not working. No rest for the wicked, as they say." He smiled at her but she got an odd feeling about him; something was different than when she spoke to him over the fence or on their street. Maybe it was the lab coat.

"Oh, I thought I had an appointment but I guess I don't, I'll have to go home and look at my calendar again. Silly me! Here I am wandering around and everything is closed." Shirley put her hand to her forehead in mock distress. "I'd lose my head if it wasn't attached." Then she looked curiously at her neighbor, adding, "Are you mistaken also, Dr. Fowler? What are you doing on the third floor at this hour of the morning?"

He kept smiling. "Sadly, I am looking for supplies. We ran out of paper for the fax machine and I remembered seeing the supply closet while discussing a patient with one of the clinicians, the office right there," he motioned. "I dashed up while my staff is getting organized for the day to see if I could locate fax paper. I have a report that needs to be faxed."

"No luck?"

"I'm sorry?"

"You're not carrying any paper."

"Oh yes, no luck, no paper."

"I guess your report will have to wait."

"We'll see. But I need to get back. May I escort you to the elevator, Shirley?" Dr. Fowler moved in that direction and Shirley followed.

"Yes, Dr. Fowler, you may. I'm sure you're a busy man. I've never seen you in a lab coat before." Shirley giggled a little. She noticed he kept his hands in the pockets of his lab coat just like the doctors she saw on her afternoon soap operas. She thought being a doctor must be intriguing.

"You also don't see me in a tie, now do you?"

"No, usually jeans. Did you have a nice Thanksgiving?"

"Yes, nice and quiet. Did Jimmy make it home for the holiday?" Dr. Fowler pushed the down button and the gears sprang into action.

"No, not this one. But he may come home for Christmas. It's so expensive to fly these days, especially with two children. But I miss him terribly."

The door slid open and Dr. Fowler motioned for Shirley to board first. "I'm sure you do. And you must miss your grandchildren as well."

"Oh, yes, of course. They're darling, and so well behaved. Jimmy makes a first-rate father and we're so proud of him."

"I'm sure you are."

The elevator stopped on the first floor and the door opened to expose an identical hallway, but with a few people moving about.

"I'm so embarrassed, Dr. Fowler!" Shirley exclaimed. "I thought since all of these offices on all of these floors are connected, they would all be open . . ."

"Yes, we're under the same umbrella, but we get to dictate some things specific to our individual practices. No harm done, Shirley. It was nice to see you."

Dr. Fowler seemed in a hurry leaving the elevator. Doctors always are, Shirley thought. Well, she'd have an early breakfast, or maybe just coffee at this hour. It was still her day.

☙

"Annie, do you have a minute?"

Ruth stood in the doorway to Annie's office; the older therapist had a look on her face that made Annie put down her pen.

"Of course, what's wrong?"

Ruth's expression was grave. She held out one hand and said simply, "This." As Annie stood and approached Ruth, she could see a small square metal box in the palm of her hand. Wires sprouted out of one end.

"I don't understand. What is it?"

"I believe it's a microphone. Someone is recording me."

Annie sucked in her breath. "A microphone! Are you sure, Ruth? This thing isn't hooked up to anything."

"My guess is that there's a tape recorder nearby. But who would want to record me? I'm not treating any Hollywood types or people of importance. I treat regular, everyday people, as you know." Ruth shook her head. "This just doesn't make sense."

"Where did you find it?"

"My last client found it, a squirrely ten-year-old with a yellow Nerf ball. I told him to put it away but instead he chucked it at the ceramic Buddha sitting on top of my bookshelf."

"What was he doing in session with a foam ball?"

"It's clear you don't treat children, Annie. Regardless," Ruth grunted, "he's a poor shot since the ball hit a basket of fabric ivy next to the Buddha. It was heavy enough to knock it down and this box fell out of the ivy and landed on the floor. I managed to grab it before the boy did, wondering what it was. He asked me what it was and at the time I didn't have a clue. But later in session it dawned on me that it must be a microphone and that I'll have to tell my patients that their sessions could have been recorded."

"My God, Ruth!" Annie exclaimed. "This is terrible! What a breach of trust, and you had nothing to do with it."

"Yes," Ruth said grimly. "Undoubtedly I'll lose patients over it. And I'll have to notify Dr. Martinez and see what he thinks. But what really bothers me is that someone is using me to get to somebody else in some way, to what purpose I can't imagine. And I don't like being used!"

It occurred to Annie that she had never seen Ruth angry before, aggravated maybe when a client failed to keep an appointment, or annoyed with the irrational demands of insurance companies, but never truly angry. This was it, full on.

Ruth's eyes flashed. "Right now, I want to find that recorder!"

"I have a half hour before my next patient. Do you want my help with the search?"

"Would you, Annie?"

"Of course. But what exactly am I looking for?"

"I guess it'll look like a regular tape recorder, probably smaller. Something the CIA would use to tape Russian spies." Ruth managed a smile.

"Is there something you're not telling me, Ruth?" Annie teased and gave her friend a quick hug.

"I'm too old to do anything covert, Annie. But let's consider this a moment. The tape recorder would need to be hidden but would need to remain accessible, since the tape probably only records for an hour or two and then would need to be changed."

"Well, our offices aren't locked, just the building gets locked at the end of the day. Prescription pads get locked in our desk drawers but I haven't noticed any missing and Dr. Martinez hasn't mentioned any problems."

"And we haven't noticed any strangers lurking about," Ruth pursed her lips, looking at Annie but not seeing her. "Which would imply that the perpetrator is . . ."

"One of us!" Annie breathed.

"Or at least someone with a key to the building. Someone who could blend in, someone we'd expect to be here."

"That new secretary looks awfully suspicious!"

"Krysten? Mother of six?" Ruth had to laugh. "She's too busy to spy on anyone. I often wonder how she gets here on time." Her expression grew somber. "This has nothing to do with prescription pads. We need to keep in mind that people in general are capable of anything. You know that as well as I do. People do the craziest things."

"So, it truly could be anyone. Okay, Ruth, I confess. It's me! I was taping you to hear how you work your magic with your patients. Except with the adolescents. I could never work with adolescents."

"Would you get serious? This is serious!"

"And I only have a half hour right now, but I can search later if we don't find anything. One thing I don't understand is how the recorder could turn on if no one is here pushing buttons."

"It could be voice activated."

"Oh . . ." Annie was at a loss, not understanding much about electronics. It seemed Ruth knew a little bit about everything.

"So, if I was an accessible but hidden tape recorder, where would I be?"

"If one of our therapists is guilty, it'd be in his or her office. Maybe I should search yours, Annie," Ruth said sardonically as she moved into the hallway. Annie followed. She scanned up and down the hallway, thinking of each clinician who shared office space at various times of the day and evening. Her eyes rested at the office supply closet at the end of the hall. It would be accessible at all hours of the day.

Ruth caught her gaze. "Do you suppose . . .?"

"It's a place to begin," Annie said firmly, and marched down the hall with Ruth at her heels. Together they scanned the shelves after moving aside a vacuum cleaner and an old file cabinet on wheels bristling with closed out charts.

"Given the size of the recorder, I'd say it's on one of the upper shelves," Ruth mused. "Annie, you're tall, can you pull down some of that stuff up there or should I move a chair in here?"

"No, I can get at some of it." Annie set to work pulling down boxes of supplies, pens, paper, folders, a phone, even Christmas decorations for the office and handing them to Ruth who put them on the floor.

Donna, the office manager, approached them from the other end of the hall, dodging a couple of people who were casting curious looks in their direction. "What on earth are you two up to?"

Annie and Ruth glanced at each other. "It's a long story, Donna," Ruth said. "Do you have a step stool?" She handed her a stack of recently closed records, overflow from the old file cabinet.

"No, no step stool."

The two women watched Annie grope high above her head where the records had been until her hand touched metal.

"Ruth! Something's here! I'll need that chair now."

Ruth disappeared into an empty office and Donna followed, placing charts on the desk and then helping her drag a heavy wooden chair into the hallway.

"There's nothing up there that you would want, I can assure you," Donna said. "Why don't you just tell me what you're looking for?"

Ruth wordlessly watched Annie position the chair sideways in the narrow space and clamber on top. Now that she was at eye level, Annie reached up and dragged out a silver metal rectangle the size of a small lunch box with two tapes embedded in it. She looked at it a moment, then offered it to Ruth.

"Your CIA recorder, Madam."

Ruth grabbed it and Donna exclaimed, "What the hell . . . ?" They both stared at the machine as Annie climbed down from the chair, and then Donna helped her lug it back to the empty office. Ruth produced the microphone she had stashed in her drawer and inserted it into the machine. The three women gathered around the desk.

"I can't believe this, someone hid these things in our supply closet?" said Donna.

"Yes, and I gather from your reaction it wasn't you," Annie replied.

"Why would anyone do such a thing?" Donna retorted, hands on hips. It was clear she took the situation as a personal affront.

"That's a mystery," Ruth said. "But it's my sessions that were being recorded." She gingerly reached out and pushed the rewind button which made a gunshot sound; the machine cooperated with a smooth transfer of tape from the right reel to the left, clicking off after a minute or two.

"Here goes nothing," Ruth said as she pushed the play button.

A soft whirring and then Ruth's voice came on. "It's good to see you, too. Have a seat. It's been a while since I've seen you."

Ruth stood transfixed, listening as a male voice responded, "I should have come in earlier," a pause, then the voice came from a different direction, but still distinct. "I guess my life has been pretty crazy."

Suddenly reaching out, Ruth snapped off the machine. "Who would do this? It's such a violation! What am I going to do? This could have been going on for weeks!"

"Now Ruth," Annie said soothingly. "I'm sure it hasn't been that long. After all, these tapes would need changing and that means someone has to get in and out of here to do that."

"Apparently that someone has access! I swear, Annie, I'm going to get to the bottom of this even if it follows me into my retirement years!"

"You're retiring?" Donna asked. "Don't let this force you into an early retirement, Ruth! Let's find Dr. Martinez and figure this thing out. He breaks for lunch soon. Come on, let's put things away and call a meeting. It'll be okay."

"If I should retire now, Donna, it wouldn't be early." Ruth smirked a little. "But I have no immediate plans to do so. Yes, let's go and show these things to Dr. Martinez over our lunch break. We can get indigestion together." Ruth gathered up the microphone and tape recorder and Donna hoisted the pile of records into her arms. "And for now, let's keep this between the three of us. We certainly don't want word to get out that sessions are covertly recorded in the Behavioral Health Clinic."

21

CONUNDRUM

From the road, Jack's farmhouse appeared to be as neglected as his truck; the peeling paint was now an indecipherable color from years of weathering. A century prior, the two-story house could have sheltered a thriving farm family, but now it served as a desolate outpost for a self-appointed soldier fighting the world.

Paul Rice turned in to the rutted dirt driveway, slowing down to a crawl in his brand new 1990 silver Buick Park Avenue, still shining from the dealership. He wondered if Jack was watching him behind one of the soulless window eyes of the house. He had strapped on his shoulder holster for safety's sake, figuring it was pretty unlikely he'd have to display his handgun, much less use it. Jack was mean, but he wasn't stupid.

Paul parked next to the truck which nearly blocked the front porch entry. "Not expecting a lot of visitors," he mused. Now that it was December, clouds amassing overhead threatened snow but it still could rain. Rhode Island weather was hard to predict being close to the ocean, and they usually got it wrong.

Without crops to tend to, Jack could be inside the house, or he could be in the barn, caring for his farm equipment and animals. In a few steps Paul crossed the porch and pulled off one sheepskin glove to knock, as the doorbell was left dangling. Peering in, he observed stacks of dirty dishes teetering on the coffee table, clothes scattered about the floor, newspapers tossed in a pile on one end of the couch, spilling over onto the tattered rug.

"What the hell are you doing?"

The angry voice from the yard was loud enough that it made Paul lurch backward, caught in the act. He dropped his hand and turned to face the older man, seeing that he was aging like he lived, kicking and screaming. Jack's winter coat was old and dirty and his greying hair ran into his beard which blew in a sudden wind.

"Hello, Jack. It's been a long time."

Jack slowly turned his head to spit. "I asked you a question. What the hell are you doing?"

"Well, I was just about to knock. Don't get too many visitors here, Jack?"

Jack looked him up and down, "Well Officer Fancy Pants, I hear you're some big shot detective now, riding around in your fancy silver car. They must pay you good money for doing nothin'."

Paul turned and descended the wooden stairs deliberately, aware of Jack's eyes on him. He didn't plan to get close to the man, but didn't want to talk from that distance. He also had taken care to let a couple of the officers at the station know where he was going when he headed out that morning, just in case. It was a crazy world.

"Let me get right to the point, Jack. You need to stop harassing your daughter. You need to respect her restraining order against you or by God, you'll wind up in jail for a good long time this time."

Jack coughed, then spat again, dangerously close to Paul's polished leather shoe. "Mary is my goddamned daughter and I'll see her whenever I goddamned want to!"

"Mary is an adult with a restraining order against you issued by a judge," Paul said evenly, "which means if you get close to her again or attempt to contact her you will be arrested."

Jack paused a minute and his eyes narrowed. "Only if she reports it and she's not going to do that. I know my daughter."

Paul took a step closer. "She reported it to me and I'm here to tell you to leave her alone! I can have every officer in town watching you, and I will arrest you if you get near her again."

"You and all of your fellow officers? Just try it." Jack smiled a little as he crossed his arms over his chest.

"Are you threatening a police officer?"

"Oh, no, Officer, Sir, I would never do that," Jack said sarcastically.

"Do you have any weapons?"

"Oh, no, Officer, Sir."

"Be careful, Jack, be real careful. I have my eye on you."

"Oh, yes, Officer, Sir."

Paul felt like he was dealing with an insolent child. He squinted as he assessed the house, the barn and the land behind.

"This could be a real nice spot, Jack," Paul said, not believing it. He wondered what kind of childhood Mary had suffered. "I'd hate to see you lose all of this."

"Lose all this?" Jack drawled.

"Yeah, Jack, just keep acting like the lunatic that you are and you could lose all this," Paul said in a more menacing tone. He hated bullies, and the thought of Jack threatening not only Elaine, but his own daughter, made his blood boil. He turned on his heel and headed for his car.

"You have a nice day now, Officer, Sir."

Paul didn't respond and he didn't look back. Some days he really didn't relish his job. At least there would be no tedious report to write after his encounter with Mr. Johnson.

22

TWISTED

Edmund didn't like it, he didn't like it one bit. In addition to Claire's repeated episodes of nausea, vomiting and perhaps diarrhea, the six-year-old was presenting in the office with headaches and swollen ankles. A delayed reaction to her seizure medication? Edmund made a mental note to talk to his favorite hospital pharmacist.

He ordered bloodwork and reviewed the cardiac consultation, knowing full well it had been normal. Now her pulse was up and she appeared weak, but not feverish. She seemed jittery and when Edmund checked her reflexes her leg nearly jumped off the table. In checking her heart, lungs and every square inch of her, Edmund found fluid in her lungs. That was it.

He left the exam room to get on the phone with Jon Con's Emergency Department. The doctor there agreed with a possible admission to the hospital and promised to order a stat EKG and keep an eye out for her lab work.

As Edmund re-entered the room, Elizabeth stood at Claire's side, stroking her long, dark hair. The little girl lay curled up on the exam table. Elizabeth's large brown eyes searched his.

"Back into the hospital, Dr. Fowler?"

He nodded in the affirmative and, given his policy of not speaking to parents about their children as if they weren't in the room, Edmund guided the rolling stool close to Claire and sat down on it. He crossed his ankles and extended his long legs in front of him, hands in pockets, trying to look casual when in truth he was feeling rather nervous.

"Claire?"

She opened her big hazel eyes and looked at him in her innocent, trusting way. Trust which in this case was undeserved, Edmund thought.

"I have to put you back in the hospital, Claire. More tests. I'm sorry."

Claire whispered, "It's okay," but she pulled her Rainbow Brite doll closer to her chest.

"It's December, Dr. Fowler. How long do you suppose Claire will have to stay?"

Edmund sighed. "It all depends on the tests we need to run. You know that, Elizabeth."

"Yes, I do, it's just that with Christmas coming . . ."

Edmund felt himself getting annoyed, even before Claire asked, "Will Santa Claus find me?" She scrunched up her little white face and Edmund had to stop himself from reprimanding Elizabeth. Instead, he said reassuringly to Claire, "It's several weeks until Christmas. I can't imagine you'd be in the hospital that long."

Claire closed her eyes again and Elizabeth resumed the hair-stroking while she answered his few remaining questions. Edmund reflected on his irritation with her; after all, her only child was seriously ill and heading for yet another hospitalization. How was she supposed to act?

Claire had walked into his office today. She was capable of walking into the Emergency Department from the parking lot but she looked so sick that Edmund got Nicole to transport her there in a wheelchair. He promised Elizabeth that he would meet them on the Pediatric Unit after they got there, for reassurance and to write additional orders for her.

When Claire's lab work arrived via fax, Edmund reviewed it in between patients. Scowling behind his reading glasses, he stared at the asterisk indicating a dangerously elevated serum sodium level.

"What the . . . ?" he hissed. The other abnormalities in her bloodwork could be explained by the sodium level, but why was it so high?

Edmund shut the door to his office and picked up the phone to call the ED. He asked for Skye, the Emergency Medicine doc that he had spoken to earlier. She was a year out from her residency in Pittsburgh and appeared nearly as young as Cheryl with a similar ponytail. Skye exuded confidence and a take-charge attitude. Edmund respected her opinion and they usually were in agreement on the cases they shared.

Claire's EKG was normal as expected and Skye agreed that the swelling in her ankles and the fluid in her lungs could be explained by the high sodium level. There was no evidence of seizure activity, despite Claire's history of seizure disorder, so the antiepileptics were working despite an increased risk posed by her elevated sodium level. She remained hyperreflexive and Skye had instituted seizure precautions.

After starting fluid and electrolyte replacement, Skye had questioned Claire and her mother regarding salt ingestion. She had determined that for whatever reason Claire had gotten into the salt and consumed a lot of it.

"Kids do crazy stuff," Skye commented. "But at least we know what to do about it. She should be fine."

Edmund clenched the phone receiver, his mind racing. "What did Elizabeth say? Claire's mother?"

"She was just as surprised as we were that Claire would do this. Given her history, this was the last thing that Claire's mother needed. Or Claire, for that matter."

"So, Claire admitted to salt ingestion? None of this makes any sense."

"She didn't deny it. Actually, yes, she did tell me at one point that she eats salt."

"Eats or ate? I can't imagine Claire forcing down salt when she feels lousy to begin with. It irritates the stomach."

"Ed, I can assure you, I've seen crazier things. So have you, especially with little kids. Let's just be grateful that we can make her better."

"Think we can avoid a hospitalization?"

"Maybe. Let's see how she does. I'll keep you posted."

As he hung up the phone, Edmund resolved to check in on Claire himself before leaving, reassured that she was in good hands but needing further explanation for what had happened.

By the time his day was done, it was past the dinner hour and Rhonda knew not to expect him on time. She told Edmund she'd wait and eat dinner with him, which he enjoyed. She wouldn't eat much but wanted to share events from their day. As he hung up, the phone Edmund envisioned Rhonda with Frank, but he immediately distracted himself and hurried to the Emergency Department nodding to people he knew.

The place was hopping and loud as he entered, with staff scurrying around calling out to each other. In the cubicles they scanned charts and talked to patients, bending over them, often shielded by thin curtains on metal rings. Friends and family either stayed or strayed into the hallways to consult with nurses and doctors, or to take a break. Gurneys rumbled with gowned patients needing testing, wheelchairs rolled, children cried, it was controlled chaos.

Edmund waved at Skye flying past but didn't approach her. She had called him earlier with her own update; Claire's sodium level was coming down and it looked like she would be discharged sometime in the evening from Room 7. Unfortunately, the timing had as much to do with the number of patients in the ED as it did with Claire's condition.

Edmund stopped by the nurse's station to review Claire's chart. Staff smiled at him but didn't stop to talk. Metal screeched as Edmund drew the curtain aside and entered Room 7. He immediately saw that Claire was better. She was sitting up in bed engulfed by her Johnnie with an intravenous tube snaking down her tiny arm, disappearing under white gauze and tape. Her color was better and she was eating a Popsicle that made her lips and mouth purple. Claire gave Edmund a slight smile.

"Dr. Fowler! Thank you for coming!" Elizabeth gushed as she stood. "Our little girl is doing so much better! But are you sure she should go home tonight? That's what that young doctor said, but do you think it's a good idea?"

For the moment Edmund ignored her. "Hello, Elizabeth! Well, hello again, Claire!" he said heartily. "You are looking better, aren't you? How are you feeling?" He sat at the edge of the bed and Elizabeth moved closer.

Claire nodded her head in the affirmative and looked at her mother, who responded, "She told me she feels better now."

Edmund kept his eyes on Claire. "Claire, I want to hear from you," he said quietly. "How is your tummy?"

"Better," Claire whispered after another look at her mother, who was nodding. Elizabeth rescued the Popsicle and plopped it into a plastic cup on the bedside table, then wiped Claire's hands with a wet washcloth. Claire didn't protest as her mother quickly swiped at her mouth.

"Any diarrhea?"

"No." A bit louder.

"Any vomiting?" Edmund had reviewed the nurse's notes and knew the answer to his questions but he hoped to get Claire talking. He needed to understand.

"No." Claire watched the Popsicle melt.

Edmund could barely hear her and leaned in, looking cheerful. "Claire, when did you eat the salt?"

Claire glanced at her mother, looked down at the bed and didn't answer.

"That sure is a mystery, Dr. Fowler, if we knew that it would answer a lot of questions," Elizabeth said.

Edmund continued. "Dr. Richardson said you told her that you eat salt. Some kids do eat salt. Do you?"

No answer. Claire started to fidget with the blankets. "Do I have to go home now?" she asked suddenly, looking at him, then Elizabeth. Intuitively Edmund knew he wouldn't get more information from his patient so he turned to her mother.

"What can you tell me, Elizabeth?"

Elizabeth thought for a minute. "I wish I could tell you more," she replied. "I'm as mystified as you are."

"You didn't find her with the salt?" Edmund was trying to picture it.

"No, she must have been sneaking it."

Edmund couldn't picture Claire sneaking salt, but anything was possible. "You never found the salt container left out in the kitchen, or the salt shaker open?"

"No, never. Like I said, all of this is a mystery."

"Her father never noticed anything?"

"Just that she was getting worse."

They gazed at Claire, who sat stone-faced yanking at her covers. She didn't look at either of them and Edmund figured she just wanted to run away. Finally, he stood and said, "Okay, well, you should be going home tonight, Claire. You'll get instructions, Elizabeth, on pushing fluids and that kind of thing. I want to do more blood work in a couple of weeks so please call the office in the morning to get that scheduled. And I think it would be wise to put the salt shaker where Claire can't reach it."

"Of course, Dr. Fowler. Her father and I will remain vigilant." Elizabeth smiled and nodded.

Uncharacteristically, Edmund reached out and rubbed Claire's head, smiling down at her. She looked surprised, but didn't smile back. He said, "It's okay, Claire, you're going to be just fine. Soon you'll be feeling back to normal."

He caught himself wondering exactly what normal was for this tiny girl with the solemn face. But Skye was right, this time they knew what to do.

Edmund said his goodbyes, suddenly exhausted. He couldn't wait to get home, home to Rhonda. Somehow talking to her about the challenges of his day put things into perspective and he could let them go. He wondered what she would think about the salt ingestion since he certainly didn't know; maybe other physicians in his practice had run into similar scenarios, but he was pretty sure he would have heard about it. He'd have to do a literature search.

༄

Pulling into what he considered to be his sanctuary, and walking in the door, Edmund smelled one of his favorite dinners. Meatloaf reminded him of his mother, and he still liked to drown it in catsup. Rhonda made meatloaf regularly during the long, harsh New England winters, knowing how much he appreciated it. She said it was an easy way to make him happy.

Suddenly starving, Edmund found Rhonda in the kitchen. She had heard him come in and was already preparing plates for the two of them. He kissed her hard on the lips and said, "I'm finally home. Let's eat!" He loved how her mass of hair fell over one eye as she worked. Feeling him watch her as he washed up, she smiled.

"I've missed you," she said. "I'm sure we have a lot to talk about tonight." Handing him his plate, warmed on top of the stove and piled with meat, baked potato and butternut squash, he saw that the catsup was already on the table, as were two bottles of Rolling Rock and salad.

"Missed you, too." Edmund sat down and eagerly picked up the catsup bottle, shaking it. For some reason the specter of Frank wasn't haunting him tonight and he relaxed. "Hey, we leave in a few weeks for El Palmar."

The Mexican resort was a favorite, as they could play tennis in addition to lounging on the beach, and it was smaller and less pretentious than the bigger resorts they had tried on their annual Christmas getaway.

For many years Edmund had covered the Christmas holiday for his partners who had children, but since he and Rhonda had lost their parents over the past ten years, they appreciated getting away from the winter weather and the forced cheer of the holiday.

Neither of them was particularly religious, a perspective which seemed uncommon in their circle. It had bound them closer together, even though Rhonda chose to believe in an afterlife. But Christmas was just another holiday, and like the others, they often spent it with each other.

"It will be nice to get some sun again," Rhonda said, sitting across from him as she had so many times. "I love the people there, the family that runs the resort."

"It does feel like coming home when we go there," Edmund commented, tucking in to the squares of meat dripping red. "And you get to whip my butt at tennis."

Rhonda ignored that. "You've been working so hard again, Edmund, look at how late it is."

"No running today," he agreed regretfully. "It's hard to go over a couple of miles when I'm so sporadic with it."

"Well, I admire you for running again. I think it makes you feel better. As I recall, the running kept you sane during your residency."

"You kept me sane during my residency," Edmund retorted, smiling. "But I wanted to tell you about Claire."

"Oh no, what now?" Rhonda wrinkled her forehead.

"I sent her to the ED from the office thinking she'd get admitted to the hospital again."

"Why? What happened?"

"She came in on death's door, with swollen ankles and fluid in her lungs."

"What? But she's only, I think you said, six years old?"

"Yes, and she looked awful. Turns out she's been eating salt. Or she ate salt once. I can't get a straight story out of her."

"Why on God's earth would she do that?"

"I can't imagine, it's really out of character for her and her mother has no insight into it either."

"So, she'll be okay?"

"Yes, she got some fluids in the ED and her sodium level came down. She's a bit anemic but her mother can work on that with her; I'm sure she hasn't been eating well as the salt is quite irritating to the stomach. Of course she never eats very well."

"I can't believe this, Edmund. What do you plan to do?"

"Well, I'll check her weight the next time I see her in the office, after she's diuresed all of the extra fluid that she accumulated with the salt. She may have lost a few pounds. Believe me, Claire doesn't have any extra weight to lose."

Edmund looked at his wife and shook his head. "Rhonda, I just don't get it. None of this makes any sense."

"Perhaps she's a deeply disturbed little girl, after all she's been through . . ."

Edmund looked at Rhonda, startled. "You think she needs to see a therapist? I sent her mother to Ruth's associate, you know. To Annie Clark just to cover the bases. It doesn't seem to be helping her much. But Claire's mother seems to carry on through all of her ups and downs. God knows how she does it."

Rhonda shivered a little. "Eating salt. Yes, I think that would qualify Claire for a psychiatric evaluation. It certainly can't hurt."

Edmund chewed absently. "Actually, it could hurt Claire. It's one more appointment, one more indicator to her parents that she's not okay. And something tells me that she is okay, really, something that I just can't explain."

"It's your intuition, honey," Rhonda said gently. "Listen to it. It's guided you before."

Edmund smiled a little. "It has? My intuition?"

"Of course," Rhonda said decisively. "I remember several instances where you used your intuition quite naturally, and it worked."

Edmund wanted to ask what those instances were, but he didn't want to stray off topic. "I don't see how believing Claire is okay is going to help. She keeps getting hospitalized no matter what I do, and no matter how hard her mother tries to help her."

He shook his head as he stabbed a piece of potato.

"I know you'll figure this out, Edmund. You always do. But sometimes," Rhonda paused. "Sometimes there's only so much you can do."

Edmund looked at her, "I'm not willing to accept that."

She smiled. "I know. That's why you're such a great pediatrician."

"I'll bring the case to my colleagues."

"Yes."

"And I'll consider a child psychiatrist."

"Or psychologist."

"Yes, I know a couple of great people in Providence."

"It may be worth another appointment, having another set of eyes. Maybe there's something psychological that's affecting Claire."

"Or maybe she's starting to crack under the strain of all these medical problems and procedures."

"Maybe she needs to go outside and kick a ball around!"

Edmund lifted his eyebrows. He really didn't know how much Claire played outside, or if she saw friends, or went to birthday parties with balloons and cake. He envisioned her kicking a ball and realized she probably needed to kick something, or punch something, or scream. A psychiatric evaluation probably wouldn't hurt. But how to get her mother to agree to it?

Edmund finished his dinner, feeling tired and satisfied. He was truly grateful to Rhonda for cooking, and loved coming home to a warm kitchen full of enticing smells. He was about to express his appreciation when Rhonda said casually, "I saw Ruth today."

"You did?" Edmund was fully aware of the appointment carefully noted on the kitchen calendar. His stomach began to churn as he remembered he had forgotten to nab the tape yesterday before heading for home, and he certainly hadn't thought about it today.

"Yes. I had taken some time off from therapy but then realized that wouldn't help anything so I've been going faithfully every week. Today Ruth informed me that some of her clients have been recorded by an unknown third party."

Edmund felt an electric shock course through his body. He worked to maintain his composure by grabbing his plate and standing.

"What do you mean, recorded by a third party?" he asked as he picked up his fork and knife. Edmund quickly moved to the adjoining kitchen, his heart beating wildly.

"Somebody has been recording her clients' sessions remotely, but for what purpose, I have no idea. Neither does Ruth." Rhonda's voice was matter-of-fact. It took a lot to throw her. "She had an antsy kid in her office with a foam ball, you know, one of those bigger Nerf balls, and Ruth asked to hold it for him. Instead, he chucked it and it brought down a basket of fabric ivy from her bookcase. Out fell the microphone."

"Really!" Edmund exclaimed. Mechanically turning on a gush of water to rinse off his plate, he reminded himself to breathe.

He could be exposed, and he knew no more about Frank than he had before. Rhonda hadn't brought him up in session and when Ruth did, she had dug her heels in, refusing to discuss him. Ruth had wisely let it go, seeing how obstinate Rhonda could be.

Edmund had mulled over every detail from Rhonda's sessions a thousand times, obsessively spinning them like a roulette wheel in some low rent, noisy casino.

Cranking the Koehler hot water handle harder than he needed to, Edmund felt like a lab rat on a wheel as his thoughts turned to fear of discovery. He reminded himself that there was absolutely nothing linking him to the tape recorder, except that he was married to one of Ruth's patients and it was Ruth's patients who were being recorded. Although he could potentially be on a short list of suspects tied to the patients who were recorded yesterday, and it would be noteworthy that he would have access to the clinic, there was nothing that could be proven. He just had to remain calm.

Edmund felt like he was sweating and he quickly dried his hands on a Santa dish towel. He ran a hand through his hair, guiding a few strands back toward the rubber band above his collar. His head was dry but his face was as damp as the dish towel. Leaning in to the upper cabinet so Rhonda wouldn't see him, he quickly sponged his face off and threw the towel on the counter.

Dammit, he was trembling ever so slightly and Rhonda could read him like a book. Gripping the edge of the counter, Edmund donned his impassive, professional persona that he used with his patients' families, especially when the diagnosis was grave. Two deep breaths later he had stopped trembling and wore a look of concerned interest.

Forcing himself to look straight at Rhonda as he crossed the dining room, Edmund said, "I'm not sure I understand. You're saying that a tape recorder was found in her office?" Then, with a masterful stroke, Edmund's face bore a dawning realization. "Wait a minute, Rhonda. Are you saying *your* session with Ruth was recorded?"

"Well, my voice was on the recorder when it was found in the supply closet down the hall, which is a little creepy. Also another patient's. It's not clear how many of us have been recorded. Ruth believes those little cassette tapes can't hold more than an hour or two. Anyway, she's telling all of her patients out of an abundance of caution. I could tell she was upset and I feel badly for her. I mean, she could lose patients over this, and she supports herself."

Amazingly, Rhonda looked interested but unperturbed. She was still finishing up the butternut squash, which she had prepared with orange juice and cinnamon, butter and a hint of brown sugar.

"Well, there's plenty of people out there doing all kinds of strange things, honey. I'm sure there's no danger." Edmund's voice came out as strong and reassuring despite his internal state, but Rhonda threw him a glance.

"Danger? What do you mean, Edmund?"

"There's a voyeuristic quality to the taping." Edmund found himself floundering, wishing he'd kept his mouth shut. "That type of individual would not likely come forward. Now that the recorder is found, I'm sure he'll simply . . . disappear."

"He?"

Edmund was taken a back. "Why yes, I guess I was assuming it would be a male who would do something like this."

"Oh, I don't know, I could imagine a woman planting a recorder. You really need to watch more TV, Edmund. *Murder, She Wrote? Hart to Hart?*"

Edmund laughed and relaxed a bit. "Even I know *Hart to Hart* was canceled a few seasons ago."

"But both shows had strong female characters figuring out what the bad guys were up to. And they weren't always bad guys," Rhonda smirked.

"I concede to your superior knowledge of human behavior." Edmund kissed his wife on the top of her head as he swooped in to take her empty plate and salad bowl to the kitchen. It felt good to move. "Thank God I deal with children; they tend to be more straightforward than adults."

"Don't you take care of teenagers, too? And don't forget sometimes you have to deal with crazy parents." Rhonda stood too and crossed her arms over her chest, still smirking.

"On occasion they get a little crazy," Edmund responded from the sink. He threw the dish cloth on the floor so as not to forget to put it in the hamper. "Usually they're responding to real or perceived worries about their children. Overall, they're not bad, especially as we live in a pretty nice community."

"Just a little surreptitious taping of someone's private psychotherapy sessions to spice it up!"

"Let's just let it drop." Edmund kept his voice even. "It's over with."

Rhonda joined him at the sink, handing him cutlery and glasses. "I'm not sure it's over with, actually. There may need to be some sort of investigation."

Edmund's stomach dropped. Of course, there would need to be someone looking into the security of the building. Working within the Health Maintenance Organization model Edmund was under the same contract as other physicians in following HMO rules and restrictions. This in exchange for a steady stream of patients. However, now some adjustments might need to be made and involving Security was less than desirable. More locks and keys. Edmund shuddered. What had he done?

"Did Ruth tell you anything about an investigation?"

"Just that she and Dr. Martinez had to report it to the HMO higher-ups and they would probably need to look into how this happened."

"Well, there probably is a security concern at this point. What a pain, I'm sure everything will get locked from now on."

"Yes, it's a real shame." Rhonda had loaded the dishwasher and was wiping off the counter. Edmund suddenly grabbed her around the waist, circling his arm around her and drawing her close. She looked at him with surprise, putting her hands on his chest to steady herself.

"Why don't we take advantage of the time – it's only nine o'clock – and escape to our beautiful bedroom retreat together? I'm not tired anymore," he said, residual nervous energy suddenly snaking its way south, leaving him hard.

"Why, Edmund," Rhonda laughed. "This is . . . unlike you."

He kissed her firmly on the mouth which made her giggle, but then the power of his expression made her pause. Being wanted was all the encouragement she needed, and looking back on their lovemaking later she marveled at its unexpected intensity. She couldn't help but wonder if the invasion of her private thoughts by a stranger triggered something in her husband.

23

UPSIDE DOWN

Stella, Shirley Nelson's Yorkshire terrier was taking her sweet time doing her business in the twilight of this gusty December morning. Shirley didn't dare upset her for fear her barking might wake up Dr. Fowler next door, who often worked late. The ground was frozen so Stella's multi-colored strands of silky hair which brushed the ground didn't pick up much dirt, unlike the summer months when she needed constant brushing. She seemed to thrive on attention, much like Shirley herself.

Although it was only 6:40 in the morning, Stella wore her tiny pink polka dot bow to hold the hair out of her eyes, pulling it up into a miniature upside down shaving brush. It reminded Shirley of her father's brush used with his Gillette safety razor every morning. Now and then he'd paint circles of musky soap on her cheeks and laugh at her squeals, then hand her an empty razor so she could shave with him, lifting her with one beefy arm to peer in the mirror.

"He never got me that puppy I wanted," Shirley muttered, stamping her feet in their silver Moon Boots to stay warm. She had gotten her own puppy, the same day Jimmy had left home, to take up some of the empty space.

Stella added energy and noise to Shirley's sizable home. She was accused of spoiling Stella who now barked at strangers, doorbells, even the TV. Shirley didn't mind, it was a frequent reminder that she wasn't alone, something she seemed to need despite the reassuring presence of her husband.

When she was out in the yard with her 6-pound, pint-sized wonder, people invariably stopped to pet her and exchange pleasantries. Shirley loved to talk to people and only wished some of her neighbors were more outgoing. And less busy. Life seemed to be speeding up and Shirley often felt left behind.

The front door clicked open at the Fowlers' and she looked to see whether Dr. Fowler emerged for early rounds at the hospital. What Shirley knew of doctoring was gleaned from personal experience and her favorite soap opera, *General Hospital*. She had followed it faithfully for years and unless she or someone in her family was ill, had never missed an episode.

In fact, Shirley could recall without regret several instances where she had propped up Jimmy on the couch during one of his fevers so they could watch it together. She would fill Jimmy in on the plot line, but being a boy it never caught his attention and before long he'd roll over, pulling the comforter over his head.

"Silly me," Shirley thought, making out Dr. Fowler's running clothes in the bleary light. "It's Sunday, I nearly forgot. He won't be going in to work today." She noticed he had taken up running again, probably to relieve stress. Doctors functioned under an enormous amount of stress and she was glad he was addressing his health.

Shirley descended on Stella, puffing a bit, to scoop her up and scurry down a walkway to head off Dr. Fowler. She wanted to say hello, but more importantly wanted Stella to sniff him so she wouldn't bark. Stella liked Dr. Fowler.

As he approached her through the heavy gloom, the doctor looked surreal in a powder blue running suit zipped high to protect his neck. Light grey gloves covered his fingers and a dark blue wool hat covered his thinning hair and held down his ponytail in back. Dr. Fowler clapped his arms in front of his chest to keep warm as he walked toward Shirley.

"Well there, neighbor, you're up early," he exclaimed, voice low, smiling and yanking a glove off to pet Stella, who strained to reach him.

"My little girl needs attention but I'm up anyway," Shirley replied, beaming. "And you're going out for a run, Dr. Fowler, good for you! I hope you stay warm in that running suit, it looks kind of thin to me. You don't have the fat layer I do to keep you from freezing!"

Dr. Fowler laughed. "I have enough, thank you. One of the joys of growing older. But don't worry, I have several layers of clothing under this suit and no doubt will be sweating by the end."

Shirley felt important talking to a doctor and could almost feel the loneliness retreating. "What is the end, if you don't mind me asking, Dr. Fowler? How far can you run?"

"I'm up to four miles, which is respectable, but I hope to stabilize at six miles, which is what I used to run. I'm already feeling better overall and especially right after a run."

Dr. Fowler seemed happy, Shirley thought, and was unusually chatty today. "Well, it's December and I know you and Rhonda like to travel over Christmas and so although you will be invited to my annual Christmas open house, I won't expect to see you there. Mexico, is it?"

"Yes, I need to get Rhonda on the tennis court again before she goes into full blown withdrawal. Maybe by getting into shape I'll have a chance when we face off with our rackets."

"So, they play tennis in Mexico?"

Dr. Fowler laughed. "Yes, Shirley, they do." He rubbed his gloved hands together and rocked back and forth. Shirley noticed her nose was getting cold.

"And how is Rhonda doing, Dr. Fowler? Everyone seems to hibernate at this time of year and she's always busy working like you are. You know, I never got to see her garden project in your backyard, although I know she and her landscaper were working hard on it for a couple of months. Is it true you have a little waterfall back there? Wouldn't that be wonderful!"

As she smiled up at Dr. Fowler his expression was thoughtful, as if he was seeing her for the first time. "Would you like to see it, Shirley? You'll have to use your imagination at this time of year, but I can describe some of it for you."

"Oh, yes, I would love that!" Shirley dropped Stella gently onto the ground and followed Dr. Fowler's long strides as he crunched over the short grass. Stella's tiny legs pumped furiously to keep up.

They rounded the bend into the back yard, hidden from the street by masses of green rhododendron bushes and the denuded branches of dwarf fruit trees. Shirley's eye traveled to the rocks arranged seemingly at random around a large pond. She had watched the construction of the whole thing from her second story windows, but couldn't see much detail. Fascinated, she moved closer.

The water and plants were illuminated at points around the pond; three tiers of light glistened off ascending piles of rock which she assumed was the waterfall, now silenced for the season. A large maple tree nearby provided for partial shade which Dr. Fowler noted was important for a future crop of Japanese koi fish that are sensitive to temperature.

"We will purchase hardy koi fish, not tropical, and we installed a heater so they can winter over in the pond. The water lilies also can remain in the pond; I guess they're tougher than I realized. The lilies provide additional shade for the fish, and we'll get frogs, toads and snails to keep insects down and control algae. Rhonda has taught me a lot about this whole thing, she found scads of books on backyard landscaping from the library and will no doubt become an expert in koi ponds."

Dr. Fowler looked like a proud peacock and Shirley hoped Rhonda knew of his feelings as men were idiots when it came to divulging them.

"Oh my, yes, I can almost see the water falling into the pond below," she said. "It must be so relaxing for you and Rhonda to sit out here in the nice weather. When your plants begin to bloom in the spring it will be spectacular! You know, I did see Rhonda several weeks ago in the waiting room of Ruth's office."

Shirley prattled on, quite certain that Rhonda had told her husband she was seeing a therapist and therefore she was betraying no confidence. "Did Rhonda tell you she saw me?"

Dr. Fowler furrowed his wide brow in thought and then smiled. "No, but perhaps she thought she shouldn't. Privacy, you know."

"What are the chances that Rhonda and I, as next-door neighbors, would be seeing the same therapist? I guess it is a small town. My husband thinks it's helping. He says I can see Ruth for as long as it takes, whatever that means. Ruth likes to say we all could use six sessions a year and God knows I've met my quota!"

Shirley's laugh sounded like tinkling glass. She grew serious and assumed a conspiratorial tone, leaning in to Dr. Fowler even though they were alone. "Did Rhonda tell you that Ruth's sessions have been taped? A microphone was discovered in her office and a recorder was found nearby. Poor Ruth had to tell all of her patients what was going on since she has no way of knowing who was taped." She took a quick breath, her voice rising. "I knew she was upset when she talked to me about it, I could tell. It's an outrage. Why would anyone want to tape Ruth and her patients?

"And you know, it was such a coincidence when I saw you outside the Behavioral Health Clinic," Shirley continued. "You were there on the Friday after Thanksgiving, remember? Like an idiot I came in when the office was closed. You were there searching for fax paper. But you weren't carrying any."

Shirley's eyes narrowed with a dawning realization as she looked up at Dr. Fowler. "You were wearing your lab coat. You looked so surprised to see me." Her speech picked up speed like a locomotive careening downhill and she felt unable to put on the brakes. "I remember thinking at the time that it was more than surprise. Sort of like a shock. And now I'm thinking, how odd, two offices in the same building without fax paper?"

Shirley should've noticed that Dr. Fowler's pleasant expression had been replaced by something else entirely. In fact he looked unlike her kindly neighbor in this moment but it didn't register with Shirley. She gazed absently over his shoulder, her penciled brow forming two half-moons as she pieced together the puzzle in her mind. Stella whined.

"You escorted me down the elevator pretty quickly that day. It felt like you wanted to get rid of me," Shirley muttered as if talking to herself. "You could have had a tape in your pocket at that very moment. You could've been there when no one else was, planting a tape. You could've been interested in what Rhonda was telling Ruth. Maybe you decided to hear it for yourself . . ."

Shirley's voice dried up as she looked at Dr. Fowler, and the twist of his lip finally registered. His eyes burned, staring into hers. She heard the guttural staccato of his words spat out one at a time. "You stupid, lying bitch!"

Shocked, Shirley's heart pounded. She had never seen this ugliness except on her soaps and her husband's cop shows.

"What do you know about me and my wife? How dare you infer anything at all about Rhonda, about me? You don't know us. Fucking go to hell!"

The menace in his tone was all the more terrifying to Shirley as he hadn't raised his voice, trying to avoid scrutiny, especially from Rhonda who must be sleeping inside. Maybe Rhonda could see them out the window and was watching them talk. Maybe she slept in on Sundays, blissfully unaware of what her husband was up to. Had she really never seen this side of him?

Feeling agitated, Shirley didn't anticipate Dr. Fowler lifting his long arms and moving at her with that terrible face. A part of her brain coldly observed him, but even if she was quicker in trying to get away, she was no match for his size and strength.

Shirley watched him close in, heard him breathe heavily, felt his gloved hands on her chest as he shoved her violently. She fell backwards, arms flailing as she tried to regain balance. She briefly saw her world turn upside down and heard Stella's furious barking before the deafening crack as her head hit rock.

"Oh, my God, what happened?" Rhonda cried as she bolted out of the house and ran to Edmund. He crouched next to Shirley, feeling for a pulse at her neck. He suspected she was bleeding where she had struck the rock but didn't want to move her head. Stella circled them, yapping and lunging at him. How he hated that dog.

Rhonda was wearing jeans and a sweat shirt and Edmund wondered if she had seen anything. He was still breathing hard but was able to conceal it, kneeling next to Shirley.

"She slipped and fell, hitting her head on a rock. I was showing her the pond and telling her about your landscaping. I feel terrible." Edmund glanced up to see Rhonda's reaction. She looked appropriately concerned, nothing else. He wondered how Rhonda would look if she saw him lose control of himself with their neighbor. The neighbor who had figured out, despite her stupidity, that he was surreptitiously invading his wife's most private moments. Rhonda must never know.

The pulse in Shirley's neck was slow to Edmund's practiced fingers. He counted her respirations; she was breathing slowly as well. Ignoring Stella, Shirley's ridiculous imitation of a dog, Edmund reached up and lifted her eyelids to check her pupils. They were uneven, and her lips had taken on a bluish tinge. In the growing light of day Shirley's face looked mottled. A series of bad signs. Maybe she wouldn't survive this, or worse, maybe she'd live but never wake up. Or maybe she'd wake up and remember everything. And start talking.

Edmund's breathing had calmed with the familiar routine of examining Shirley. He carefully removed her hat to check for bleeding. It was a decent bleed, but head wounds always bled a lot. Taking longer than he needed to, Edmund began to hope that if he stalled long enough, Shirley would never incriminate him. If it was his life against hers, given that he would lose everything, he would have to win out.

He was necessary, after all. Shirley's life was simply less of a priority, even to her family, as he suspected she drove them all crazy with her vacuous chatter and her inane ideas. It was a miracle that her husband Jim hadn't left her already. Edmund was certain her son had purposely moved as far away as he could.

"My God!" Rhonda repeated. "Should I call 911?" Not waiting for an answer, she turned and ran to the back door and disappeared into the house. By making the phone call it looked as if Rhonda had more sense than he did, but Edmund figured she would chalk it up to his distress at seeing Shirley injured.

Instinctively guarding her neck, he moved Shirley slightly away from the offending rock, which cupped a tiny pool of blood. Then he gazed down at her. Shirley looked peaceful, as if she had decided to take a nap on the frozen ground in his backyard.

Maybe she'd wake up with amnesia and he'd be off the hook. Could he hope for that? If he believed in a God, now would be a good time to pray. But he knew better. Standing up and stretching a little, Edmund knew it was now him alone against the world when it used to be him and Rhonda.

As if on cue Rhonda flew out of the house again, this time carrying a quilt which she used to cover Shirley. Edmund had rehearsed his story a few times in his mind to make sure there were no inconsistencies. He was ready for the rescue truck and the inevitable curious neighbors, ready to play the concerned physician neighbor who had tried to help but ultimately was unable to, given Shirley's accidental fall and head injury.

Edmund gently took Rhonda's arm. "You'd better go and fetch Jim, Rhonda. He'll want to accompany her to the hospital."

"Yes," Rhonda breathed, looking down wide-eyed at Shirley's death mask face and motionless form. She lifted Stella and sprinted toward Shirley and Jim's house as a faraway siren pierced the early morning stillness. As it grew closer, Edmund decided it would look better to resume his kneeling position, despite the fact that Shirley was probably bleeding into her brain and there wasn't much anyone could do except alert the local emergency room. Rescue would do that.

Jim beat the ambulance by a few minutes, running across the yard with short steps as quickly as his rotund belly would allow. It spilled over the belt of his wrinkled pants. He was clearly distraught, and for a moment Edmund felt sympathy for him. Jim was basically a nice guy. Rhonda stayed close to him, jogging slowly with a grave face. There was no sign of Stella, thank God.

Panting loudly, Jim reached his wife and exclaimed, "Mother! What happened to you?" Glancing at Edmund, he wheezed, "Dr. Fowler! Rhonda said she fell? Thank God you're here!" He started to kneel, swiping at his brow with the back of his pudgy hand.

Edmund warned, "Don't move her, Jim, in case she injured her neck." He could hear the ambulance cut its siren in his driveway. He watched Rhonda as she hurried to meet them.

Edmund stood and Jim awkwardly knelt down next to his wife, looking like a lumbering black bear. Jim plopped himself down Indian fashion and took one of Shirley's pale hands in both of his. He crooned, "I'm here, darling, I'm here. Oh, my darling, my darling. . ."

Watching him rock back and forth in anguish, Edmund wondered if Jim would need help getting up.

The ambulance crew had jackets with South Coast Rescue along the back. They moved swiftly over the icy ground, bringing a gurney. The older of the two said, "Excuse me, sir" to Jim, who looked up in surprise.

"Oh! Oh!" Jim stammered. He had been oblivious to the clattering metal of the gurney, now silent and waiting like some enormous insect preparing to fold its legs underneath it. Unwrapping his own legs, Jim rolled onto his hands and knees to get up. Edmund fought an impulse to grab his upper arm and pull.

The ambulance crew quickly ascertained the gravity of Shirley's condition. They handed Rhonda the quilt and rolled Shirley log-fashion to one side after applying a cervical collar to protect her neck. They pulled a back board close and carefully rolled her onto it, maintaining body alignment to prevent a spinal cord injury. Head, chest and leg straps ensured stability as the men prepared to lift Shirley onto the gurney.

As the scene unfolded, Edmund introduced himself to the crew as a physician who had witnessed the accident and assessed the patient. He tried to make his expression as somber as Rhonda's but inside him a flicker of hope had been fanned into flames. He clung to the possibility that she'd never wake up, or that Shirley would display such mental impairment that she wouldn't be believed even if she remembered him attacking her.

Grabbing the end of the backboard, Edmund helped lift the still form. Jim wiped his eyes, talking to his wife as if she could hear him.

"I won't leave you, darling. I'm staying right here by your side. You're gonna be okay." It was a tender moment as the crew secured her to the gurney and covered her with a blanket.

"Sir, do you want to follow us to the hospital?" the senior crew member asked Jim.

"Yes, yes!" Jim answered and Shirley's gurney rattled away. He started to cut across the yard to his property. "I'll just grab my wallet and a jacket and be with you in one minute!" he yelled. "I drive a red Mazda. I'll follow you."

"Jim, I can drive you," Rhonda called to him. He paused thinking. "No, I'm fine, Rhonda. I can drive. I'll want my car there."

"We'll meet you then," Edmund said emphatically. "We'll grab some food and coffee and meet you at the emergency room."

"Thanks, Edmund. Thanks, Rhonda. God bless you both!"

Jim took off, arms pumping, and Rhonda and Edmund returned to the warmth of their kitchen. Edmund realized he was shivering. Rhonda put her arm around his waist and leaned in to hug him.

"It wasn't your fault," she said quietly, looking up at him. Edmund felt her words slicing into him. The irony of it . . . He thought of how witnessing Shirley's exit must have been traumatic for Rhonda, given her kind heart and inexperience with medical emergencies.

"You don't have to feel guilty," she continued. "They call it an accident for a reason."

Edmund kissed the top of her head as he wrapped his arms around her and held her. Then a strange thought entered his mind; what he did to their obnoxious neighbor could actually bring Rhonda closer to him. An unexpected benefit.

"Well, honey, I'm sure I do look guilty," he replied. "What a terrible morning. Let's get dressed and stop at McDonald's on the way to the hospital. Maybe Jim can eat an Egg McMuffin and I'm sure he'd appreciate a cup of coffee. I know I could use one. It's the least we can do."

24

Opportunity

Daydreaming about Mary, Tony gripped the handle of his beer mug and lifted it to wash down the soggy mass of pretzels. The pretzels filled wooden bowls along the bar and Tony was hungry. The beer and free pretzels were enough to stave off hunger pangs and he was beginning to feel happy, a rare and desired effect of the alcohol. He smiled at his work friend Steve who was laughing at his own joke.

Tony flirted with confiding in Steve about Mary but he and Steve weren't really that close and it was a small town. Mary ran into half its population at the diner and he couldn't take the chance that they, he and Mary, would become part of the local gossip. He was married, after all.

Tony fervently desired a romantic relationship with Mary. He loved their talks, he loved looking at her; her interest in him got him all hot and bothered.

Talking was something he and Elizabeth had long ago surrendered. Tony missed the intimacy with his wife. She could be such a bitch! Elizabeth felt cold between their sheets and he figured Mary would be a lot warmer.

It was late but Steve kept talking and Tony had no desire to leave. Cigarette smoke curled and wafted up to the plastic stained glass lamps above the bar. The bar stool was less comfortable than a booth but Tony like watching the bartender with her unabashed cleavage and hair knotted loosely behind her back. On occasion he caught her eye and she smiled at him, even when he didn't need anything.

Tony leaned on his forearms, nodding in agreement with whatever Steve was saying. He thought maybe the deep V neck and the smiles were a ploy to get more tips, but you never knew. Maybe the bartender was interested in him. Maybe he could strike up a conversation with her, later, when the customers dropped off for the night. If Steve left before he did it would give him the opportunity to try.

Risking a hangover and the wrath of his wife seemed worth it. A hard-working man like himself deserved more than a sick kid and a wife who slapped his hand away.

Tony laughed because Steve was laughing as warmth spread out from his belly, but he was distracted with his own thoughts. Mostly he avoided thinking about Claire.

It was around the time that Elizabeth got pregnant that she turned on him after only a year of marriage. It was like he had finally given her what she wanted and so she was done with him. Some days it seemed like he should be grateful to sit at his own kitchen table and eat the food he had provided for his family.

Tony also avoided thinking about the fact that Elizabeth earned more at the hospital than he did at the garage, despite the fact that he worked more hours. It just wasn't right. But in truth he liked being at the garage with his buddies who listened to what he had to say and respected him as a man.

If thoughts of Claire floated into Tony's mind, he'd fix his eyes on the bartender or contemplate his relationship with Mary. He had to admit the bartender was curvier. His eyes slid slowly down her frame – ample breasts half exposed, nice hips, rounded buttocks reined in by tight black jeans.

As if reading his mind she approached, looking Tony straight in the eye. Putting both of her hands at the edge of the polished wood of the bar, her bracelets jingled. She leaned in and smiled.

"You boys have another?" Her tone was low, alluring as her eyes flitted briefly from him to Steve.

"I don't know about my friend here, but I'm in," Tony said, pushing his empty beer glass toward her. "What's your name, sweetie?"

Throwing the covers aside, Mary bolted out of bed and stood shaking next to it, her heart threatening to bound out of her chest. It took a minute to realize she was safe and in her own bedroom at Aunt Elaine's. Sweating and panting like a dog, Mary had an impulse to run into Aunt Elaine's room. She quelled it, reminding herself that if her own mother couldn't help her in the middle of the night, nobody could.

The red glow from her digital clock showed it was a few minutes after midnight. Just like a horror movie, she had been awakened at midnight.

Mary remembered the grounding technique of counting things that Annie had taught her for when she was coming out of a vision. It worked for nightmares, too. She needed to focus on ten things. Eyes adjusting to the moonlight spreading into the room, Mary groped for the light switch, temporarily blinded as she snapped it on. She needed to count ten colors out loud. Then she focused on the feeling of her bare feet on the rug, how her Patriot's shirt felt on her skin, her hair on her cheek. Ten feelings.

Counting sounds proved more difficult in the night with everyone sleeping, but she counted her hollow breath tones, her slowing heart beat and the clock ticking on her bedside table. The wind outside pushed dry leaves around on the ground, making a skittering sound. She counted the sound of the wind and the leaves separately and realized she was calming down. But so cold.

Picking up the thick, luxurious robe Aunt Elaine had bought for her, Mary balled her fists and stuck them deep into the sleeves, shivering. She shrugged it on and tied it tight around her waist, wrapping her arms around herself for warmth. The robe was another reminder that she was no longer on the farm as Daddy had said they were a waste of money. Folks got out of bed and went right to work, even on a Sunday, so there was no lollygagging around in a robe and slippers like some goddamned panty-waste.

Mary shivered again. Damn these visions, these nightmares, this "family gift". If this was a gift, she'd take punishment. Suddenly furious, Mary said out loud to herself, "Grow up." The venom in her voice further angered her. It was about time she started finding her own way in the world. She was a woman, not a child.

Fully awake, Mary couldn't go back to sleep even if she wanted to and she knew what she had to do. She reached for the brand-new skinny jeans that were slung over a chair. Wrangler jeans, never in style in her lifetime, were what she had always worn.

Once in awhile as a child Mary had seen her parents from the landing at the top of the stairs getting up and dressing in the early morning hours. Her mother would slide out of bed in her extra-large tee shirt and with her back to her husband would pick up her ratty blue jeans from the floor and pull them on. She'd dig a bra out of the ancient oak bureau drawer and keep her breasts covered while hurriedly putting it on, then snatch a flannel shirt from the closet as if she were in a race. Mary noticed her father never looked at her mother and he also didn't look at her as he pulled on pants and socks and brushed past her like he was the only one living there.

The jeans felt cold on her legs, so she hurriedly put on slouch socks and rescued her Champion sweatshirt, turtleneck and sports bra from the floor. The sports bra was a godsend for someone small like Mary, not that she was into sports. She had never learned how to play anything but checkers, and her parents never watched sports on TV. Daddy said it was all about money, not competition. And he could never play sports, so why would he watch other men playing when they should be working?

Mary remembered seeing kids in town dressed for soccer, baseball, cheerleading. She would watch them banter easily back and forth, laughing without a care in the world, and Mary would feel envy pushing up her throat. Sometimes it choked her.

But the farm came first in all of their lives and her mother was her constant companion. At least the work had made her strong, and she hoisted heavy trays at the diner without thinking much about it.

Fully dressed but freezing, Mary wrapped her robe around herself and made her way downstairs to locate the woolen hat jammed into the sleeve of her new down winter coat.

Aunt Elaine had insisted that Mary donate the bulk of her clothing to the Goodwill after buying her what she called more appropriate clothing for a woman Mary's age, especially an outfit for job interviews. It had seemed Aunt Elaine enjoyed the buying spree as much as Mary did; Mary felt like somebody else in her interviewing clothes and contemplated going to church just to wear them again.

Brushing her hair back as she pulled on her beret, Mary thought about telling Aunt Elaine where she was going. She reached down to her knees to zip up her coat, thinking she'd leave a note, just in case. Just in case . . . what? In truth Mary had no formal plan, but felt compelled to do something. She had to go to the house that kept creeping into her visions and dreams. She had to find Claire before it was too late.

Mary backed out of the driveway as fast as she could, hoping the headlights wouldn't wake her aunt. There was little traffic. Bare tree limbs waved goodbye along the road, ghostly pale in the moonlight. Driveways with white crushed stone seemed to light up as she passed by.

The air blasting in the Land Rover turned warm, then hot, and by the time Mary reached the center of town she had turned it down and removed her driving gloves. Streetlights made it easier to see but cast an eerie yellow glow over the familiar landscape.

Mary was used to silence but she clicked on the radio. Hits from the Seventies came on with the reassuring voice of Dan the DJ giving a weather update. Expect snow flurries. No accumulation.

She came upon the Rise and Shine with its large windows black, their metal outlines weakly reflecting the light from a lone halogen poised over the parking lot. Mary half expected to see her father's truck positioned there, waiting for her early morning arrival.

"Don't be an idiot," she said out loud to herself as her heart picked up. It was creepy enough to be virtually alone in town at this hour and she didn't need to make it worse. For some reason it helped to talk out loud, as if someone else were calming her down.

Wakefield flowed into Narragansett, a tourist destination due to its location along the coast. Modest homes from the 50's and 60's competed with large ones built by wealthy Rhode Islanders and sprawling estates attributed to rich New York City types who confined their use to the brief summer months. Mary was pretty sure she'd never encounter the New Yorkers in the diner.

Pickens Street was not in the best section of town; she had located it on the way to the market one Sunday but hadn't traveled it. As she peered at the street sign in the shadow of a massive oak tree, Mary considered turning around and returning to the shelter of her new home. She desperately wanted to retreat to her bed and wait for morning to come.

The memory of little Claire lying on top of her canopy bed kept Mary right where she was. She gripped the steering wheel hard and focused on the houses with the tiny yards, the chain link fences, the beater cars parked on dirt driveways or pulled up on patches of grass.

Mary sensed rather than saw the small ranch house with the yellow siding and the red brick. In the moonlight it could have been some other color but she knew this was the one. Loosening her grip on the wheel, Mary swung the Land Rover into a spot along the street a few houses down.

Her aunt's vehicle looked out of place, a Goliath. She slipped the keys into her front pocket for quick access, got out and eased the door shut. The loud click was swallowed by the wind which caught her hair and threw it across her eyes, blinding her for a moment as she waited to see better in the dark.

Absently tucking her hair into her hat, Mary looked down the street at the little house, deceptively ordinary in appearance. Since there were no sidewalks, Mary set off resolutely down the street.

She approached the darkened house with its compact car in the driveway, glancing over her shoulder and scanning the area. Cutting across the lawn to a side window Mary ducked underneath it, remembering to pull off her white hat.

Clutching the window sill for balance she slowly brought her head up to peer through the glass. Mary had to stand on her tiptoes and once again wished she was taller.

Heart hammering away, Mary made out an empty double bed with the covers pushed back as if someone had gotten up in the middle of the night. The room was quite ordinary with a chest of drawers in the corner, a shaker chair next to it, two bedside tables with mismatched lamps.

The faintest of lights were discernible from beyond the open bedroom door, a red glow which reminded Mary of the fires of Hell, as Daddy put it. Her intuition nudged her to turn back, to get away.

Instead, she crept quietly to the back of the house where she could see more red light shining through a window. Mary had never seen red light in a private home before and it struck her as not only garish but creepy. She hoped it would make it hard to see a face in the window.

Slowly, slowly Mary raised herself until she could see in, prepared to run if discovered. With a gasp she took in the canopy bed, the still figure lying on it, uncovered with blankets heaped at the foot. A woman, probably Claire's mother, attended to her.

The grotesque hue illuminated a cascade of dark hair as her mother lifted Claire's head and forced the blunt end of a large syringe into her mouth. She pushed the plunger to squirt some type of liquid into her. It seemed an eternity as her mother waited for Claire to swallow before pushing more in.

She didn't appear to speak to the girl, lying motionless on the bed. The window faced the back yard and Mary was pretty sure she wouldn't be seen as Claire's mother was focused on the matter at hand. What that was, Mary was certain, was poisoning her daughter.

Mary lowered herself below the window and crouched in the cold, mind racing. What could she do? How to get Claire out of there? Was Tony a part of this, a silent accomplice? Somehow, she didn't think so, but he certainly wasn't protecting his daughter. Nobody protects the children, she thought bitterly.

Above the wind Mary heard an engine a few blocks away, a truck engine, and she scrambled to peek around the corner of the house thinking it was her father, looking for her. As the sound grew closer Mary began to panic. She couldn't catch her breath in the cold. Nearly crying, she told herself sternly, "Don't be silly, he doesn't know where you are at this hour of the night. He didn't follow you. You would have seen him."

The truck finally came into view and swung into the driveway, parking behind the small family car. Mary recognized Tony's truck. Of course. He was simply coming home late. Probably avoiding his wife.

Sprinting around the house, she ran up to Tony as he got out of his truck. He stood for a minute, trying to see after extinguishing his headlights. Mary realized he was hanging onto the door to prevent himself from falling. Tony jumped as Mary came at him from the dark.

"Holy shit! What the fuck . . .?"

"Shhh," Mary said in a low tone. "It's me, Mary. Be quiet, Tony!"

"Mary, what're you doing here in the middle of the night?" Tony had trouble getting the words out. Mary saw him smile. "You looking for me? You wanted to see me?" He laughed and Mary smelled beer and cigarettes. It nauseated her.

"Shhh!" she said again, angry that he was drunk when she needed him to take action. "Don't wake up the neighborhood, Tony."

He reached out for her and she ducked, getting angrier. "I'm here because of Claire."

That stopped him cold and Tony squinted at her. "Claire! What are you talking about, Mary? Claire's asleep in the house with her mother." He gestured at his house and then grabbed the truck's mirror for balance. Mary wondered how he had driven himself home from whatever bar he was at.

"Claire's not asleep, Tony, she's barely conscious and her life is in danger!" Saying the words, Mary was aware of how crazy she sounded.

"What the hell, Mary!" He kept squinting at her. "I still don't know what you're talking about." Tony had only a jacket on but didn't seem to feel the cold. "All I know is its 1 o'clock in the morning and you're standing in my front yard."

Mary took a deep breath. "I see things, Tony. I see things and then they happen. They're not dreams, they're visions. I've had them since I was Claire's age. I know it sounds crazy, but I've been seeing Claire, Tony."

He stared at her.

"I see Claire in her little pink canopy bed, and she's sick, real sick."

Tony snorted. "Well, that's no surprise, Mary. You knew she was sick."

"I knew it before I ever met you, Tony. I've been seeing Claire for a while now." Mary gently took his arm and moved closer.

"And tonight I had a vision of her funeral, Tony. You were there, crying, and Claire was in this little casket, it was terrible . . ."

Tony shook off her hand and stepped away. "You're crazy, lady!"

Mary kept talking. "I can sense things, Tony, and I know Claire is in danger. In fact, she's been in danger for some time but now it's worse. She could die."

Tony shook his head. "So, you saw her mother, too? Elizabeth? Describe Elizabeth for me, Mary."

"I haven't seen Claire's mother in my visions, Tony. And I only saw you once, at her funeral. But tonight I saw her for real, Elizabeth, forcing some kind of liquid down Claire's throat. She used a large syringe with the needle off. I saw it."

"Syringe?" Tony ran his hand through his long hair with his free hand. "How did you see this, exactly?"

May bit her lip. "I saw it through Claire's bedroom window, just now. The window at the back of the house."

"You're spying on us? Sneaking around and looking in our windows at night?" He sounded like he just couldn't comprehend it.

"I saw the red light in Claire's bedroom. It was bright enough to see what Elizabeth was doing. You have to call an ambulance, Tony. Claire doesn't have much time. It looks like she's being poisoned."

Eyes on Tony, Mary held her breath. After a minute he slapped his forehead. "Oh yeah, I get it now! You were never interested in me. You were just tryin' to get to Claire. I should've fuckin' known!"

He got louder and pointed a finger at her. "You're crazy! You're a witch! You leave me and my family alone!"

Suddenly a halo of light extended from the porch and Mary's heart sank. The door swung open and Elizabeth stepped out onto the cement steps dressed in robe and slippers. Her thick, almost black hair fell to her shoulders and in the yellow light Mary could see the resemblance to Claire.

"Tony? What's going on out there?"

Mary briefly wondered what had attracted Elizabeth to this man and then was overcome by a sense of evil. Instinctively she drew herself up, standing as tall as her 5-foot 2-inch frame would allow.

Tony contemplated his wife through slit eyes as if surprised that she was there, then bellowed, "Well, Elizabeth! You're up! Meet my almost girlfriend Mary. I told her what street I live on and here she is. We were just talking."

"Keep your voice down, Tony, for God's sake. People are sleeping." She looked from him to Mary. "I see you're drunk," she said contemptuously.

"Yeah, well, you'd be drunk too if . . ." Tony's voice trailed off. "If you lived with you."

He seemed to gather his courage and tried to sling his arm over Mary's shoulder. Mary stepped aside. "I went looking for a woman who'd heat up my bed, Elizabeth! Mary's not real big but she's a hell of a lot warmer!"

Elizabeth paused. "You're drunk. Get in here," she said calmly, reaching for the door. "And you," she sneered to Mary, "get off our property before I call the police."

Tony looked from her to Mary. He hesitated and then shuffled awkwardly toward his wife, head hanging in defeat.

25

ANNIE

Annie's pager blinked and screamed in the night. It seemed like she had just fallen asleep. Fumbling for it, Annie sat straight up in bed. She pushed the button and the number lit up; it wasn't a phone number she recognized, not one of a handful of patients who would wake her when they were in crisis.

The pager showed the time: 1:15 AM. Grabbing her sweatshirt, she remembered an 18 year old male patient who had called her in similar fashion a year or two ago. He had called just to see if she'd call back, he had told her, and then said, "I can tell you what's wrong with me. I'm spoiled." She suspected he was high. And spoiled.

As she headed for the kitchen, Annie sighed. That 18-year-old was long gone. She dialed the phone after putting the old family kettle on for chamomile tea, just like her mother had so many times. Annie lived in a small Cape Cod and it seemed most everything was in reach, just like in her office. One phone in the kitchen was plenty since she avoided the damn thing at home.

It was cold in the kitchen but Annie resisted turning up the heat as heat was expensive in New England, and hopefully she wouldn't be up too long. She pulled up the hood of her Keaney blue URI sweatshirt and tucked the phone receiver inside it awaiting an answer, while rummaging through her tea bags. Like the teapot, her pink slippers came from her mother; Annie resisted all things pink after growing up in a cherry blossom bedroom with wall-to-wall dark pink shag. Not her idea. The phone stopped ringing, "Annie?"

At first she didn't recognize the voice, distraught and high-pitched.

"Yes, who is this, please?"

"It's Mary. I'm so sorry to call like this."

"Mary, what's wrong?"

"I didn't know who else to call."

"It's okay, Mary." Annie waited for her to collect her thoughts. The phone cord reached to the stove, and Annie placed her free Rhode Island Blood Center mug proclaiming SIX GALLONS next to the tea kettle. Annie found chamomile to be calming when she got calls like this.

"Annie, I had another vision, well, more like a nightmare, they don't often come at night. Maybe I was awake, I don't know. It was midnight. I came out of it in a panic; I had seen her funeral, Annie! Instead of a canopy bed she was lying in a little white casket and her father was moaning and sobbing . . . it was horrible!"

Mary was crying. Annie poured boiling water over the tea bag.

"Take a deep breath, Mary. I'm here," Annie said soothingly.

"But Claire was dead because of me! I'm the one who can see the future! I need to save her!"

Annie was bewildered. "You know her name?" She herself knew of one little girl named Claire; how many sick little Claires could there be? In the pause that followed she could hear Mary taking the deep breath while Annie held hers.

"Yes, I met her. I saw her in the MOB and followed her to the lab and spoke with her father."

"You followed her?" Now Annie's voice was higher; she couldn't believe what she was hearing.

"I followed them," Mary said pointedly. "Her father told me how she was sick and the doctors didn't know what was wrong with her and they have a ton of medical bills. But now I know what's going on, Annie, her mother is poisoning her. Claire's mother is poisoning her!"

Annie absently put the hot tea down on the counter. Mary was talking about Elizabeth. Obviously, she had no idea that Annie treated her as well. But what was this about Elizabeth poisoning her own daughter?

Mary needed to feel believed and Annie had to tread carefully, but what if she was delusional? Maybe Mary needed Risperdal after all . . . not that it worked all that well for delusions.

"Okay, just slow down, Mary. What makes you think Claire's mother is poisoning her?" Amazed at how reassuring she sounded, Annie tried to slow her mind.

A pause. "I saw it! I saw it through Claire's bedroom window. I was there. I went tonight and tried to get her father to do something but he didn't believe me."

"You went to Claire's house?"

"Yes, I had to, Annie, it's the same nightmare house I've been seeing! I've been seeing it at night in my visions and tonight it looked just the same!"

"And you looked in Claire's bedroom window?" Annie curled her fingers around the handle of her mug, trying to keep her tone even, as if this was any other piece of information about the puzzle that was Mary. She played a scene in her mind of Mary peeking through somebody's bedroom window in the middle of the night. She just couldn't comprehend it.

"I just had to do something, I saw her funeral, Annie! I had to go there!" Mary sounded like she was ready to break down. It really seemed to Annie that her patient was coming unglued.

It was fairly unusual for one of her patients to talk about another, especially making accusations. Not that Elizabeth would likely continue therapy. She hadn't had a session in weeks.

"How did you know it was Claire's bedroom?"

"I . . . looked in the parents' bedroom first. The bed was turned down and no one was around. Then I saw Elizabeth in Claire's room."

"Elizabeth?" Annie interrupted her.

"Claire's mother. Her father told me her name. There was this awful red light on in the bedroom so I could see in without Elizabeth seeing me."

Annie gripped the receiver. She had been visualizing Elizabeth in her office, talking about her sick daughter. Now she could see the red nightlight and Elizabeth tending to Claire, not knowing she was being observed.

Mary continued, speaking fast. "She was lifting Claire's head and forcing some kind of liquid into her mouth with a large syringe. That little girl didn't even move, Annie! Her arm dropped onto the bed as if she was already dead! It took her forever to swallow, and I just know she's being poisoned!"

Annie lifted the mug to her lips, mind racing. It would be highly unusual to give a child medication in the middle of the night, especially if she was minimally responsive. She really should be in a hospital. What could her mother be giving her?

She recalled Dr. Fowler telling her that Elizabeth brought Claire in to his office frequently, sometimes for minor things despite knowing better with her medical background. She seemed to need a lot of reassurance. Why wouldn't Elizabeth bring Claire to the hospital now?

Annie could understand why Claire's father hadn't believed Mary, she must have looked like a lunatic approaching him in the middle of the night about his wife poisoning his daughter! He barely knew Mary.

"So, you rang the doorbell and the father answered?"

"No, I heard his truck coming down the street. I spoke to him in the driveway."

"He must have wanted to know what you were doing there in the middle of the night."

"I explained everything."

Annie got the feeling Mary was hedging. "I guess it would be a lot to take in," she offered.

Mary hesitated and Annie could almost see the wheels turning in her head. "He had come in to the diner once," she said. "We talked about Claire. I knew him a little bit. But he still didn't believe the visions and told me I was crazy."

Another pause. "He was drinking tonight. I'm sure that affected how he reacted."

Annie considered this. "How come you never told me this, Mary? I see you every week. It would seem to be important enough to bring up."

"Oh Annie, I don't know . . . I just didn't."

This explanation was less than satisfactory but Annie didn't want to push it over the phone with Mary at this hour.

"Tony, that's Claire's Dad, told me Claire had been in the hospital after eating salt," Mary said. "She was really sick and could've even died.

Does that make any sense to you, Annie? Why would a 6-year-old girl eat salt? But after what I saw tonight, it makes sense!"

"She ate salt?"

"Enough to land her in the E.R. Tony couldn't understand it either."

The realization hit Annie like a blow to the head and she gasped despite herself: Munchausen by proxy. It was entirely possible that Elizabeth was poisoning her daughter if she had Munchausen's . . . which is a rare condition but certainly in the realm of possibility and would explain Claire's constant illnesses without a discernible medical cause.

Elizabeth, as a respiratory therapist, would be credible with Dr. Fowler and able to research ways to harm her child enough to get the attention she likely craved so desperately. At least that was Annie's understanding of it. She had never dealt with this before and she didn't know any colleagues who had encountered Munchausen by proxy.

Annie realized the complexity of the situation. Technically Elizabeth was her patient, even if she no longer came to the office. Annie had not yet closed her record. It seemed clear enough that Elizabeth had never intended to get help from Annie, but came for a couple of appointments to appease Dr. Fowler. And he had no idea what was really going on.

"Annie?" Mary's voice brought her back to the present, to the phone clenched as hard as her jaw.

"I'm here, Mary, I'm just thinking."

"What can we do, Annie? We have to do something!" Mary was insistent.

"Listen, Mary, leave this to me. I'll have someone check on Claire."

"Check on her?" Mary sounded incensed. "We have to get her out of there!"

"We have to be careful. Claire is in the care of her parents and they have every right to her at this point. For all you know, Tony looked in on her and she's on the way to the hospital." Annie sounded sure of herself but wasn't. "I'll make some phone calls. Let me handle this."

"Now? Right this minute?"

"Yes, Mary."

"Will you call me back? I have to know Claire's okay."

"Yes, I'll call you back. Give me your phone number again."

Hanging up, Annie glanced at the time. 1:43 in the morning. God, calling Dr. Fowler at this hour . . . maybe Claire was in the E.R. already. Annie would call there first. But if Mary was right, it might be too dangerous to wait until morning.

"Dammit!" Annie muttered as she dialed the hospital operator. She doubted there'd be much more sleep for her this night.

26

AT THE BEDSIDE

It was late and Rhonda had long ago retired for the night. Edmund couldn't sleep. He paced about the downstairs living space, grateful for its modern, vaulted-ceiling open concept which allowed him room to move without feeling like a caged panther at the Roger Williams Park Zoo. That exhibit always fascinated him, watching the outline of the animal's muscles as he slinked back and forth, his slit eyes surveying those who gawked at him as if waiting for an opportunity to strike.

Tonight, Edmund had a real appreciation for caged animals as he padded back and forth in his bare feet, chewing a thumbnail. Rhonda was right to be worried about him, he thought, but she attributed his mental state to misplaced guilt over Shirley's accident.

In truth he had been obsessed with Shirley in the couple of weeks since he assaulted her but not in the compassionate way that Rhonda imagined. In visiting Shirley in the ICU Edmund made certain that Jim was there so he could convey a false sense of caring concern for her. It wasn't hard to do as he did care about Jim and he felt himself growing closer to him despite their differences.

When Edmund consulted his ICU colleagues as well as the unit nurses about Shirley's condition, his apparent concern for her came through. In fact, he received a good deal of strokes and kind words from them but it became increasingly clear to Edmund that he couldn't deal with the uncertainly of Shirley's prognosis. It was a cosmic crap shoot, and although he was pleased that he had taken Shirley out of the game, he wished to God he had done it more thoroughly to eliminate her clinging to life at all costs, refusing to just die and get it over with.

Edmund managed to put on a good performance when Jimmy arrived with his wife and kids. He had always called Jimmy James, partly in jest but also to avoid further emasculation, and he liked the young man as much as he liked his father.

James had reiterated his gratitude that Edmund had been there when his mother fell and hit her head and Edmund accepted this humbly and graciously, by now a well-rehearsed bit in this macabre play that was his life.

Repeat EEG's showed brain activity and Edmund was certain Shirley would continue on, draining an already burdened health care system in her need for 24-hour care. She'd be removed from all aspects of life save everything medical and her family would continue to grieve. In fact, pretty soon she'd be removed from her community, transported from the Jonathan Conrad Hospital to a rehab facility. The closest one was a half hour away.

Edmund ran his hand through his hair as he strode about his spacious home. It was starting to get to him. Lack of sleep was the first sign, with irritability and anger to follow. Edmund knew the pattern well; it had taken years to put it behind him after Viet Nam.

He stopped dead. The war had nearly claimed his marriage and Edmund would be damned if he allowed this thing with Shirley to destroy it. Now was the time to act.

In speaking casually with the ICU staff Edmund had confirmed that there was only a skeletal crew after midnight. He could show up tonight, unable to sleep, seemingly wracked with guilt and sit at Shirley's bedside awhile. It would be just him and Shirley. He could almost hear the click of the IV pump, the claustrophobic sound of the ventilator forcing air into her lungs, the tick of the wall clock counting down the minutes of her miserable existence.

All he'd have to do was wait for the nurse to finish her assessment and give Shirley her meds and do whatever else nurses do before leaving the room for a few minutes. Edmund could lean over and disconnect the respirator hose. He could watch as Shirley slipped away from her vegetative state. She wouldn't even be aware of the need to breathe as she passed on to something else, or perhaps nothing.

Either way her family would be free to move on without her. Shirley would be free. Being atheist, Edmund believed only in the here and now and he was hell-bent to preserve it for himself and Rhonda. And he'd be the first to arrive at Shirley's funeral.

Edmund found himself staring at the old wooden clock standing nearly as tall as Rhonda, inherited from his grandfather. Plain and a little beat up, it didn't really fit with their modern décor, but Rhonda had insisted on placing it in their living room, not in his study or her office. She had wanted to show it off.

There had been great affection between Rhonda and his grandfather, a man who always seemed to know what the right thing to do was. He treated Rhonda like a granddaughter, and Edmund would find them laughing together after his grandfather leaned in to whisper something. The warmth of that would spread across the room.

When Edmund had come back from Viet Nam his grandfather told him how proud he was to have a true war hero in the family. The dissonance hit Edmund like a sucker punch, worse somehow than people at the airport screaming "Baby killer!" while he was in uniform.

With his grandfather, Edmund had managed a feeble smile to cover up the gulf between them. His grandfather was just another old man who didn't get it. He should have expected it.

Tired of tormenting himself, Edmund hurried to get ready to go the hospital. He slipped into his role of concerned physician and friend like it was a second skin; he was beginning to believe it himself. He could stop Shirley's suffering and make everything go back to the way it was.

The drive to the hospital was desolate as it was already one o'clock in the morning, but Edmund didn't mind. The fewer people out at this hour the better as it provided less distraction from the task at hand. Edmund looked forward to finally sleeping again.

The hushed tones and lights of the hospital units didn't bleed over into the Intensive Care Unit, which was nearly as active as any other time of day. The lack of true sleep affected the sickest of patients, contributing to what was called ICU psychosis. While imprisoned in a bed, the constant beeping of machines combined with pain medication and tranquilizers was enough to literally drive some people mad.

Because of Shirley's vegetative state there was little concern over her messed up circadian rhythm, and the harsh lighting set Shirley into stark relief.

The better to see you with, Edmund thought, looking down at her pudgy face misshapen by the ventilator mask pressing on her cheeks and chin. How ironic that over the many years he had known Shirley, Edmund had never seen her without coral lipstick and little black mascara sticks encircling her eyes. She looked like a caricature of herself sans makeup with her brown hair pulled back and splayed across the pillow.

Shirley's nurse was checking lines and entering data on a clipboard while she made small talk with Edmund. She didn't really know him as pediatric cases were shipped to Hasbro Children's Hospital in Providence. Edmund never visited Shirley on the night shift and he didn't know some of the staff.

Luckily there was only one respiratory therapist covering the entire hospital at night. Edmund could return the ventilator hose to its proper position after Shirley was gone; he didn't want any meddling from an RT.

Feeling as calm as the night he went into Ruth's office, Edmund waited for the nurse to leave. He decided it might hasten things if he focused on Shirley and quit chatting with Nurse Julie, or whatever her name was.

Edmund turned his full attention to the form in the bed and made his expression grave, watching her chest lift with the onslaught of air. He wished he was enough of an actor to well up with tears, but that might be overkill.

The nurse paused in the doorway, telling Edmund she'd be back in a few minutes and if he needed anything to please go to the nurse's station. Her voice was soft and kind. He nodded, not turning to look at her and mumbled a thank you but inside of him a ripple of euphoria signaled the end of his two weeks of hell. It would finally be over.

Incredibly, at that moment his pager sounded an alarm. Edmund happened to have it with him out of habit but he wasn't even on call. Automatically he shut it off and noted the number. It was the idiot answering service. They had screwed up and their mistake could cost

Edmund his opportunity to act. If he put off answering the page and Shirley was dead a few minutes later it would look suspicious.

Anger welled up in him and he tensed, his mind searching for a way out. It was a struggle to keep an impassive expression so he kept looking at the pager. Nurse Whoever said in her soft voice, "Dr. Fowler, you can answer that at the station."

Not knowing what else to do, Edmund followed her out of Shirley's room, the rhythmic swish of the respirator receding as they walked down the hall. The nurse's station was located in the middle of the hallway for easy access to all of the patient rooms but Shirley was now farthest away as her condition had stabilized. Hopefully it wouldn't be stable for long.

The short walk gave Edmund time to take a couple of deep breaths. He smiled at the unit secretary who was on the phone with the lab looking for stat bloodwork. Waving his pager at her Edmund picked up one of four phones nestled in a whirlwind of papers and metal charts along the long desk. Photos of the unit secretary's grandchildren smiled behind her phone, a promise of life outside of the ICU.

Steeped in his role as compassionate pediatrician, Edmund dialed the service and got a young, fresh voice. She had to be young to be fresh at this hour.

"Dr. Fowler here. I was paged?"

"Yes, Doctor, sorry for the late hour. I have a call here from Annie Clark? She says you know her and it's urgent. I have her phone number when you're ready."

"Annie? She asked for me specifically?" Edmund couldn't believe it.

"Yes, sir, I know you're not on call. She was very insistent. I'm sorry."

"Okay, go ahead." Edmund took the outstretched Bic from the unit secretary who was arguing with a lab tech about a requisition. He jotted down the number on a Post It note, wondering what it was all about despite his distress at being interrupted.

As he dialed, Edmund decided nothing had changed. He'd take care of this and go back and sit with Shirley and wait for the next opportunity. He'd sit at her bedside all damn night if he had to, certain that none of the ICU staff, the hospital staff, or anyone who knew him would entertain a notion that he had anything to do with Shirley's death. It would simply be a relief to say goodbye.

But Edmund wasn't stupid. He'd have to get out of the room quickly after making sure she was dead, maybe buy some time before anyone else entered. He could search out the nurse and talk to her for a minute. He could ask about what she thought about Shirley's condition, being a seasoned ICU nurse. Then he could ask her to check on Shirley as she wasn't looking good. He was just a pediatrician and unaccustomed to ventilators but it was a feeling he had. Looking concerned, he could accompany the nurse back into Shirley's room and together they would find her dead. Yes, that's the ticket, Edmund thought.

He hadn't been aware of the ringing of the phone but now it stopped with Annie's crisp, "Hello?"

"Hi, Annie, Dr. Fowler here."

"Yes, hi, I'm so sorry to call this late." She continued rapidly, her words tumbling out. "I got a call from one of my clients, one of my patients, Mary. She's convinced that Claire, your patient, is critically ill and needs to be hospitalized."

"Claire?" Edmund furrowed his brow, staring at the little yellow sticky note.

"Yes, Elizabeth's daughter. She saw her and became extremely concerned."

"Recently?" Edmund tried to recall when he had last seen Claire. It had been ten days, maybe two weeks. She had looked okay then, at least pretty close to her baseline.

"Yes. Tonight."

"Did she talk to the parents?"

"One of them, Claire's father. He brushed her off. Unfortunately, he was inebriated."

"Inebriated," Edmund repeated, concerned. "What about Elizabeth? I'm quite sure no one has contacted me about Claire. Even if Elizabeth spoke with my colleague on call, I would've been made aware of it. The family is . . . known to the practice."

A pause as Annie seemed to collect her thoughts. She was professionally bound not to disclose more about her patient than Edmund needed to know. The only reason they were talking like this was because it seemed like there was some kind of emergency.

"Elizabeth appears to be the perpetrator, according to Mary. She's convinced that Claire's mother is out to harm her and in fact appears to be poisoning her."

"Poisoning her!" Edmund exclaimed. The CNA at his elbow looked at him sharply. She was middle aged and it took a lot to throw her.

Annie spoke rapidly again. "I've been thinking about this family, Dr. Fowler, and especially about Elizabeth. Given this information I think it's entirely possible that Elizabeth could be diagnosed with Munchausen by Proxy. I've been recalling the variety of Claire's illnesses and symptoms, and her lack of real improvement in the face of a consistently negative workup, despite excellent care from you. Of course, you know Claire's situation better than I. But Munchausen's really makes more sense than any of Claire's previous diagnoses, wouldn't you say?"

Edmund was silent as his thoughts whirled crazily; it was like a searchlight had been flipped on to illuminate a shadowy landscape.

Munchausen's did make sense. It was the only thing that made sense. He felt like a damn fool. Elizabeth had played him, time and again, played him for a fool. He should have seen it!

As if anticipating his reaction, Annie said in her no-nonsense way, "I feel like I should've figured this out, Dr. Fowler. I'm the psych specialist that you referred Elizabeth to and I missed it entirely."

Cold comfort, Edmund thought. *Nice try.* Gripping the phone, his mind conjured up a picture of Elizabeth forcing salt on little Claire. He shivered despite himself and caught the CNA glancing at him again. Looking down at the desk, Edmund pictured Tony drinking, getting drunk, maybe to manage his guilt? *Was he in on this? How had Claire's father let this go on?*

"Well, I've seen this little girl for a couple of years, Annie. You just saw her Mom a few times." The bitter taste of revulsion crept up his throat. He wished he could confront Elizabeth right now, unleash his fury at being duped and in fact coerced into actively assisting her in hurting her only child. A child who trusted him implicitly.

"So the question is, what do we do about it?" Annie's matter of fact tone irritated him. Who was the doctor here, anyway?

"It seems reasonable to send an ambulance to pick up Claire," she continued. "She should be evaluated. I imagine you'd want a thorough toxicology screen to try to identify a poison. Of course, Elizabeth would fight it and Tony could be a problem since he's been drinking. We probably need police involvement."

Edmund could see Annie had thought this through. She had more objectivity, being less closely involved with the family. *Maybe to her this was just another interesting case.*

"That's not it," he chided himself silently. Edmund knew Annie cared deeply about her patients. She might be feeling betrayed just like he was.

"I know the police captain from a previous situation and could make the call on behalf of both of us," Annie offered. "The police in this town are pretty good when I send them to check on clients. They're trained to defuse potentially violent situations."

Edmund figured that Annie knew he was aware of all of this but she was taking him through the steps because he was too upset to think rationally. That made him even more furious, but his measured words belied his feelings.

"Actually, I'm at the hospital right now, Annie. You make the call and I'll be in the ER waiting for Claire. You said she looks critical?"

"Nearly unresponsive." Annie sounded worried but relieved.

"Okay, I'll go talk to the doctor in the ER. We'll be ready for her. You make the call."

"Thanks, Dr. Fowler."

"No, Annie, thank you. Thank you very much."

27

CONFIDENT

MARY WAS EXHAUSTED, running on only a couple hours of sleep. Her mind kept replaying the events of the previous night despite Annie's reassurance that she'd get Claire to the hospital. They both had done their parts, Annie had said. Now it was time to leave it alone.

But she couldn't leave it alone. It was a slow work day for some reason and Sally was in a mood to gossip. Mary never had any idea who the cast of characters were that paraded through Sally's mind, but she often learned something about how their world operated and how people functioned, so she paid attention.

Today Mary found herself nodding without really listening, absently chuckling at Dennis's antics in the kitchen; he loved to flip the spatula in the air and catch it after dishing up pancakes or French toast, or just when he felt like it. When Cindy caught him, she'd yell DEN-NIS! as the thing clattered to the dirty floor. It slowed him down.

On this Saturday Mary's insides were all balled up like a clump of sheets pulled hot from the dryer. Her throat ached as if she wanted to cry, and the extra cup of coffee she had taken time to pour herself threatened to show up again.

Because business was slow, Mary observed the comings and goings of the diner, so when John Smith showed up mid-morning in his blue jeans and running shoes, hair still damp from his shower, she knew it right away. Her eyes widened and she looked down to still the sudden pounding of her heart, scrubbing an already clean table in the corner.

When she looked up, he was coming right toward her, smiling, eyes crinkling just like she remembered. He seemed taller somehow, and moved gracefully down the cramped aisle, dodging Sally with a heavy tray.

For a moment Mary relaxed, forgetting Claire, forgetting the nightmare house and Tony. Without thinking, she slid into the booth with the wet Formica. John Smith followed and they sat facing each other.

"Can I get you something, sir?" Mary said, lifting an eyebrow and smiling back. She forgot about her stomach.

"Oh, I would never ask you to get up, Mary," he teased her. "It would seem I have everything I need right here. Except maybe for a glass of orange juice."

"Oh!" Mary exclaimed, jumping up. "I'll be right back."

Mary felt like one of the cheerleaders she had pretended not to watch when she came to town as a teenager, the ones with the boys hanging on them. Boys with letter jackets, girls with short skirts and bulky sweaters they wore to cheer the games. In warm weather the girls shed the sweaters to expose tight white T shirts that melted into the curves of their young bodies. The boys were all over them while trying to act nonchalant, and the girls would giggle coquettishly, a word from one of her mother's old romance novels.

As Mary hurriedly poured John Smith's juice into the bigger juice glass, not the 6-ounce size, she said to herself, *Okay, you're over thirty but maybe it's your turn. It's finally your turn!*

Back in the booth, Mary could think of nothing to say except to ask John Smith if he needed something to eat, except he had told her to call him John. She was acutely aware of her awkwardness as he looked at her . . . John.

He said he was fine. Not hungry yet. Then John said, "You know, Mary, I've been in here a couple of times when you weren't working. I didn't stay long."

Her heart leaped and Mary twisted the rag she had left on the table. His blue eyes never left her face.

"Maybe it would work better if you gave me your phone number," he said. "If you want to, that is. I'd really like to take you out sometime."

Her throat felt too dry to speak but she managed to croak, "Yes. Yes, that would be nice."

Grateful to move, Mary slid to the edge of the booth. He looked worried, like she was running away, so she said, "I'll get a piece of paper."

"You'll be right back."

"Yes." Mary couldn't help but laugh, then sprinted for the cash register, not worrying if she looked too eager. A party of six could show up at any moment and pull her away from him.

Sally approached her as she rummaged around for a slip of paper and said, "Don't you worry, honey, I can handle this crowd. You go talk to that nice young man."

Sally's low tone was discrete; Mary wondered if she'd be the next topic of conversation in the diner. She realized for once she didn't care.

Scribbling the phone number with the pencil from her apron pocket Mary thought about how this wasn't even her house number, it belonged to Aunt Elaine. How could she explain it if her aunt picked up the phone? And what if he asked about her family?

Mary shrugged and scooted back into the corner booth with its modicum of privacy. Extending the paper, Mary said impulsively, "I don't expect to see this on the bathroom wall."

She stopped, surprised at herself, and John laughed. It felt good to make him laugh. Maybe she could be amusing . . . another romance novel word.

"Rest assured, I will keep this in a very safe place," John said as he pulled out his wallet and tucked it in. He rested his arms on the table and looked at her again, as if he liked looking at her. That felt good, too.

"Have you worked here long?" John asked, lifting the glass. She decided he had a strong chin and looked even more attractive with a day's growth of beard.

"No, not really, a couple of months."

"Do you like it?"

"Oh, yes, the owner and the other employees are wonderful and . . . I like serving people."

Mary remembered her musings about what he did for work. It was probably more interesting than her waitress job.

"What about you, John?" She liked using his name. "What do you do when you wear that suit?"

"To earn a living, you mean?"

"Yes, to earn a living." Mary liked him teasing her but decided she could give it right back.

"I started a home security business here. I'm actually from the Midwest."

"Really!" Mary didn't know anybody who wasn't local, but then she didn't know a lot of people.

"Really."

"How does Rhode Island compare? I've never been anywhere else. Do you like it here?" She really hoped that he did.

"Well, yes, I like it here. It's taking me longer than I expected to meet people, so I'm glad I'm getting to know you."

Under his gaze she felt flustered again and looked down, noticing an ad on the paper place mat for a free oil change. Mary traced it with her index finger, wondering if it was Tony's garage.

She looked up. "I'm glad I met you, John."

They didn't speak for a minute or two. Then he said, "Well, one good thing about moving to a new location is I can shed my old name. I never liked being called Jack but John was my father's name. Now it's mine."

Mary felt like she'd had the wind knocked out of her. She honestly hadn't connected his name to her father's, since the two men were worlds apart. But now she felt it hard to breathe and her heart resumed its thumping, propelling itself out of her chest. Mary feared she would start sweating, feared she'd panic, feared the fear rising up in her.

Twisting the rag, she focused on the buttons of John's Polo shirt beneath a V-necked sweater as she tried to calm down. As if from a distance she heard him say, "Mary, are you alright?"

She didn't know what to say. That she was having a panic attack? That his name was the same as her father's and that drove her into a panic? That she was her father's daughter so she was crazy too, in fact, crazy enough to have visions?

Mary slid over on the seat again, preparing to flee before she really lost it. John took her hand. "Whatever it is Mary, it's okay. I'm here. Don't leave."

Instinctively she looked into his eyes and saw compassion. It seemed like he really was there for her, like he somehow understood. He tightened his hand around hers.

"Just breath."

She did. She searched his blue eyes and breathed deeply, shaky at first and then stronger, slower. The battering of her insides eased. She wondered what to say but knew it didn't matter.

Mary whispered, "You're the only one outside of my aunt who can calm me down when I get like this."

"My pleasure," John replied with a smile.

"I live with her, my aunt, I mean," Mary continued bravely, looking for a sign that John would think this was odd in some way or that she was odd, since she wasn't a kid any longer. Mary felt her hand in his reassuring grip. Maybe he wouldn't let her go.

"It sounds like she's great," John said. "I hope to meet her some day."

He looks so relaxed, Mary thought. He has no clue what this is all about. Regardless, she felt relieved and smiled back.

"I think you will. Meet her, I mean. Her name is Elaine, but . . ." Her smile died. "You'll never meet the rest of my family. I mean my father. He's all I have and we don't speak."

"I'm sorry to hear that."

"Actually, it's more than that. He's dangerous," Mary heard herself say. *What was she doing? Did she want to drive him away?* But she couldn't help herself, she felt that before John got involved with her, he needed to know that she carried baggage. Some day it could affect him.

Run away now, Mary thought as she studied his kind face, *before you get sucked in to my mess.* She already liked John too much to watch it happen. Maybe this wasn't going to work. But the look on his face tugged at her.

"Dangerous?" John repeated.

"Just to me," Mary replied hastily, as if to reassure him. "It's because he can't keep the family farm going without me. My father needs me, and I'm not going back. I even took out a restraining order against him which infuriated him. I've never stood up to him before."

John's expression turned cold. "He's hurt you?"

Mary cast her eyes down as shame colored her face. She didn't need to respond.

"His name is Jack," she finally whispered, eyes filling up.

He seemed to understand even this, Mary saw, as she wiped her eyes with the back of her hand. *But how could he understand?*

"Your father can't keep you on the farm against your will, Mary."

"He made it impossible for my mother to leave," she said. "He ripped out the phone in one of his rages right before she got sick. And the farm is too far to walk to town." She could tell John was picturing it.

"There's only one vehicle," Mary continued. "It's my father's truck, and he keeps the keys."

"How did you buy groceries? Supplies?"

"I was allowed to use the truck because Daddy knew I would come back. I would never leave Mama. It never occurred to him that I would leave for good, but I did after Mama died. My bag was packed the next day," Mary said defiantly. "I went to my aunt's house, and that was the end of it. Except . . ." her voice trailed off.

John waited for her to continue. Mary had trouble getting the words out. "Except that it wasn't."

He seemed to consider this. "But Mary, if your father hauled you back to the family farm, wouldn't your aunt call the police?"

"I guess so." She hesitated. "My aunt had one of her friends who's a police detective talk to him, but I know it won't help. I know my father. He doesn't quit."

"If he tried to take you, he'd go to jail for kidnapping and it wouldn't be a short sentence."

Mary felt surprised, like she hadn't considered this before, even though she and Annie had discussed this very thing. Maybe she really was stupid.

"Okay. I guess."

"He won't want to hurt you, if he needs you to work the farm."

Eyes flitting across the diner, Mary worried their time was short. "There's all kinds of hurt," she said nervously.

It was John's turn to look surprised. She started to squirm, wondering how much he really understood. She felt incapable of explaining the fear that grabbed her by the throat, that defied logic. Her father was larger than life, the devil himself, and if he got hold of her, he'd make her pay. God knows what could happen before Aunt Elaine realized she was missing and called the police.

"I know." He took her hand in both of his. "I want to help you."

He really does, Mary thought to herself. He really does.

Suddenly she withdrew her hand and leaned against the stuffed red leather behind her back. "John, I don't want to involve you." Mary tried to look at him but couldn't. "It's okay. I'll be fine. I just appreciate your company."

'Your company'? Mary realized nobody talked like this anymore. Did she look like a fool?

John smiled at her. "I'm already involved, Mary. I was involved the first time I saw you flitting around with the coffee pots. It made me want to drink coffee. When I saw you had no wedding ring, I decided I'd have to ask you out instead."

He reached across the table and gently took her hand back. "I can take care of myself, Mary. You don't have to worry about me."

They sat in silence until Mary realized the front door bell had rung again and the place was filling up. God bless Sally for giving them this time together.

"I need to get back to work," she said, not moving.

"Yes," John said. He didn't move either.

Mary took her hand back and he asked hastily, "Are you working Friday night?"

"No, I think I get off at 2PM." Mary stood and reached for her rag.

"Dinner?"

"Yes. Absolutely." Mary spotted Sally greeting a family of four at one of her tables, pulling out her order pad.

"Call me," she said over her shoulder as she hurried down the aisle, feeling like she was in a movie. John apparently saw something in her that she was blind to, and it made her stand a little taller. Energized, Mary approached Sally as she dug into her pocket for pad and pencil.

"Thanks, Sally, I'll take over," she said.

28

Uncovering

Waiting in the windowed, central room of the ER which served as a physician work room was a privilege afforded Edmund because of his status as a Jonathan Conrad Hospital staff physician. As he discussed Claire and her likely condition with Mike Morrissey – that of being poisoned by her own mother – Edmund took in the morbid curiosity of the nurses as he was laying out the whole sordid affair.

Mike was experienced, an old hand like Edmund, and didn't react outside of reviewing out loud what he'd look for in toxicology testing and lab work. He considered the possibility that Claire might need assisted ventilation as the poison took hold.

"Coffee, Ed?" Mike asked, acting like a good host to a weary traveler. "It's under 4 hours old."

Edmund realized he was exhausted. "Oh no, no. I'll have to get to sleep pretty soon. But thanks."

"Dr. Morrissey!" A nurse Edmund didn't recognize charged into the room, brandishing a chart. "Our friend in two is cranking up. Could I get some more Haldol?"

"Is he the one yelling?"

"Yeah, he yells at me, he yells at people who aren't there. But he hasn't taken a swing at anyone. I hope to prevent that. He's a pretty big guy."

Looking through the window at the rooms reserved for psych patients, Mike shook his head. "The cop who brought him in, didn't he stay?"

"Nope, he got called away. He said since this guy isn't under arrest, he really couldn't hang around. The officer was nice about it, though.

Said to call him if we got into trouble with our Mister, uh," she flipped the chart open. "Mr. Nugent."

"How much Haldol has he had?"

"Ten milligrams in the last hour. It should have kicked in."

"Any Ativan?"

"Two milligrams an hour ago when he came in."

"Okay, give him an additional ten of Haldol. I can't have him beating up the staff. Is Psych on the way to see him?"

"It'll be a while. Full moon."

"Yeah, yeah, great. We'll be filling up with psych patients." Mike spoke while glancing through some labs. "Our friend here may be even less coherent by the time Psych sees him. Can't be helped."

"He'll still get a bed at Westbrook when one becomes available. Mr. Nugent is clearly off his meds."

The nurse wheeled around grabbing her key for the locked medication room. Edmund heard a patient retching in the hallway, waiting in a wheelchair for a bed while his wife tried to comfort him. In a nearby room a woman moaned nonstop and somewhere a baby cried. Staff shifted like pinballs, dodging lab techs, X-ray techs and transport personnel. Edmund watched dispassionately, feeling like a third wheel as he observed Mike, careful not to let himself get triggered.

This was nothing compared to Viet Nam and Edmund certainly didn't need reminders of that. He didn't want to resume medication for the nightmares. As it was, he was lucky to get a couple hours of sleep before facing a full day in the office.

Left to himself, Edmund's thoughts shifted from Claire to Shirley. As he played out the details of her impending death in his mind, he had an odd thought – was he pulled away from Shirley's room by some kind of divine intervention? Edmund realized the urge to end it with the demise of his neighbor was receding like a wave that slapped the shore before pulling back.

Maybe he was just tired, but Edmund had no desire to do anything more. His impulsive lashing out when he pushed Shirley was understandable, he mused. But who could comprehend him pulling the plug on her? Wasn't he the compassionate physician sworn do no harm?

Edmund glimpsed Rhonda's stricken face upon hearing he was charged with . . . murder? Betraying Rhonda, have her see him as some kind of monster, would be the worst thing. Worse even than a couple of years in prison, which is what he could get if Shirley woke up and talked. And of course, the demise of his career.

Edmund rested his head in one hand, shielding his eyes from the light. His head hurt. All he wanted to do was go home, crawl into bed next to Rhonda and sleep. Let Mike deal with Claire.

Edmund recognized Leslie, a nurse who intercepted Mike in the charting room. "There's a report coming through from EMS," she said.

Mike moved to the EMS radio motioning to Edmund to follow him. Mike picked up the radio and said, "Yes? Dr. Morrissey here." He held it out so staff could hear.

The voice on the other end was punctuated by the "Whoop, whoop!" of a siren followed by its two-note blare. The EMT spoke loudly and Edmund detected a note of panic.

"Doc, we're in route with a six-year-old girl found unresponsive at home by police. No known trauma. Respirations are depressed. She's requiring us to bag her to keep her oxygen above 90. We're working on an IV but currently no access. Her blood pressure is low, 60 over palpation. We're about five minutes out."

"Got it," Mike replied calmly but the furrows in his forehead deepened as he turned to Leslie. "We need to set up room 10 for intubation. Where's the pedi code cart? Sounds like this six-year-old will need a tube. Call respiratory stat. I want them here." The unit secretary picked up the phone.

"Gabby," Mike continued, "we're going to need an IV in this kid. Just get access. Bilateral would be best. She's hypotensive. We'll give a 20cc per kilo bolus of fluid."

"Okay, 20 cc per kilogram," Gabby repeated. "Normal saline, right, Mike?"

"You got it." To the unit secretary, "Barbara, get security here." Barbara picked up the phone again.

Turning to Edmund, Mike said, "How well do you know this inebriated father?"

"Not well since I dealt with the mother," Edmund said ruefully. "I saw the father once, briefly. He could be complicit. God knows if either one of them will show up. I'd have a few choice words for the mother."

"Well, that mess is not our concern right now. Let's keep everyone safe and take care of this little girl."

The staff scattered and Edmund wished he had something to do.

"Ed, I want you to help with whoever shows up from the family. We don't have Social Services at this hour and Security will have no idea what's going on. You'll have to put your feelings aside." Mike looked at Edmund who nodded with more assurance than he felt.

After a minute the hiss and click of the automatic double doors in the ambulance bay signaled Claire's arrival. The EMTs moved quickly, bathing the tiny slip of a girl as they rolled her in. The ambu bag concealed her face. Edmund's heart leaped in his chest, seeing her motionless body strapped in, a blanket pulled up to her chin.

"Room 10!" Gabby called, hastening to join them with IV equipment. The crew rolled Claire into the room where Leslie was setting up. They transferred Claire to the jacked-up hospital bed quickly and efficiently, huddling around her in the middle of the room. Another nurse pulled the blanket off gently, exposing Claire's pink rosebud nightgown which she addressed with scissors.

The respiratory therapist showed up looking short of breath herself, and slid into position at Claire's head. Resting her arms on the bed, she took the ambu bag from the EMT and gently squeezed it to avoid overinflating Claire's lungs. The RT watched her chest rise and checked the ambu bag's seal around Claire's mouth.

Mike looked at her. "Betsy, any trouble bagging her?"

"Nope, it's okay."

"What's her sat?"

"90."

"Check a sugar. What are the pupils?"

"Dilated bilat."

"Any evidence of tongue biting? Maybe she seized?"

"No, Doc." One of the EMTs responded from the doorway, paperwork in hand, looking shaken since it was fairly unusual to transport a child in this condition.

"Do we have access?" Mike's machine gun questions reminded Edmund of himself, so many years ago in Viet Nam. His mind pictured Claire's recent trip to the ER, so ill with salt ingestion. Salt! He should have known she would never eat a lot of salt, and the vision of Elizabeth forcing it down made Edmund want to vomit. He told himself to stay in the moment. He focused on the team hovering around Claire.

"Got it!" Gabby reached for the adhesive tape she and had stuck to the bed. She secured the IV and opened the line, watching the needle site to make sure the fluid went into Claire's vein.

Janet, a nurse that Edmund recalled had two young kids of her own, showed up at the door. She swiftly assessed Claire and the unfolding nightmare, impassive, wearing her professional face. Edmund wondered how she dealt with this stuff as Janet took paperwork from the EMT, leading him to the desk. He wondered how they all dealt with it.

"Dr. Fowler!" Barbara said, approaching Edmund from the desk. "The father is here. He wants to speak to someone about his daughter. Security is standing by."

Mike glanced at Edmund as if to ask whether he could handle this before his eyes reverted back to Claire.

"Just the father? Not the mother?" Edmund was shocked but not surprised.

"He was brought in by the officers who went to the home. No sign of the mother."

"Can I use the Family Room?" Edmund inquired coolly, disguising a flash of anger.

"Yes, of course. He's already there waiting for you."

As Edmund turned on his heel, he heard Mike announce, "Okay, we've gotta intubate. Number 5, please. Betsy, I'll take over."

Not wanting to witness Claire's intubation, Edmund kept his back turned and grimly prepared to deal with Tony. He was intent upon keeping his feelings in check while interrogating him about Elizabeth, that pathetic excuse of a mother. Not pathetic, he reminded himself. Deadly.

The family room was located just before the automatic doors leading to the waiting room, a small space where loved ones gathered to hear good news or bad. In one corner sat Tony, clutching his greasy head in his hands. For a moment Edmund felt sorry for him, wondering if he was losing his wife as well as his only child.

Maybe not, Edmund thought. Perhaps he'd stay with Elizabeth, no matter what she had done to their daughter. A feeling of revulsion crept up his throat and a blackness took over his mind.

"Tony," Edmund croaked. He cleared his throat as the smaller man looked up. Edmund took in the bloodshot eyes, the smell of beer, the slight sway.

"Doc," Tony whispered. He grabbed the arms of the chair as if to rise and Edmund held up an authoritative hand.

"Don't get up." He turned to shut the door, feeling sick as the stench of the sweat and alcohol permeated the room.

Taking a seat, Edmund stared at Tony, hoping to make him squirm. Tony blinked, waiting, then finally asked, "Is she okay? Is my little girl okay?"

"Your little girl," Edmund repeated contemptuously, fighting to maintain control, "is not okay."

Tony looked at him wide-eyed, blinking.

"She could die." Edmund wanted to hurt this man as Claire had been hurt. "Where is Elizabeth?" he continued, lip curling. Tony looked confused.

"She's at home. She couldn't handle seeing Claire like this. She wants me to call her when we know what's wrong with her."

"What's wrong with her, Tony," Edmund's voice rose, he was furious, *"is that she's been poisoned."*

Tony shrank back into his chair, eyes bulging. "No!"

"Yes! And it happened with you there, Tony, right under your nose! But you were drunk, weren't you, Tony." Edmund jabbed a finger at him. "And somebody else had to call rescue, somebody so worried about your daughter that she called the police as well as an ambulance, and now Claire is getting a tube shoved down her throat to breathe!"

"No, no, no!"

The Family Room door swung open to reveal a portly man in uniform with grey hair combed back off his face. He stepped in, looking from Edmund to Tony and back to Edmund.

Edmund stood up, unable to contain himself. "And her mother isn't even here with her, knowing this could be the last day of her life, knowing she's been poisoned, because Elizabeth is the one who did it!"

"Is everything okay in here?" the security guard asked.

Edmund tried to slow himself down. He was aware of how this must look, and how it had sounded.

"It's okay, thanks. We just have some tough decisions to make."

Tony started to cry, not taking his eyes off Edmund, who sat down and casually crossed his legs.

"I'll call for you if you're needed." Edmund gestured toward the phone on the wall.

The guard paused, then nodded. "Well, Doc, I'll be down the hall." It sounded like a warning.

Edmund offered a weak smile. "Thank you." He watched as the guard gently closed the door, keys jingling.

Bent over and sobbing, Tony covered his face with his hands. Edmund watched him. He waited for Tony to take responsibility for his child. As a mental exercise Edmund tried to find something to relate to in this man and failed. *Grease monkey,* he thought scornfully, looking at Tony's hands.

His sobs eased. Playing the good doctor, Edmund moved closer to offer a box of tissues. Tony took the box while he ran his sleeve across his nose. He took off his glasses to mop his face, blew his nose mightily and leaned back in his chair.

Edmund gestured toward the waste basket. Tony threw the sodden ball of tissues, missed, and got up to retrieve it. He blinked as if to see better and shuffled toward his goal, hanging on to the couple of chairs. As he bent over, Edmund wished Tony would topple but he managed to properly dispose of his tissues. Edmund thought of the cops who had brought Tony in; they dealt with alcoholics all the time. What a miserable job.

"What was it?" Tony asked suddenly.

"What?"

"What was the poison?"

Edmund looked at Tony and saw a glimmer of what he was looking for. "We don't know yet. We're running a toxicology report."

"How do you know what to do if you don't know what poison it is?"

"We treat her symptoms. Like her inability to breath," Edmund couldn't resist saying. Tony looked at the floor.

"Remember when Claire came in to the ER with salt ingestion, Tony?"

"Yeah."

"Didn't you think it was strange that Claire would eat that much salt? Enough to poison her? With her mother right there?" Edmund didn't want to say he had thought it strange at the time but believed Elizabeth anyway.

Tony was silent, staring at Edmund. "Jesus Christ," he breathed. Edmund figured he was getting the same mental image of Elizabeth forcing salt on Claire. His anger ebbed.

"You really didn't know, Tony?"

"I should've been there," Tony said more to himself than to Edmund. "I could've been home more. Elizabeth drove me away but I should've . . . been more of a father, I guess."

Edmund remained silent.

"She just took over," Tony said slowly. "She took over Claire and she seemed to do it right. What do I know about raising a little girl? Elizabeth was educated and she always had the answers, every time. Every single time. If I said anything, I was the dummy. I couldn't even let the girl outside to play without hearing about it."

Tony's fists were clenched and he breathed heavily. "I should've seen it but all I saw were the bills coming in, all those medical bills that had to be paid. Shit, I didn't make enough money to pay all those bills. Elizabeth made more than me." He snorted. "So maybe it was Elizabeth who got us into debt, huh, Doc? Maybe she made Claire sick all the time!"

"I think she pretended Claire was sick, in the beginning."

"Why would she do that?"

"For attention, I guess." Edmund ruefully recalled the feedback he had gotten from the nurses when Claire was hospitalized. He had ignored that as well.

"She sure as hell wasn't coming to me for attention!" Tony spat out. It seemed like Tony had caught Edmund's rage.

"Got it Tony." Edmund realized he was done, spent; he desperately needed sleep. He rubbed his head, wishing he had asked Janet to get him some aspirin. Now that Claire was here and in Mike's capable hands, Edmund decided his part was over. There was little to be gained from talking to Tony, and Elizabeth wasn't here.

"Thank you for speaking with me, Tony," Edmund said dismissively. "You can go back to the waiting room and one of the nurses will fetch you when there's more information about Claire. Dr. Morrissey is in charge of her care. He will speak with you as soon as he is able."

"I can't just stay here?"

"No." Edmund felt perverse pleasure from sending him out. He stood, and Tony stood, and they looked at each other with an odd kind of kinship.

"Thanks, Doc," Tony said. "Thanks for everything you've done for my little girl." He stuck out his hand and Edmund remembered the wet wad in the wastebasket. He shook Tony's hand as the smell of cigarettes and beer overtook him. At least Tony had a good grip.

"You're welcome." Edmund tried to recall where the nearest sink was to wash his hands as he reached for the door knob. He'd wash very thoroughly.

29

Taken

Mary marveled at how easy it was to talk to John over dinner. She wanted to know every detail of his life and was held transfixed as he traveled from one crazy story to another. Never having had a sibling and not knowing anything about boys, Mary reveled in John's tales of boyhood adventures with his brother, Matt.

She tried to picture Wisconsin's rolling farmland, corn fields that stretched as far as the eye could see. She envisioned John and Matt digging a snow fort from the snowplow's remains after a blizzard that dumped over a foot of snow.

Mary told John about Rhode Island's Blizzard of '78, always capitalized in the Ocean State and referred to in reverential terms. It was a freak nor'easter that left thousands stranded for nearly a week; stories of dramatic rescues, governmental failings and neighbor helping neighbor continued to dominate the local culture.

"It dumped over 27 inches of snow, and Rhode Island had never seen anything like it," Mary explained. "We didn't have the plows or the manpower back then. There's a funny newspaper photograph of snowplows from Massachusetts turning around at the Rhode Island border, and all you see is solid white beyond them. Nobody traveled for days. People left their cars and holed up wherever they could. At the farm, we couldn't even shovel a path to the barn."

Her face darkened. "We lost a lot of chickens," Mary said, "and our dairy cow. She didn't get milked or fed." Mary had often wished she had been stranded in a restaurant, a hospital, anywhere but home with her father. She looked down at her plate, seeing Daddy's rage, as he shook a fist at the storm which left them powerless. Mary saw Daddy outside, screaming over the freight train wind telling Mama and her to work harder, as the three of them struggled with their pathetic little shovels. Mary had even dared to hope that this could be it, they might lose the farm and would have to move to town, where maybe something else was possible. Anything else.

She looked up to see John studying her face, not like a puzzle to be figured out but like a compassionate friend who wished for all the world he'd arrived on the scene earlier.

"I can't imagine it, knowing you can't get to your livestock," he said.

"Yes, knowing they were starving, and dying in pain. And eventually no eggs to sell, no milk to drink."

John took her hand and rubbed her unadorned fingers. She thrilled at his touch. Maybe he noticed because he smiled.

"It's nice to see you out of that waitress uniform," he whispered.

Mary didn't tell him the angst of picking out her red dress from Aunt Elaine's closet for the first date she'd ever gone on in her life. Thank God it was stretchy and it fit her and seemed to be in style; her aunt had advised her about investing in quality clothing as she helped pull the fabric over Mary's head and bent to tug it to a few inches above her knee.

Aunt Elaine had laughed at Mary's nervous anticipation as she helped dab a bit of make-up to emphasize her eyes, flesh out her lips and color her cheeks. "When I was dating," she had recalled, "it took me forever to do my hair, but yours is perfect just the way it is. You look beautiful."

Looking at herself in the mirror, Mary had chosen to believe it. The dress clung to her shapely arms and exposed her long neck. With earrings even her plain bob looked flattering. Mary reminded herself that John had picked her. Maybe a little bit of make-up could do a little bit of magic, on this night, anyway.

She had never been to a restaurant like this, at a well-known historic inn in Westerly. They were sitting at the edge of the ocean with soft background music and candle light. Mary noticed the waitress was friendly, attentive but unobtrusive, leaving them to talk undisturbed.

John slid the candle aside after they finished and leaned in. He seemed as eager to hear her stories as Mary was to listen to his. He winked and wondered aloud if their coffee was as good as the Rise and Shine Diner's.

Focusing on her mother and her forays with Aunt Elaine seemed to satisfy John for the moment. Mary decided to hold off any discussion of her family for as long as possible, and in truth she knew precious little about her father's family anyway. He never talked about such things, especially with her. When she was five, she remembered asking her mother why her father seemed to hate her, or worse yet, why he treated her like she was one of his animals. Her mother had brushed it off. Mary went to Aunt Elaine for information about grandparents and cousins, not that there were any left, and decided that she took after that side of the family.

It feels alien to be this happy, Mary thought as John held the door for her on the way out. She had decided her long, grey down coat would have to do. They headed down the walkway and then across the grass toward the dimly lit dirt parking lot in front of the inn. The occasional overhead orb weakly illuminated the shapes of the few remaining cars.

"It seems the parking lot hasn't been updated since the Shelter Harbor Inn was built," John commented . "And this is an old building!"

"I imagine it takes a lot to keep up a building this old," Mary commented, feeling like she should defend Rhode Islanders' efforts to preserve historical sites. She felt safe with John and focused on what he was saying while doing her best to remain upright in heels on the grass. An icy breeze gently slapped her cheeks.

A step away from the smooth terrain of the parking lot, and woefully unskilled in the art of the cat walk, Mary suddenly lurched sideways, one arm flying up.

"Whoa!" John exclaimed and grabbed her hand.

Mary laughed. "I'm not used to heels, I guess." She looked up at him, feeling the strength of his hand, barely able to make out his features as the moon sliver peeked through outlines of Burr oak and ash. She was aware of how close he was.

"Maybe you're not used to that much wine?" John asked. "Then I should apologize." Mary could sense his smile.

"Oh, no," Mary said emphatically. "You have nothing to apologize for." And then, true to her mother's romance novels, John cupped her chin and leaned in, instinctively tightening his grip on her hand. He had to bend over a bit but Mary had gained a couple of inches in heels and this thought occupied her mind until she felt the firm, warm pressure of his lips. All thought left her; it was as if Mary had practiced all her life for that first kiss.

Suddenly a familiar, harsh cackle erupted from 20 feet away. Mary pulled back from John. Eyes wide, her head whipped sideways to view the threat, assess the risk. She felt her heart convulse; she wanted to run.

Jack stepped from the shadows of the parking lot, hair hanging down to his shoulders, beard a dirty mess of grey that seemed stuck to his filthy jacket as his mouth moved. "Well, well, ain't this the sweetest thing!" Jack sneered. "Mary's gone and got herself a boyfriend. Ain't you gonna introduce us, Mary?"

Frozen, Mary didn't notice John's jaw hardening and his frame tensing. She felt horrified that he would now link her, genetically at least, to this apparition, while wondering at the same time what her father was up to. She desperately tried to imagine how he had found her here.

Facing her father, Mary found the strength to shout, "Leave us alone!"

Jack laughed and spit casually. "No, darlin', I need you to come home. Enough of this nonsense, it's been long enough. You come with me now." Jack's voice was calm, but Mary knew he was anything but. Her father was outraged that she continued to defy him.

"You know that's not going to happen," John said matter-of-factly. "Mary's with me now. Why don't you just move along and leave her alone."

Jack folded his arms in front of his chest and widened his stance. "Who's gonna make me?"

It occurred to Mary that her father was looking psychotic. John tugged her hand and they started walking to his car at the back of the lot, keeping an eye on Jack. Mary noted John's air of calm authority, but her heart didn't slow down.

Jack moved to his truck parked close by, deep in the shadows. Mary hadn't seen it there. He reached into the back bed and pulled something out. Stepping into the light, he rang out, "Not so fast!"

They stopped cold and Mary felt dizzy staring at her father and the rifle. *Where had he gotten a gun like that?*

Now it was happening. Her worst nightmare. She'd go back to the farm and never get away. Knowing he had won, her father's abuse would get worse. He'd treat her the way he had treated her mother, night and day. It all flashed before her eyes in a second. And what if John got shot trying to protect her? He could be killed. Mary didn't know if she loved him, but she couldn't let that happen.

Breathing deep, all at once she shrugged off John's hand and stepped forward. "I'll go with you," she said firmly. "Don't hurt anybody."

"Mary!" John exclaimed as he tried to grab her arm, but she shook him off hard and bolted to the truck. Her father's body odor reached her as she got close enough to look into his crazy eyes; Mary wondered what had happened to him after her mother died. The sight of him grinning, the smell of him, set her stomach to churning.

Resolute, Mary opened the cab's passenger door and clamored in, brushing empty beer cans and pork rind bags onto the floor. As she glanced over her shoulder, she glimpsed John standing alone helplessly, fists clenched at his sides. Mary was grateful he hadn't done anything stupid and her father had no cause to shoot him.

Instead, Jack clutched the weapon as he got in to the driver's seat. It was shocking to see it up close in the feeble dome light. Mary had never seen a gun before, and it looked huge and dangerous. Jack held it awkwardly as he turned the key and the engine roared. Mary had forgotten how loud it was but the clattering of coins and screws in the ashtray and the stink of old floor carpet made her feel like his child again as they lurched backward.

Jack slammed the gear into drive, and they took off as if someone was chasing them, but nobody was. They rattled down the Shelter Harbor's long, dark driveway, bouncing over potholes and coming out onto the smooth highway. Jack drove recklessly, fast, with a triumphant air. After several minutes he turned off the highway onto a patchwork of sparsely populated back roads. One of them ended with the tiny farm she had never called home.

∽

It was late when the call came through, and Paul Rice had been soundly asleep. As he awoke, disoriented, to the shrill insistence from his bedside phone, he glanced at his watch: nearly midnight. Calls at this hour were uncommon and he leaned over to snatch the phone from its cradle.

"Paul Rice here."

"Paul? It's Captain Nelson. Sorry to call at this hour."

"Ken? What's going on?"

"It seems like there's been a bona fide kidnapping in Westerly."

"What?" Paul sat straight up in bed.

"Yeah, that crazy loon Jack Johnson has gone and kidnapped his daughter. Guess he's been harassing her and now he's forced her into his vehicle with a goddamned rifle, for Christ sake! Her boyfriend John Smith called in the plate."

"Jesus! Where did this happen? Were there any patrols that responded?"

"Yeah, it was at the Shelter Harbor Inn, in the parking lot. Appears he was waiting for them to come out. Two patrols nearly caught up with him but kept their distance as the daughter was in the passenger seat."

Paul was silent a minute. Elaine had been afraid Jack might do something, and Paul had kept an eye on Jack as promised. *But I never imagined anything like this. What the hell is Jack thinking?*

"Where are they now?"

"Holed up in that farmhouse, you know where it is. Jack's been yellin' to leave them alone. The officers are awaiting further instruction. We already notified the Chief."

"I'm on my way." Paul slammed down the receiver and reached for his pants on the floor before shoving aside the bed covers. He kept it cold at night to save money. Well, he'd be earning his paycheck tonight.

Paul backed out of his garage fast. *This could get ugly,* he thought as he drove toward the farm. He was very aware his department had never dealt with an erratic gun owner holding a hostage. The hostage being Elaine's beloved niece. He hoped to God they didn't screw it up.

The deep ruts in the driveway to the Johnson farm forced Paul to slow down and he cursed. Up ahead a string of pulsating lights atop four police vehicles lit the night. As Paul finally swung into the yard Chief Bradbury, holding a bullhorn, approached him. He scratched his forehead underneath his hat, a sign that he was thinking. Paul rolled down his window.

"The men are in position," he said. "I figure you know the bastard the best, so maybe you can talk some sense in to him."

Paul snorted, pulling on his gloves. "Jack? He doesn't know the meaning of the word. He's really gone off the rails this time. Does it appear his daughter is okay?"

Chief Bradbury stamped his feet. "Goddamn, it's cold. He dragged her out of the truck and into the house by one of her arms, but she didn't seem injured. Dragged her all dressed up in her heels, lucky she didn't twist an ankle. We notified the Providence FBI office. They're on the way. But," the Chief emphasized, "they don't know him. You do."

"So, the officers have been here, maybe fifteen minutes? Any movement in the house?"

"No, none. Figure he's holed up next to a front window. Vinnie saw him pass by once."

Paul got out of his vehicle and waved away the bullhorn. He squinted at those farmhouse windows with their bedraggled curtains and rotting frames, thinking, *how do you negotiate with a head case?* He moved to the police car closest to the front door and squatted behind it.

"Jack!" he called, his deep voice carrying across the yard. "It's Paul Rice. Put down the gun and come on out and we'll talk. Nobody needs to get hurt."

"Top o' the morning to ya, Paul!" Jack hollered out a downstairs window, sounding like a bizarre leprechaun. This made Paul furious. What game was he playing?

"Just send out your daughter, Jack. She doesn't need to be part of this. Let's talk, man to man."

Paul heard Jack's derisive hoot through the window crack. "Oh, Paul, you're so wrong! She's the reason we're all together tonight. I had to bring Mary home."

The lines in Paul's forehead deepened. "Coffee, Jack? You want some food? We can get you something."

Nothing.

"It's not going to work, Jack! Just look around you! Give up now and we'll get you a good lawyer!"

More laughter.

Paul glanced back at Chief Bradbury who was shaking his head. Crouching above the frozen ground, knees aching, Paul knew it was going to be a long night.

30

Resolution

Mary slumped against the wall next to a low window looking out onto the front porch. Flashing red and blue strobed across the room. Her father had initially switched on one of the small end table lamps flanking the couch before thinking better of it. The circular glow illuminated the living room mess and exposed the wallpaper, now yellowing with fading flowers. *Funny*, Mary thought, *I'd never noticed the state of the wallpaper.*

On the floor Mary tucked her stockinged feet beneath her, chilled to the bone. She hardly noticed she had lost her heels as she sat beneath her father, leaning against the wall. Paul Rice had stopped talking, and Jack was quiet as well. Mary didn't consider the irony of being seen by her father only after she left home. But she longed to be invisible once again.

She pulled her coat closer, oblivious to how long she might have to sit there. The movement caused Jack to glance down at her and grab her by the hair. He twisted it, pulling her close.

"Keep still," he growled. Mary whimpered and he let go. She could feel him looking down at her in the half darkness. Jack bent over and his free hand fumbled at the collar of her coat. Mary didn't, couldn't, look up. She sat frozen. Finding the opening, he slid his rough claw silently down, found the scooped red neckline and entered, fingering her bra, then plunging lower to encompass her breast. Jack gently rubbed Mary's nipple, and she heard him suck in air like an animal in heat. She couldn't make a move to stop him.

A sudden flashback vaulted Mary to the past, and she was the young girl lying in her twin bed upstairs, with him on top of her, heavy and hot, moaning softly in her ear as she gasped in pain. He shifted and pushed, plunging his weapon deeper, causing her to cry out. He clamped her mouth shut with his T bone hand and she struggled to breath. Mary wondered if she'd leave blood behind to stain her sheets, wondered if Mama would notice this time. Dizzy and sick under his heaving, sweaty weight, Mary feared this time he might really suffocate her.

A surge of vomit brought her back to the present, filling her mouth; she bent over, gagging, and he pulled back. She barely missed Jack's boot and left a pool of partially digested rice and fish where the fake Oriental rug met the wood.

Wiping her mouth, clutching the neck of her dress, Mary didn't see the butt of the rifle as Jack viciously sideswiped her; rather, she heard it crack against the side of her head, pitching her onto the floor with blood coursing into one ear. The pain of it caused the room to spin and Mary saw her mother on the floor after taking a punch. She saw Claire with her mother hovering over her, bathed in red. She saw herself with her father on top of her.

"No!" Mary screamed. She scrambled to her feet and lunged at her father, the beast with the gun, tackling him at the knees. The force of the impact caused him to flail, nearly letting go of the gun to break his fall. Mary landed on top of him in a rage and ripped the shotgun out of his hand. She brought it up, his head a matter of inches from the barrel. Her right hand found the trigger.

The kickback threw her backwards onto the floor, ears bloody and ringing from the explosion, rifle clattering softly to the rug. His blood filled her eyes, her nose; it was sprayed across her neck, her torso.

Mary lay vaguely aware of glass shattering, men shouting. Flashlights joined the circus of colored lights as heavily armed police rushed in. Mary wiped at her eyes, trying to see, trying to breathe through her mouth. She looked up stupidly as Paul Rice knelt at her side. Somebody switched on the overhead light which blinded her. She felt him take her hand but had a hard time hearing him as she made out his kind face, looking concerned, mouthing words. She felt exposed on her back on the floor in the light, covered in blood. She wanted to ask what had just happened, but a part of her knew. She had just killed her father.

31

DISAPPEAR

TONY RESTED HIS head on the scratchy white sheets of his daughter's pediatric ICU bed. He couldn't sit up another second. The warm buzz of the alcohol had turned into a sledgehammer headache. He usually took three extra-strength Tylenol and a couple of aspirin with coffee to take care of it before work. If it was a weekend, he downed the whole pot just to stick it to his wife. She bitched about his drinking beer and then bitched about him drinking coffee until he could pull himself together enough to leave the kitchen and find something that needed doing. *My wife.*

Hearing steps behind him roused Tony, who at first thought it was Elizabeth, come to take charge like she always did, so he wouldn't have to talk to these nurses who looked at him like he was a piece of shit. But it was just the cleaning lady, here to run a dry mop over the floor, eyes firmly fixed on the mop and equipment in her way.

Tony glanced at the clock positioned high over the jungle of IV poles and machinery surrounding his daughter. 9 AM. She was so still he would check every now and then to make sure she was breathing.

One of the nurses, kinder than the rest, had gotten him a cup of coffee in a little Styrofoam cup, maybe less than a cup, and not up to the job of his headache. He had asked politely for aspirin and been told it was against the policy of Hasbro Children's Hospital to dispense medication to family members. *Medication. Jesus, all I want is some aspirin. Maybe four would do the trick.*

A breakfast cart rolled quietly by in the hallway. Who ate breakfast in the ICU? Tony wondered if he could buy a bottle of aspirin nearby.

There had to be a store he could walk to. He'd ridden the ambulance with Claire from Jonathan Conrad and his truck was at home. He'd been told he was in no condition to drive but by the time she was transferred to the city, he probably could have driven himself. Elizabeth hadn't shown up last night and hadn't answered the phone. Shit, she still wasn't answering the phone. His anger from the previous night had burned itself out but now he was pissed that he was alone in this rotten hospital and couldn't even take care of his headache.

"*Elizabeth, what a bitch,*" he thought. *I should've left her years ago.* But a part of him knew that he got something out of the deal. He could be a father, a husband, a respectable homeowner, and avoid a return to the dinky apartments he could afford on his salary. He could talk to the neighbors, fix their cars, mow the lawn. He could even have an affair someday, he thought, why not? Men did it. Make his life with her a little more tolerable.

Mary intruded into his thoughts, and he pictured her at his house last night in the dark, peering in his windows, for Christ's sake, watching Elizabeth through Claire's window. Watching Elizabeth give something to Claire, some poison, poisoning her own daughter. And Mary had tried to warn him about it.

Tony didn't like where his thoughts were taking him, but he forced himself to look at Claire, really look at her. The rosebud lips forced open with a plastic tube carrying air into her little lungs. The rhythmic whooshing sound of the ventilator. Her skin the color of the sheets. Eyes closed as if she were sleeping late, something she never did, even when she was sick.

I could lose her, Tony thought. *I could sit here next to my little girl and watch her die.* He wasn't an idiot. He knew that the more the nurses hovered, adjusting IV drips, pushing medicines into the lines, the worse it was. The stream of doctors continued.

Elizabeth is a respiratory therapist, Tony thought. *Where the hell was she?* A coldness spread across him and his mind cleared enough to finally take it in, the reality of what Elizabeth had done, of what she had been doing. For months, maybe years. Right under his nose. And now the reality that Elizabeth had disappeared.

Tony felt shaky as he gazed at Claire, but he steadied his hands with a sense of determination. *Now it's up to me to raise my little girl on my own. If she lives.*

32

Aftermath

Annie checked in with Jane, the staff nurse assigned to Mary before she entered the hospital room. Jane said Mary was awake and preparing for discharge after an overnight stay for observation. She was apparently doing okay, considering the previous evening she had been taken hostage at gun point. Despite a confidentiality mandate, Annie figured the whole sordid affair had leaked out from either police personnel, ambulance crew or hospital staff. She figured Mary was aware of this as well.

Annie paused at the doorway, relieved to see a polished older woman who she took for Aunt Elaine fussing over Mary. Jane strode past her to obtain vital signs and check Mary's head dressing.

"Thank you for everything, you've been wonderful here at Jonathan Conrad, but I just want to get her home," the woman said to Jane. Mary looked up at Annie and her face brightened.

"Annie!"

"Hi Mary," Annie moved in with a reassuring smile. "I had to stop in to see you! How are you doing?"

"Well . . ." Mary rubbed her eyes. She looked exhausted and seemed at a loss.

"She's been through hell and back, this one," Aunt Elaine said brusquely as she kissed Mary's forehead. "But she'll be fine, I'm sure. I'll see to it. I'm Elaine, by the way." She stuck out her hand. "I've heard a lot about you, Annie, and I want to thank you for all you've done for my niece."

"It's my pleasure, Elaine. And I've certainly heard about you, as well. I'm sorry for the loss of your sister," Annie said.

Elaine nodded, and Annie saw that she also looked exhausted. Jane pulled off the blood pressure cuff with a loud ripping sound that startled Mary.

"Sorry," Jane said, touching Mary's arm briefly. "All I need is a pulse, and you'll be on your way. Your doctor wants you to check in with her in about a week."

"I'll see that she does," Elaine said.

"And perhaps you'll want to schedule an appointment with Annie as well?" Jane asked. All of this was a bit out of her league, Annie thought, and Jane looked relieved to defer to her.

"Can I see you soon, Annie?" Mary asked.

"Of course, I'll save you an appointment for later in the week, so that you have a few days to rest up. Unless you want to see me earlier. Will you need a note to take some time off from work?"

"Oh, the attending physician has already taken care of that," Jane said, showing Mary where to sign the paperwork. "He's given Mary five days off. Any longer than that will be up to you, Annie, or her primary care doctor."

"Then we're all set," Elaine said, grabbing large plastic bags from the bed holding the stained red dress, coat and muddy heels. A smaller hospital bag contained toiletries and a couple of sterile dressings for Mary's head wound. It looked like Elaine had gone on a grotesque shopping spree and Annie wondered how she'd attack the bloodstains. No doubt the inability to look at those clothes again would come up in Mary's sessions.

Annie watched Mary slide off the bed, looking frail in a sweatshirt and jeans. She wondered if Mary's new boyfriend would stick around after all of the drama. Thank God for Aunt Elaine.

As if reading her mind, Mary said softly, "John left, Annie. You just missed him. Aunt Elaine sent him home to get some sleep."

"Oh!" Annie said, smiling.

"Yes," Mary replied, and smiled back.

Watching the two of them, Elaine introjected, "Annie, Mary will need to speak with police later at the station. Hopefully she can get some sleep before she needs to do that. But rest assured, I'll be with her every step of the way."

Mary put on her jacket while Annie pulled Jane aside. Ambien had been ordered for her but Mary had refused it. She had been quiet but awake most of the night, with Elaine and John staying close.

"Give me a call if you have trouble sleeping at home," Annie said to Mary. "You have a prescription for Ambien, but let me know if it's too sedating or causes side effects."

"I'll see that she does, Annie," Elaine said.

Mary stopped in her tracks, looking bewildered. "I may have to talk to the FBI."

"It'll be okay, honey, we'll get through this," Elaine said soothingly, putting an arm around her niece's shoulders. "And then we can get back to our normal lives. This won't last forever."

"I'll second that," came a deep voice from the hall. He was middle aged, well dressed, and seemed to fill the doorway. "Paul!" Elaine looked surprised.

"Detective Rice," Mary smiled at the two of them.

Edmund awoke with sunlight sneaking around the blinds in his bedroom. He knew it was late, as he usually got up long before the December sun rose. He could smell bacon, one of his favorites, and heard Rhonda clanking around in the kitchen. He loved their weekends together when he wasn't on call and his pager was banished to the closet, stashed in the pocket of his lab coat. This Saturday was especially precious.

The scrape of Rhonda's energetic egg-beating and the crackling of frying bacon enabled Edmund to a surprise her, grabbing her from behind and holding her tight. Rhonda jumped, and laughed, reaching to turn off the burner. He lifted her hair to nuzzle her neck as she put down the whisk. She turned with a perplexed look.

"Doctor Fowler, I do declare!" Rhonda exclaimed in her Scarlet O'Hara imitation. Messy hair, no makeup, and wearing a twenty-year-old sloppy white robe, Edmund thought she had never looked more beautiful. The gentle lines around her eyes deepened as she smiled up at him.

"It's the bacon, isn't it?" she teased. "Maybe I should give it to you more often."

He kissed her quickly, mindful of his breath, and returned the smile, feeling liberated, happy. Savoring the moment, he didn't speak, and just held her in their beautiful kitchen, in their gorgeous home, feeling like the luckiest man in the world.

Rhonda looked thoughtful. "Edmund, what is it, really? You've been acting rather odd lately. I thought it was you reacting to everything, you know, Shirley, and now Claire in the ICU. I understand you take these things hard, you always have. Maybe you care too much."

Edmund saw that he couldn't escape her. He couldn't lie or dodge the truth, she was too good. He'd have to come clean.

"Actually, honey, it is about us." Edmund was pleased with his gentle tone and he knew he looked as earnest as he felt. There was relief in his words. "I was pretty sure you were having an affair with the landscaper. Maybe not physically, but emotionally. And frankly, I'd rather you have sex with him than fall in love with him."

Rhonda sucked in her breath and her lovely brown eyes widened. Edmund could see he had hit his mark, but he felt no anger.

"It sent me over the edge a little," he admitted. "But then I realized that whatever happened, it was my fault for abandoning you. For making you feel like you needed something, or someone else. For not appreciating every blessed thing you do for me."

Rhonda gasped, her eyes filling, and clasped Edmund hard, murmuring into his chest, "Oh no, Edmund, no, there's never been anyone but you!" She shook her head. "Frank was just a stupid flirtation; I would never betray you!"

Edmund took Rhonda by the shoulders and pulled her back so he could look at her. Now she was really crying, still shaking her head, with a stricken look like she had stabbed him with her kitchen knife. He brought Rhonda to him, and she clung to his robe like she was drowning. They rocked as he whispered into her hair his love, his regret, his determination to do better.

Finally, Rhonda lifted her head. "I'm using your robe as a handkerchief, but I promise to wash it."

Edmund laughed. "It probably needs a good wash anyway."

She wiped her eyes with his sleeve. "Now I'm a mess. But I needed that. Oh, God, Edmund, I don't deserve you. Oh my God, I love you so much!"

"I love you, too, Rhonda. I guess we deserve each other, warts and all. You're stuck with me."

He had no intention of telling her about Shirley as she clearly had no need to know. *Let her think the best of me, and be happy.* A shadow crossed Edmund's mind, and his chest constricted, but Rhonda didn't notice.

The jangle of the phone intruded, and she moved to pick it up. "Hello? Oh, hi Jim, how are you doing? What? Oh, yes, yes, that's wonderful news! Thank you so much for letting us know. Yes, of course. Bye, now."

Rhonda turned to Edmund, her face shining.

"Shirley woke up."

Author's Note on Munchausen Syndrome:

The illness that led Elizabeth to poison daughter Claire has a medical name. It's known as Munchausen Syndrome and was first described in 1951, named for the German "Baron of Munchausen" who exaggerated his exploits. The term is used interchangeably with Factitious Disorder which describes the fabrication of illness for psychological gratification. In 1977 Roy Meadow, a pediatrician, used Munchausen Syndrome by Proxy (MSBP) to describe two cases of mother-induced illness in their children.

Currently four medical terms are used interchangeably for it: Medical Child Abuse coined by Roesler and Jenny (2009), Paediatric Falsification Syndrome (interchangeable with Medical Child Abuse) and Factitious Disorder Imposed on Another (interchangeable with MSBP).

Such cases overwhelm clinicians who are already burdened by dysfunctional health care systems. The persistent focus on the pathology of the perpetrator, almost always the mother who is assumed to have mental illness, lets the medical establishment off the hook for participating in the abuse with unnecessary surgeries, procedures, hospitalizations, medications and the like, all of which complicate efforts to protect the child.

Prevalence of the disorder is unknown with estimates of 1% of hospitalized patients. Victims are generally children, but any vulnerable population is at risk. Unfortunately, we seem to have made little progress in grappling with the disorder.

About the Author

Jill S. Moretti, APRN, CNS is a licensed Advanced Practice Registered Nurse and a Clinical Nurse Specialist whose career spans 45 years, 31 of which have involved specializing in adult psychiatric/mental health nursing. She is a graduate of both the University of Wisconsin and the University of Rhode Island.

She utilizes psychotherapy and psychopharmacology (prescriptive authority) in her evaluation and treatment of adults ages 18 through the lifespan. She is a Certified Public Health Nurse who has worked in a variety of clinical areas including consultation to both hospitals and long term care settings. Her areas of expertise include anxiety, depression, mood and personality disorders, schizophrenia, bipolar disorder, obsessive compulsive disorder, and panic disorder.

White Lies and other Colors is Moretti's debut novel.